Once Beyond A Time

by
ANN TATLOCK

HERITAGE BEACON
FICTION

ONCE BEYOND A TIME BY ANN TATLOCK
Published by Heritage Beacon Fiction
an imprint of Lighthouse Publishing of the Carolinas
2333 Barton Oaks Dr., Raleigh, NC, 27614

ISBN: 978-1-941103-90-6
Copyright © 2014 by Ann Tatlock
Cover design by writelydesigned.com
Interior design by Karthick Srinivasan

Available in print from your local bookstore, online, or from the publisher at:
www.lighthousepublishingofthecarolinas.com

For more information on this book and the author visit: www.anntatlock.com

Brought to you by the creative team at LighthousePublishingoftheCarolinas.com:
Eddie Jones, Rowena Kuo, and Michele Creech.

Library of Congress Cataloging-in-Publication Data
Tatlock, Ann.
Once Beyond A Time/Ann Tatlock 1st ed.

Printed in the United States of America

Praise for *Once Beyond a Time*

Wow. I can't remember the last time I was so absorbed in a book. I LOVED this novel. I've always been taken with the idea of God existing outside of time and this book captured that so beautifully. Utterly engaging.

Sarah Loudin Thomas
Author of *Miracle in a Dry Season*

Ann Tatlock is a remarkable writer. I have not enjoyed reading a book this much in a long, long time. I was sucked along by the characters and their lives, by the uniqueness of the setting, and by the beauty of her language and storytelling.

Holly Lorincz
Editing and publishing consultant
Lorincz Literary Services

Once Beyond A Time is a novel less about time and more about healing and forgiveness. Even as the house transcends time, the themes Tatlock weaves transcend decades. We see, very clearly, how enduring our pain can be, and how sweet forgiveness can be. Highly recommended.

Aaron Gansky
Author of *The Bargain,*
Firsts in Fiction, and *The Hand of Adonai Series*

This is the best book I have read in a long time and I read a lot! The characters became a part of my life and I wanted to step into the pages and become a part of theirs. The story was intricate but not confusing, deep but not underwater, weaving together several plots, mysteries and truths in a natural and fun way. You don't want to miss this one!

Robin Prince Monroe
Artist and author of *Devotions for the Brokenhearted*

Ann Tatlock has served up a truly great story! *Once Beyond A Time* tugs at your imagination, pulls you into a captivating world of "what ifs," and confronts very real conflicts in a very surreal manner – I thoroughly enjoyed it!

Denny Brownlee
Actor, voice artist and comedy writer

Once Beyond A Time is a window into the soul of every human; it's a picture of what it is to live and love and hurt and struggle and triumph and rejoice. Hauntingly honest and beautifully written, I found myself emotionally drawn in to the lives of the characters.

Mike Dellosso
Author of *Fearless* and *Rearview*

There is nothing sweeter than the gentle hand of words when written by Ann Tatlock. *Once Beyond A Time* is no different. In this story, Tatlock draws you into her world and allows you to wander from age to age with her characters. A read that is "timeless."

Cindy Sproles
Author of *Mercy Rains*

Part 1

Time is what keeps
everything from
happening at once.

———Ray Cummings,
The Girl in the Golden Atom

1

Meg
Friday, July 12, 1968

MY FIRST THOUGHT now, of course, is that Carl will never come home.

Not really, anyway. Not to the home he left only a short time ago. When my son comes back from Vietnam—and please, God, let him come back—he'll return to a place he's never been, and where none of us really wants to be. Not Sheldon. Not I. Certainly not Linda, who makes no effort to hide her anger. Digger is the only one at peace with the move, and that's because at eight years of age he's simply too young to know any better. To him, leaving the familiar and landing in some remote corner of North Carolina is just another adventure.

That's not to say this place is without its charms. I stand here on the wide front porch of the old house and look out over the mountains. Because we are up high and in a clearing, I can see for miles and, yes, the mountains, layers of them, are oddly blue. The Blue Ridge Mountains. After a lifetime spent in the flat farmland of southeast Pennsylvania, I have the same feeling of hushed awe I got every time I stepped into the Cathedral Basilica in Philadelphia. The ceiling was so high, and there was so much open space! I almost longed to sprout wings and soar upward to touch the pinnacle of that domed ceiling.

But here, the ceiling is infinite and endless and untouchable, for the dome is the sun-streaked sky, and the walls are a living landscape formed by the mountains. I think I might find it beautiful, if only I could see it without the pain.

But I can't. Because the pain is at the heart of why we're here.

Sheldon had an affair. Two months I've known, and yet I can scarcely bring myself to believe that this is *my* life, that *I* am the woman scorned. It's something that happens to other women, not to me. I didn't even suspect, though it was happening right under my own roof with a young woman who is my own cousin. I was so certain of my relationship with Sheldon, so secure, so proud of our twenty years with scarcely a bump in the road that I couldn't even see what was playing out in front of my eyes.

Not until the whole thing was over, and Sheldon came to me in tears, did I know. The night he confessed, his words literally knocked me off balance, and I had to stumble to a chair and sit. My hands shook, and I couldn't catch my breath. What was he saying? What was he asking of me? I shut my eyes, rubbed my temples with my fingertips.

He knelt at my feet, his hands folded in my lap. "Forgive me," he said.

Forgive you?

I felt myself breaking apart like an old star giving out and floating off, bits and pieces, into space. Which part of me should forgive you, Sheldon? Which broken part?

Finally, I managed to string six words together and spit them out. "When did you stop loving me?"

I opened my eyes. He was shaking his head, looking horrified. "I never stopped loving you, Meg. I swear, that's the truth."

I didn't believe him. You don't cheat on someone you love. You couldn't do that to someone you love.

From somewhere inside me, a scream rose up that seemed to go on and on. I pushed Sheldon away. We fought. Bitterly. For hours. That night he moved into the den.

The next day, the deathly silence fell over us. The marriage which just twenty-four hours earlier had been my whole life, was now gone. Just like that. But there was more to come. Not only did the affair ruin our marriage, but Sheldon, in some misguided act of penance, allowed it to strip him of his life's work. Quietly, without explanation, Sheldon resigned from his job as pastor of First Baptist Church of Abington.

"What will we do?" I asked.

"We will start over somewhere else," he said.

I thought of leaving him. I thought of finding a job and an apartment and raising the kids on my own, but in the end, I couldn't muster the strength and courage it would take to do it. And when finally Steve called and said, "Listen, Sis, one of my salesmen just quit. I'll give the job to Sheldon if you all want to come down here. Just wait till you see this place; it's beautiful. You'll love it"—I went along with it. Sheldon took the job, and we left our home state of Pennsylvania to come down here to Western North Carolina where my brother ended up eons ago when he married a southern girl. Steve loves it here, and he thinks everyone should love it here. As I stand on this wide porch and look out over those far blue hills I think, maybe I would love it here too if I weren't already as good as dead. I can hardly pull any of this mountain air into my lungs, much less allow the beauty to enter my soul.

I thought I had proved Mother wrong, but she was right after all. "Love always ends," she said, "and men always leave." Those were her words to me when Daddy left her for wife number two, whom he later left for wife number three and number four. It's a wonder Steve has stayed with Donna all these years. How is it he didn't end up like Daddy, while Sheldon did? Not in the leaving, but in letting love die.

My jaw clenches. I can't give in to the anger right now. Steve and his family will be here any minute. I move down the porch steps and find Digger playing in the drive, digging in the dirt with his shovel and his bucket, making a race track for his Matchbox cars. He's smiling, laughing to himself. He's the only untroubled soul around here. It gives me a moment's pleasure just to watch him; Harrison, my last-born, the surprise. Linda was nine and Carl ten, and next thing I know, I'm pregnant. A surprise, yes, but never "the mistake." Never.

Harrison Benjamin Crane. From the day he was born, he's been my joy.

Steve and Donna came up the summer he was two, and when Donna saw him digging in the garden, she exclaimed, "Well, look at the littlest Crane, out there digging in the dirt! He's building himself a whole little town!" And then Steve added, "But isn't that what cranes do? Work in the dirt and build things?" And we all laughed, and ever since, he's been Digger. Now, it seems hardly anyone remembers his real name. Except me. Harrison Benjamin Crane, the only real joy I have right now.

A car horn honks and Digger jumps up and waves. The drive is so long I can't see the beginning of it from the porch steps, but in a moment, there's Steve's car—a Chevy, of course—pulling up to the house. The car stops, and they all pile out: Steve, Donna, Jeff, and Marjorie. Come to welcome us on our first day in Black Mountain, North Carolina.

"Hey, y'all!" Donna calls.

Yes, we are in the South. Best get used to it, I suppose. I step off the porch and greet Donna with a hug.

"Welcome, Sis," Steve says. He kisses my cheek and shakes hands with Sheldon, who has just stepped out the front door. Steve settles his hand on my shoulder, giving it a gentle squeeze. If he weren't my older brother—and a man at that—I'd almost think he understood.

2

Linda
Friday, July 12, 1968

OH GREAT. I'VE died and gone to hell. Dad—oh yeah, that great man of God—turns out to be a hypocrite, and now all of us have to pay with our lives. The old man can't keep his hands off Mom's pretty, young cousin, and next thing I know, I've got to do my senior year down here in Barney Fife country, where the best-looking guy in class is probably as ugly as sin after ten generations of family inbreeding. I mean, if they're all like those two bozos Uncle Steve sent up here this morning to help us unload the U-Haul, I'm as good as in a nunnery. One guy had brown teeth, and the other had an Adam's apple the size of Texas.

My senior year! I was just starting to make some headway with Brian, too. I mean, at least he'd talk to me when he was high, and that's something anyway. Another few weeks, maybe a month, I bet we'd have hooked up. I'd finally shed that preacher's daughter stereotype stuff and was hanging out with the right people, the cool kids, and I bet I had a pretty good chance at homecoming queen this year and what happens but Dad announces we're pulling up stakes and heading to hillbilly country. He wouldn't say why we were moving, but later Mom told me the whole creepy story about him shacking up with Charlene. Yeah, Dad was pretty miffed about Mom spilling the beans and all, but hey, when it comes to

being mad, I'd say Dad doesn't have a leg to stand on. What he did to
Mom is way worse than her telling me what he did.

I begged Mom to let me stay in Abington and live with Monica for our
senior year. Monica's parents even said it was all right, but Mom wouldn't
give in. She's already lost Carl to the war, she says, and she's not going
to give up another child right at the same time. Like we have this close
mother-daughter thing going on or something. And anyway, Carl's just a
company clerk, for crying out loud. Like, what, he's going to die of too
much typing? Bleed to death from too many paper cuts? It's not like he's
out on the front lines where the killing's going on. Plus, he wanted to go,
the psycho. He's seventeen when he graduates, and then he goes and works
at that two-bit Woolworth's job until his eighteenth birthday so he can
sign up for the war soon as he's old enough. I mean, there's guys out there
burning their draft cards and running off to Canada, and my brother the
weirdo wants to go to Vietnam like he's signing up for some sort of cruise
ship vacation or something. Anyway, Mom's wasting her time worrying
about him. He's probably having the time of his life, smoking all the weed
he wants and meeting pretty little Vietnamese girls in the back streets of
Hanoi. That's more than I can say for myself, down here in Hicksville. Oh
man, my life is ruined.

So this dump is supposed to be my bedroom? At least we're not in
some church manse for the first time in my life, but that's about the only
good thing I can say about this house. This place is so old it looks like it's
falling apart around our ears, and the furniture hasn't been changed since
the last century. It's been sitting here, moldering, for decades. I mean, I
wonder how many old geezers have slept in this very bed. I don't know,
but I think I can still smell their sour sweaty flesh like they just got up
and didn't bother to change the sheets. And look at that old chair—it's
got doilies on the arms! And the dresser— sheesh—the mirror's so bad, I
can hardly find a spot in it that shows my whole face at once. That might
be fine for some old lady who doesn't want to see herself anyway, but it's

not going to work for me. I mean, putting up with the furniture in all those manses was no picnic, but this takes the cake. I got to get my boxes unpacked and get my Grateful Dead posters up on the wall. Maybe that'll help. But I doubt it.

There's a door here in my room, leading out to the upper porch. We got a porch downstairs and a porch upstairs. "Well, isn't that nice," Dad says this morning when we pull up in front of this oversized shack that's supposed to be our new home. Yeah, so, whoop-de-do. We can all sit out here in our rocking chairs like the bunch of hillbillies we are now and smoke our corncob pipes and drink moonshine from a jug. Like two porches make up for an entire senior year. It'd be all right if I could step out here at night and hear Brian calling to me from down behind a tree, and then I'd sneak off … but, no, forget it! Brian's a thousand miles away, along with all my friends and every other good thing that used to be my life.

Good grief, look at Digger, will you? Down there playing in the dirt. That's all he ever does. He's like Pig Pen in that Charlie Brown comic strip, the guy with the dust cloud following him around. Dirt up to his elbows, on the back of his neck, down his pants. If he's dirty, he's happy. That's my kid brother. How embarrassing.

"Hey, Digger," I yell down to him. "Why don't you go play in a riptide somewhere."

Digger stands and looks around. Then he looks up at me. His face is all scrunched up because he's squinting against the sun. "I didn't know there was any ocean around here," he says.

Stupid kid.

He goes back to playing in the dirt. Mom is on the porch below me. I know she is. I can hear her footsteps. I hear her sigh. She is big-time mad at Dad, and I don't blame her. "Why don't you just divorce him, Mom?" I asked. I mean, anyone else would. But Mom? She doesn't even answer. She just looks at me like I've told her to go jump off a cliff. I guess she thinks she has to play the devoted wife, like this is The Donna Reed Show or something. Of course, if this were The Donna Reed Show, Dad wouldn't have been sleeping around.

Oh great. Look who's here. It's the Clampetts. Jed, Granny, Jethro, and Elly May. Okay, so Aunt Donna doesn't look anything like Granny, but she waves her hand and yells, "Hey, y'all"and I know I'm not in Pennsylvania anymore.

Well, I for one am not in the mood for company. I slip back into my room and plop down on the old stuffed chair with the doilies on the arms. It smells musty, and it's all lumpy like it's stuffed with a sack of potatoes. I let my head drop against the back and shut my eyes. Oh God, if you're up there, just kill me now.

I open my eyes, and there's cousin Jeff, standing in the doorway of my bedroom. I haven't seen him in a couple years, and he's grown about a foot and sprouted a boatload of pimples since we were last together. He smiles and shrugs like I asked him a question or something. "Hey," he says.

"Is that how you say hi around here?"

He shrugs again. "I guess so."

He's not a bad-looking kid, except for the acne, but he's two years younger than me, and he's still a year away from getting his driver's license, and he'd better not get any ideas that we're going to be friends or anything. I'm in a place where there's not going to be any friends. But just one year, I tell myself. Just one year and I'm outta here.

"So what do you do for fun around here?" I ask, not bothering to get up from the chair.

For a minute, he just stands there looking stupid, like he has no idea what fun is. I was afraid of that. "Well," he finally says, "lots of stuff."

"What? Like, go to hoedowns and have coon-dog howling contests? Shoot varmints to make stew? Attend public hangings?"

He looks confused, the poor dweeb. Then he laughs a little. Like he's not sure he should, but he's afraid not to. Then he says, "Well, I don't think we do that anymore."

"Do what?" I ask, egging him on.

"Hang people. Anyhow, I haven't heard of any hangings around here lately."

"That's too bad," I say.

His eyebrows try hard to meet his hairline. "You do that in Pennsylvania? Hang people?"

"Only during leap years."

He doesn't know whether to believe me or not. He fidgets and sticks his hands in the pockets of his overalls.

"So," I go on. "Back to good times in Black Mountain. You folks smoke weed?"

He finally looks alive. "Oh sure!" he cries. "Yeah, we do that."

My head springs up. Maybe we're getting somewhere. "Really?" I ask.

"Sure! Corn silk. Grapevines. Rabbit tobacco."

I feel my eyes turning into slits. Jeff looks scared.

"I mean," I say through clenched teeth, "marijuana. You got any marijuana down here?"

His eyes widen even as mine grow narrower. "You mean, that illegal drug they do out in California?"

I don't bother to answer. Far as I'm concerned, this conversation's over.

How am I going to make it through this year? I want to kill myself. No, better yet, I want to kill somebody else. And I can hear him downstairs right now, talking to Uncle Steve about the Chevy dealership. So let's welcome Sheldon Crane, Birchfield Chevrolet's newest used car salesman.

Dad, the big liar, should fit his new role just fine.

3

Sheldon
Friday, July 12, 1968

FATHER, FORGIVE ME, for I have sinned.

Father.

Forgive me.

For I have sinned.

No matter how many times I say it, I know I have to say it one more time, because the forgiveness is always just beyond my reach.

Meg, I know, has not forgiven me. Can I blame her? If the tables were turned, would I forgive her? I'd like to think I would. I'd like to think she *will*—someday. That's my prayer, anyway.

Linda is as angry with me as her mother is. Won't talk to me, barely looks at me. Is it because she's seventeen? Would she have hated me anyway, just because she's seventeen, and I'm a pastor? Was a pastor. Was. Past tense now.

Carl writes to me from Vietnam, telling me to forget it. "These things happen," he says. "Just forget it and move on." It is hard to move on when the one you're supposed to be traveling with refuses to budge.

The Birchfields came this afternoon, bringing greetings and food. Casseroles, canned goods, fresh fruits and vegetables, cookies, and other baked goods—all pulled out of the back of their Chevy like it was some sort of welcome wagon. They've been good to us. Heaven knows, Steve was good to me, offering me the job. Not that it's the kind of job I ever imagined myself doing.

"You look worried," he said to me after supper.

"I really have no idea how to sell cars."

"Nothing to it!" he said cheerfully. "I can tell you in an afternoon everything you need to know."

His smile was full of confidence. He is a man who doesn't worry. "Listen," he said, nodding toward the porch, away from the women who were cleaning up the kitchen. Steve and I stepped outside. He pulled a pack of cigarettes from his shirt pocket and lit one, throwing the match into the grass at the foot of the steps. "Listen," he said again. "I know things are ... tense ... right now, between you and Meg. But she'll come around."

I found myself sighing heavily.

"I mean," he went on, "you're not the first guy to ever—well, you know. Women get over it."

I looked at him for a long while. I've seen Steve only a few times in my life, whenever he and Donna came up to Philly to visit. We never came down here, never could afford a real vacation on my pastor's salary. So I don't know Steve well, but he's my brother-in-law, my wife's brother, and he's already extended his hand to me. He's bailed me out. I need his friendship, and so far he's been friendly.

It felt awkward, but I went ahead and asked, "Were you ever unfaithful, Steve?"

"Me?" He tapped his chest with the hand holding the cigarette. "Yeah. Once." He shrugged, like he was telling me he'd once gone fishing.

"Donna know?"

"Sure. Yeah, she knows everything. It was a few years ago."

"So what happened?"

"I was in the doghouse a couple of months, you'd better believe it. I mean, she wouldn't cook for me, do my laundry, nothing. And as far as ..." He paused, looked at me, took a long pull on his cigarette. "Well, let's just say, I got pretty well acquainted with the guest room before I ever laid my head down on my own pillow again."

He said it like he shouldn't be talking about such things with a pastor, because everyone knows pastors are different. Not quite human. No, more than human. Holy, somehow. Incapable of *being* human. Incapable of sin.

I am a used car salesman.

But for the moment, Steve seems to forget that. To him, I am still a pastor. He must be careful.

"So what happened?" I asked again.

"Well," he said with a smile, "you know, after a while it gets old for both of you. If you just go on working and bringing home the bacon—and a few roses don't hurt either—you eventually fall back into the old routine. You don't even have to say anything, you know. She just starts making your dinner again and washing your socks. And then someday it's almost like it never happened."

Like it never happened? For me, it will never be like that. In this house, there are four bedrooms. One for Linda, one for Digger, one for Meg, one for me.

I am no longer married. What I wouldn't give to be married again. Not just to anyone, but to Meg, my wife.

It's heading toward twilight and I'm in my room now, a spacious square at the back of the house next to Digger's room. The girls have the front rooms that open up onto the porch. I thought they'd like that. But I don't know. Obviously, neither of them seems very happy about anything right now.

I look out the window and see Digger jumping from that big rock in the backyard. His arms are raised toward the sky and he's holding a stick in one hand. He jumps, he yells, he climbs the rock, and jumps again. Oh, son. You have it all ahead of you. Don't mess up. It's easier to make a tangle of things than I ever imagined, but maybe, if you're very, very careful, you'll be all right.

I had prided myself in my goodness. Funny, isn't it? How can one be proud that one is good? The one negates the other. So yes, maybe I too believed a pastor is somehow more than human. Somehow immune to sin. And yet I did something I thought I couldn't—and wouldn't—ever do.

Her name was Charlene McMurphy.

"She was engaged to be married, and now her fiancé has gone and called off the engagement," Meg explained. Meg had come to my office at the church, Charlene's letter in hand. "Now she wants to leave Des Moines and make a fresh start somewhere else. She says she's hoping to get a job in Philly. Can she stay with us for a short time, just until she finds her own place?"

Of course! Of course she can. She's family after all. Meg's cousin on her father's side. Meg's younger cousin, only twenty-two, but yes, of course she can stay with us. What, with Carl gone, we have a spare bedroom. Tell her to come right away; we'll leave the light on for her.

And so she came.

At first I pitied her because of the broken engagement. None of us spoke of the ex-fiancé by name, though he was always there, hanging around, making Charlene weep at the oddest times. She used to play the piano and cry, tears running down her face, her mascara two black streaks that she dabbed at with crumpled tissues. Meg tried to comfort her—"There are plenty of fish in the sea"—and, who knows, maybe it did some good because as the days passed, Charlene grew less and less somber and occasionally even ventured a laugh. And often, very often, she smiled at me.

I asked her how she could coax such beautiful music out of an out-of-tune piano, and she said one has to love the instrument, love what it can do in spite of how broken it is. If one loves and respects the instrument it will do great things for you. I told her she was a talented musician, and she said she wasn't yet, but one day she hoped to be. I told her she could come next door to the church any time and play the organ, and she said she'd like that.

She was a beautiful girl: young and lithe and blonde and perfect. She didn't spend much time trying to find a job or a place of her own, but neither Meg nor I rushed her. She had, after all, a broken heart and needed time to mend.

I should have run, somehow. That was my mistake. I should have helped her find an apartment, but I didn't. Of course, I couldn't admit to myself then what I readily confess now: I didn't want her to leave.

I still loved Meg, and for that reason I tried at first to toss off the desire Charlene aroused in me. And there was that pride again; I had prided myself on being strong enough to resist temptation. I believed myself impervious to the charms of Lorelei! But, in the end, I couldn't resist the siren's song that lures men to shipwreck on the rocks.

The day came when she found me alone in my office at the church. She approached my desk where I sat reading the sermons of Spurgeon. She wore that orange mini-skirt and white sleeveless blouse, her long hair hanging around her shoulders in gentle waves. She smiled at me as she said, "You know, you don't look like a pastor to me anymore."

And startled, I replied, "I don't?"

"No," she said, touching my arm with her fingertips. "You just look like a regular man."

And so as easily as that, I was. A regular man. My grip let go the wheel of the ship, and I was lost.

Father. Father.

Forgive me, for I have sinned.

Forgive me.

4

Digger
Friday, July 12, 1968

YEE HAW! I'M Daniel Boone! I got my rifle, and I'm going hunting, and I'm not coming back till I got the biggest buffalo ever! I'm not afraid of nothing!

Oh boy, this is great. This is the best thing ever. I wish we'd had a rock like this in the backyard up home. I never saw a rock this big for climbing on and jumping off. It's just like flying.

Yee haw! Pow, pow, pow! This might look like a stick, but it's the meanest rifle you'll find anywhere in these mountains. I can shoot a tin can at sixty paces. Pow!

Boy, I wish Marjorie and them could have stayed a little longer so she could go on playing the Indian maiden I rescue from the bad guys. Aunt Donna said Marjorie had to go to bed, but what I want to know is, who can go to bed when it's not even hardly dark yet? Yeah, I guess she's only seven and I'm eight, and I can stay up longer.

Look out below! Here I come! And I'm the roughest, toughest, rootin' tootin'est …

Hey! What's that?

I must have said it out loud because some voice behind me says, "It's a lightning bug. Haven't you never seen one?"

I turn around, and there's a boy standing there with his face all freckled and his bare feet all dirty. Wow, lucky kid! Ma says I got to wear my sneakers in the grass in case of bees.

"Haven't you never seen a lightning bug before?" the kid asks again.

I shake my head. "Nope, I don't guess so." Now they're everywhere, little lights flashing all over the backyard. "How do they light up like that?"

"Austin says they got little gas lamps in their tails they can turn on and off, just by thinking about it."

"No kidding!"

"Yup. How come you never seen a lightning bug before?"

"Guess we didn't have them up in Abington."

"Abington? Where's that?"

"Pennsylvania. We just moved here. You live around here?"

"Yup." He points over one shoulder with his thumb.

"Here in Black Mountain?"

"Yup." He points with his thumb again at the house we just moved into. I think he must mean he lives down the mountain from us somewhere.

"What's your name?" I ask him.

"Malcolm. But everybody calls me Mac."

"Hey, that's funny! My name's Harrison, but everybody calls me Digger."

"You wanna catch lightning bugs in a jar?"

"Sure! You got any jars?"

"Don't tell nobody, but I took some of Ma's canning jars. Just a couple. I hid them up there in the woods." He points to the woods that Dad told me was off our property and if I went up in there I'd have to be careful. Aunt Donna said maybe don't go in the woods at all because there's black bears all over these mountains. When she said that, it looked like Ma was going to faint, but Uncle Steve said don't worry because if you bang a couple pots together they run away pretty fast, and anyway, it's been a while since the last time they heard of anybody being clawed up by a bear. So when Mac says, "Come on! I'll show you where they are," I say, "All right!" and we start running.

I run on ahead of Mac, even though I should be following because I don't know where we're going. But I always was a good runner, the fastest in my second-grade class last year, even faster than Marty Higgins, who always bragged he was best at everything. But he wasn't faster than Digger Crane. No siree!

I'm running across the grass and into the woods behind our yard, and then I think I better slow down and let Mac show me where those jars are. I stop and turn and start to tell Mac to go ahead, but he isn't behind me.

"Hey," I holler. "Hey, where'd you go?"

I'm looking everywhere, but he's gone. I can't believe it! He went and snuck off without making a sound, the way the Indians do when they're walking through the woods. I'm sorry he did that because I don't know where the jars are and now I can't catch any lightning bugs and besides I wonder why Mac didn't want to stick around. Maybe he heard his Ma calling or something, but he could have told me he had to go and maybe said good-bye. Oh well. He'll probably come back. Next time I see him, I'm going to ask him to show me how to disappear into thin air just like he did.

5

Meg
Saturday, July 13, 1968

How QUIET IT is here in the early morning. I step out onto the upstairs porch and hear nothing but birdsong. No voices. No traffic. Only the whistles and trills of a thousand birds.

In the distance, a mist rises from the mountains, as though the sun is gently lifting a blanket off a sleeping child. Time to get up now. For all I know, this might be the dawn of the world. There is nothing here to tell me otherwise.

Donna says that in the winter, when the leaves are off the trees, we'll have a better view of the town in the valley below. But for now, with few signs of human life, we might as well be the only people living in these hills.

While Sheldon and the kids are still asleep, I go downstairs to the kitchen to make coffee. A large stone fireplace nearly fills the whole of one wall, and there is actually a blackened kettle dangling from a wrought-iron crane on the hearth. I wonder who last used that kettle. No telling. This house is filled with all sorts of odd things. Chamber pots under the beds. Hat pins on the dressers. Framed photos of unknown people on the walls. A spinning wheel in the living room. I am used to living in houses that are not my own, filled with furniture bought by somebody else. But this time

I almost feel as though I'm intruding, as though I've moved into a house that has never actually been vacated. The owners will be coming home any minute now and will be surprised to find us here. That's how it seems to me as I stand at the kitchen sink filling the coffee percolator with water. Perhaps I will hear someone at the door, a key in the lock, and I will know the family who lives in this house has come home again.

Steve, who arranged for us to live here, said it would be the perfect place for us, since it was already furnished and available to let right away. The man who really does own the house—his name is Ronald Simpkins, or maybe Simmons, I can't remember now—at any rate, he bought the house in 1959 with the idea he and his wife would retire here someday. For now, he lives over the mountains in Tennessee and rents this place out, as he can. Apparently, he has trouble keeping his renters, though certainly the place is under-priced.

"What seems to be the trouble, far as renting this place out?" Sheldon asked last night at supper.

"Don't know for sure," Steve responded, "but I suppose people are anxious to buy rather than rent. The price of real estate is always going up around here, you know."

"Yeah," Jeff added, "that and the fact that people say this place is haunted."

"Oh right," Linda said, rolling her eyes.

Sheldon actually laughed. "Well, Jeff, we don't have to worry about that," he said. "We don't believe in such things."

Jeff shrugged. "I'm just telling you what I hear."

I was afraid Jeff would frighten Digger, but Digger was so intent on eating, he seemed not to have heard.

"Well," Donna rushed to add, "I've lived here in Black Mountain almost all my life, and I can tell you there aren't any ghosts in this town. I've never actually been in this house before, but I can tell you I've never heard anything about it being haunted. When I was growing up it was owned by a widow who more or less kept to herself and didn't much welcome company. But now that I've seen the place, I think it's lovely."

Steve, sitting beside me, gave off a guttural sound, wiped his mouth with his napkin and said, "Well, I think we can agree it's got potential. Could be fixed up real nice someday."

We fit easily around the large table in the dining room, one of two rooms at the back of the house, the other room being the kitchen. The dining room is large and airy, full of light and filled with a curious mix of furniture: a china buffet, a commode table with a porcelain washbowl and pitcher, a fainting couch, a Singer sewing machine with a foot-operated treadle, and several small serving tables, one of which holds a phonograph and a dozen or so albums. The widow must have enjoyed listening to music while she ate. The floor is bare, the wood smoothed and dulled by decades of footfalls. Of course, there is no wall-to-wall carpeting anywhere in the house, only the occasional woven rug. Some of the items cluttering the rooms are so old, like the phonograph and the commode table, that surely they must have already been here when the widow moved in.

"I wonder why the widow didn't will the place to her children when she died," I remarked.

Linda, with that indelible teenaged smirk of hers, sneered, "We should be so lucky."

Donna smiled at Linda, then explained, "She didn't have any children. She didn't have any will, for that matter. The place was auctioned off by the county after she passed away. It's just as it was when she lived here, furniture and all."

"No kidding," Linda said. "I never would have guessed."

"That's enough, Linda," Sheldon said.

"When she died," Jeff sputtered, so eager to tell the tale that little missiles of spit shot from his mouth, "she lay dead in her bed for a week before anyone found her."

Linda stared at her cousin for a moment in disgust. "Oh great," she finally said. "And I know just which bed it was too." She then glanced at her father, daring him to reprimand her. He didn't.

"You're gross, Jeff," Marjorie piped up.

"Yes, Jeff, we really don't need your comments," Donna added. "And you know not to talk with your mouth full."

"So," I said, smiling around the table and trying to keep the conversation light, "do you know when the house was built?"

Donna shook her head. "I don't know for sure. You could check with county records over in Asheville, though, if you really want to know."

"Sometime before the fall of Rome would be my best guess." Linda, of course. Why can't she just be sullen and silent rather than sullen and sarcastic? It gets to be so tiresome.

"Well, listen," Steve said brightly, "tomorrow's Saturday. Normally I'm working, but I can let my people handle things alone for one day. Why don't we come pick you up in the van and show you the town?"

"Sure, Steve," I said, "that'll be fine."

"We might as well start to learn our way around," Sheldon added.

"Ho boy, I can hardly wait." Linda again. Of course.

So later today, they will come and show us the town. For now, while the coffee percolates, I sit in one of the rocking chairs in front of the fireplace. My mind drifts to Carl, and I wonder what he is doing right now, there on the other side of the world. I cannot begin to picture where he is. But then, neither can he begin to picture where we are, here in this strange and solitary house high on the side of a mountain. Funny, isn't it, the places we end up, the places to which human folly takes us?

6

Sheldon
Saturday, July 13, 1968

BLACK MOUNTAIN IS a pretty little town. Built on the banks of the
Swannanona River, it fans out across the valley and slopes upward toward
the hills. Steve, from his perch in the driver's seat, rambles on about the
place with obvious pride, pointing out historic landmarks like we're a
group of paying tourists on a sightseeing expedition.

In fact, it was tourism, Steve explains, that caused the town to
mushroom in the first place. It wasn't long after the white settlers arrived
in the late eighteenth century that word of the valley and its beauty spread
eastward across the Piedmont. Soon, the well-to-do started arriving
from the lowlands in search of fresh air, pure mountain water, and relief
from the summer heat, with a host of hotels and inns springing up to
accommodate them. These tourists came by stage at first, and then, after
the Civil War when the track was finally completed, they came by train.
When the health benefits of the mountain air were realized, sanitariums
appeared for the treatment of tuberculosis, attracting the afflicted from up
and down the East Coast and as far west as the Great Plains.

"That's one of them right there," Steve says, pulling over and pointing
to a two-story building set back from the road. "See those screened-in
porches? They wrap around the whole building like that. That's where the

patients slept, summer and winter. Rest and fresh air—that was about all they could do for TB back then."

"What's the building used for now?" Meg asks.

"Reform school for juvenile delinquents," Steve explains.

"Oh, so that's the high school," Linda mutters in the back seat. Jeff, beside her, gives a frustrated sigh for the umpteenth time since we started out, but other than that, no one responds to her latest quip.

Steve rejoins traffic and heads down the road again.

We are all of us squeezed into the van, the four Birchfields and the four Cranes. Marjorie sits on Donna's lap and Digger on mine. It was a year or more ago when Digger started saying he was too big to sit on my lap anymore. I'm glad to have an excuse for him to sit here again. He has absently thrown an arm around my neck, and I would like to keep it there forever.

We wind through the outlying streets of Black Mountain, passing every kind of dwelling imaginable—from single-wide trailers to modest homes to larger Victorian-style dwellings. A number of the latter have been turned into inns or bed and breakfasts. We drive by Town Hall and the combination police and fire station, then on out toward a recreational area called Lake Tomahawk.

"We've got everything here you could want," Donna assures us. And as she begins to list the attractions of the park—swimming, boating, tennis, fishing, picnicking, golf—I turn slightly in anticipation of another comment from Linda. But I see that she is slouched down in her seat with her eyes closed. I can only imagine what is going on in that thorny head of hers. Perhaps it's best I don't know. The not-knowing leaves me with a modicum of hope.

"Well, we'll have to come out here for a picnic," Meg says. She's trying very hard to sound cheerful. I admire her for that.

Steve makes a gravel-crunching U-turn in the road and heads south toward the center of town. The heart of Black Mountain is a small patchwork of intersecting streets with only sporadic traffic. The main thoroughfare, State Street, turns into Route 70 just beyond the west edge of town. If you stay on Route 70 for twenty minutes, Steve says, you end up in Asheville.

A couple of cross streets bisect State Street and slope downward toward Sutton Avenue, which parallels the railroad tracks and, in some spots, the Swannanona River. This place is quintessential America. Small store-front shops of red brick, plate glass, and awnings. A general store, a furniture store, a couple of cafes, a bakery. A barbershop and a beauty parlor are right next door to each other. The street that meets Sutton at the train depot—that's Cherry Street. The next street over is Broadway. Up this way are antique shops and second-hand bookstores, the post office, a drug store, a shoe store. At least that's what I take in as we drive through town.

Digger drops his head to my shoulder and squeezes my neck. He would rather be outside playing. I don't want to be anywhere other than right here with my son on my lap.

"Okay, folks," Steve announces, "let's go on over to the car lot. See where you'll be working come Monday, Shel."

My mood suddenly drops by a dozen degrees. Not that it was very high to begin with.

"That'd be great, Steve," I manage to say. I glance at Meg in the front passenger seat. She doesn't look at me. But then, she hasn't really looked at me for a couple of months now.

We drive back down Broadway and bounce over the railroad tracks. Digger, who's been shifted by the bump, inches back up in my lap. He raises his head and looks around.

In another moment, Steve pulls off onto a side road that leads eventually to the seemingly massive encampment known as Birchfield Chevrolet. We ease into a lot decked out with pennant streamers and filled with rows of cars glinting in the mid-afternoon sun. In every windshield is a sign that begins with the word "Only" and ends with an exclamation point, with a number in between that is greater than any number I have ever once seen in my bank account.

"This is the lot for new cars," Steve says. "This is where I work and where we do most of our business. Now on the other side of the building"—he points to the glassy, flat-roofed building that is obviously Birchfield's main office—"is the used car lot. That's where you'll be, Shel."

We wade through the sea of multi-colored 1968 models and head over to the older vehicles around the back. Steve parks in an empty slot but leaves the engine idling and the air on. This lot is just as big as the new car lot, but the cars on this side of the office are a little less shiny, less expensive, less inviting. Here they are, endless rows of them, my new congregation, and my four-wheeled metal-and-chrome sheep. These cars will be my responsibility now, my life's work.

"That's the used lot's office," Steve says. He points again, this time to a pale yellow trailer propped up on a cinder block foundation. "You'll share that space with Ike Kerlee, the other used car salesman. Ike's been with me fifteen years. Nice guy. He'll be able to answer any questions you have."

I should say something. I know I should. But I can't think of a single response.

Undeterred, Steve goes on, "I've got twenty employees here, counting the salesmen, the service and parts managers, the mechanics, a couple of secretaries, and a bookkeeper. We do a good business, with people coming from everywhere to buy our cars, some coming from as far away as South Carolina, Tennessee, even Georgia. Now we like to have a bit of fun around here too, Shel. Every month we tally up the sales and see who's brought in the most in the way of profits. Top salesman for that month gets a free pass for two at one of the restaurants here in town."

Behind me, I hear Linda say quietly, "Lucky you, Dad."

Yeah. Lucky me.

"Now, the first thing we're going to do Monday morning is fix you up with a couple of Chevys," Steve says. "One for you, Shel, and one for Meg.

The first one you can consider a fringe benefit of the job. That one'll come off the used lot. The second one'll be new, but it'll come at a good price. We'll take the payments right out of your paycheck, Shel. Come Monday, you can get rid of that junk heap you've been driving around ever since I've known you."

I am slightly taken aback. "The Pontiac's only nine years old, and it still runs well, Steve."

"Yeah, well, you can't work for Birchfield Chevrolet and still be driving a Pontiac. See what I mean?"

I acquiesce and nod my head. My life is in Steve Birchfield's hands.

"We'll get you something nice. You'd like that, wouldn't you, Sis?"

He turns and looks at Meg, who smiles. "Sure, Steve. A new car would be nice. Anything new would be nice."

I'm stung by the slap of her words. I have seldom been able to give her anything new.

Steve turns as far around as he can in his seat now, shining his benevolent smile upon us. "So," he says cheerfully, "what do you say we go get some ice cream? Right up on Cherry Street is the best ice cream parlor in the whole of the Blue Ridge Mountains."

Well, I guess this means I have a lot to be thankful for, doesn't it? An office in a yellow trailer, a Chevy I don't need, and the best ice cream in this entire area right at my disposal. What more could a man want?

7

Linda
Saturday, July 13, 1968

POP'S ICE CREAM Parlor. Holy Toledo, just look at this place. Antique junk everywhere and radio and movie stuff from when my *parents* were kids. Or maybe even longer ago than that. How tacky can you get? I mean, just check out the posters. "Gone With the Wind" and "It's A Wonderful Life" and "Little Rascals" and "The Wizard of Oz." This place is one totally uncool sentimental journey with not a single thing from the sixties. I ought to sneak one of my Grateful Dead posters in here and tack it up on the wall beside Scarlett O'Hara—yeah, or maybe one of Jimi Hendrix burning his guitar on stage while he's high as a kite. That ought to knock some hillbilly socks off.

Everyone's standing at the counter trying to decide what they want and saying there's just too much to choose from. You've got to be kidding me. You'd think we were at Howard Johnson's trying to choose from twenty-eight flavors, instead of at this no-place hole-in-the-wall that has three flavors besides vanilla. I mean, look at everyone. All excited because they have mint chocolate chip in the freezer. Like that's something to throw a party about.

There's a really fat lady behind the counter scooping up a chocolate cone for Digger. Every time she takes a stab at the ice cream her arm wiggles back and forth like Jell-o. I think she must have been eating a whole lot of her own ice cream on the sly to get that fat.

Uncle Steve decides to introduce her to Mom and Dad. He tells the lady we just moved to town, and the lady hoots and hollers like it's the best thing to happen to her in a long time. "Well, welcome!" she says. "Glad to meetcha. I'm Gloria Reynolds."

She holds out a hand to shake, and it must have been sticky because afterward Mom takes a napkin and tries to wipe her palm without anyone noticing.

"Hope y'all will be real happy here in Black Mountain," Gloria Reynolds says.

"I'm sure we will," Dad says while he flashes her this really fake smile. The big liar, at it again. Can't even make small talk without lying through his teeth.

"I'm happy!" Digger yells, and everyone laughs at him because he's got ice cream all over his face and dripping from his chin. Stupid kid.

Finally, everyone except me decides what they want, and Gloria's arm is flapping like a flag in a hurricane because she's working so hard filling the orders. Finally she looks at me and says, "So what can I get you?"

A one-way ticket out of here, I want to say, but instead, I tell her to give me a plain vanilla. While she's scooping it up she glances at me and says, "And what's your name, pretty miss?"

The hair on the back of my neck bristles. This lady's giving me the creeps. I make sure I'm not smiling when I tell her my name.

"Well, Linda," she says, waving the ice cream scoop and throwing vanilla raindrops all over the counter. "Would you by any chance be looking for a job? I could use some part-time help around here."

Holy cow, lady, do I look like I'm looking for a job? I thought this was an ice cream parlor, not an employment agency. I shrug. "I don't know," I say. "Maybe."

"You could work full-time till school starts. After that, you can work after school and weekends."

"Weekends?"

"Saturday nights, mostly. We're closed on Sundays."

"Saturday nights, huh? Well, I don't know. It might interfere with my dating life."

"I can offer ten cents over minimum wage."

"Yeah? Wow, I'd be rich."

"Well, you think about it and let me know."

She hands me the ice cream cone with a smile. I take it and mumble thanks. I'm about to join everyone else at one of the tables when Digger comes back up to the counter. "What do you want now?" I ask him because I can see he's finished his cone.

"I just want to ask this lady a question," he says, pointing with his thumb toward Gloria Reynolds.

She's wiping her hands on her apron, but she stops and looks at Digger. "Ask away, little man," she says.

"I'm just wondering," Digger says. "Do you happen to know where Mac lives?"

Gloria's face scrunches up like she's tasting something sour. "Who's Mac?" she says.

Digger shrugs. "Just some kid I met. His real name's Malcolm and he lives around here somewhere."

"Where'd you see him?"

"Up at my house."

"What'd he look like?"

"I don't know. Like a regular kid, I guess."

I've been licking my ice cream cone, but I stop long enough to say, "There hasn't been anyone at the house besides us and the cousins."

"Well, Mac was there too," Digger says.

"He was not," I say. "You're making that up."

"Am not."

"Yes, you are."

Next thing I know, Gloria Reynolds is hollering across the room at my cousins, "Hey Jeff, Marjorie! You two know a boy by the name of Mac?"

They shake their heads and shrug. They don't say anything because they're too busy eating their cones.

Gloria looks at Digger and gives him that I'll-play-along-with-you kind of smile that grown-ups are always giving kids. "You'll see Mac once school starts, I bet," she says.

"But that's a long time from now," Digger says. "I was hoping he could come over and play sometime."

"Well, now he knows you're here, he'll show up again. Don't you worry. And if a boy named Mac ever comes in for ice cream, I'll tell him you're looking for him."

"Thanks, lady."

"Now what's your name again?"

"Digger Crane."

"All right, Digger. Listen, you like Wrigley's spearmint gum?"

"You bet!"

"Here." She picks up a pack from the display and hands it to him. "It's on the house. Sort of a welcome gift. But you got to share it with Mac."

"Thanks, lady! I will!"

I roll my eyes and wander off to pretend like I'm looking at the movie posters. The thing is, though, I just don't feel like sitting with my cousins the Clampetts and the bunch of circus freaks who are supposed to be my own family. I mean, can my life get any worse? Dad's a two-timing hypocrite, Mom's a gutless pushover who won't divorce him, and now my kid brother has an imaginary friend named Mac. Criminy. If somebody put a bullet through my brain right now, I'd thank him before I died.

8

Meg
Sunday, July 14, 1968

SHELDON INSISTED WE come to church this morning, though he didn't bother trying to extend his authority as far as Linda. He knew it would do little good—might even make matters worse—to force her to come with us. She was still in bed, asleep, when we left for Valley View Baptist Church. Steve and Donna had invited us to the Presbyterian Church with them, but Sheldon declined. A lifelong Baptist, he has never been a fan of Calvin and predestination.

Valley View is a quaint little church, white clapboard built upon a foundation of fieldstone. As the name implies, it's cradled in a valley. The side windows are open to let in the air while the large window over the altar is a stained glass recreation of the resurrection of Christ. He stands there in a white robe showing us his upturned palms, his nail-scarred hands.

A sign outside says the congregation was established in 1893. Most of the congregants here look as though they are from among that original group. Oh, I know, it's unkind and sarcastic to say that, even to myself, and yet the pews are swimming in gray hair. We are drowning in age. It was beginning to be like this in Abington too. The church everywhere is dying out. In fact, judging from the size of the cemetery rolling through the surrounding fields, I'd say a far greater number of congregants are out there than in here.

As the preacher climbs up to the pulpit, I glance sideways at Sheldon. His skin is ashen, his mouth drawn down. A muscle in his jaw twitches. I wonder how he feels, being down here rather than up there. Humiliated? Possibly. Like a failure? Probably. In my opinion, he had no business being a pastor in the first place. He certainly wasn't one when I married him.

When I married him he was a junior executive at a plastics plant. He was on the bottom rung of the corporate ladder, but he was poised to work his way up. We were already comfortable and things could only get better … but then he came home from work one day and told me he'd gotten the call.

"What call?" I asked.

"The call to serve God," he said.

I didn't even know what that meant, but next thing I knew, I was a cashier at Woolworth's, working to put Sheldon through seminary, and when he was done with that, I was a pastor's wife, ready or not. Like it or not. Cut out for it or not.

Through it all, I loved him. And I tried to be the best pastor's wife possible, in spite of the frailty of my own faith.

Digger sits between Sheldon and me, bored, fidgeting, swinging his feet back and forth beneath the pew. I put a hand on his knee to still the double pendulum he has made of his legs. He looks up at me and smiles his irresistible smile. I can still count on him to love me. For now, at least.

But someday he'll grow up, like Carl, and that will change his devotion to me. Oh, he may still love me, as Carl does, but he won't need me anymore. If only I could stop time and keep Digger this age forever, at least then I'd have one person I could count on.

Linda, it seems, is completely lost to me. How did that happen? If I shut my eyes, I can still experience it perfectly: she as a very small child, sitting in my lap, her head resting gently against my shoulder as I read to her at bedtime. I kiss the wispy curls on the crown of her head and tell her I love her. "I love you too, Mommy," she says. We were bonded then, heart and soul. And now?

No matter what I say to her now, it's the wrong thing. If I ask a question, she responds with sarcasm. If I make a suggestion, she responds with rage. If I say, "I love you," she rolls her eyes.

Where did my little girl go? Does any part of her exist anymore? If so, how can I find her?

Yesterday, our tour of the town ended at Steve and Donna's house. Their new house. That incredible dwelling they built for themselves. Afterward, when we got home, Linda followed me into the kitchen where I'd gone to get a glass of milk for Digger. She didn't even have to speak. Her eyes said it all: *See what you got for marrying Daddy? If you'd married someone else you could be living in a palace like Aunt Donna.*

I poured the milk and put the bottle back in the fridge. "What's the matter, Linda?" I finally asked.

She crossed her arms and scowled at me. How does one slim body hold so much anger? "You should have divorced Daddy," she said. "Then we could have stayed in Abington instead of coming down here and living in this shack. We'd all be better off, if you'd just left him."

"You know," I said, trying to sound calm, "most kids don't want their parents to get divorced."

"Yeah?" Her eyes narrowed the way they do so often now. "Well, I'm not most kids."

"Listen, Linda, I know you're unhappy about the move, but I wish you'd get that chip off your shoulder and try to make the best of things. Anyway, I know you better than you think. You've always loved Daddy, and you love him now, whether you're willing to admit it or not."

We stared at each other for a long moment, neither willing to look away. I waited. Finally, she said, "Sure, I love him. But right now, I don't like him very much."

With that, she turned and went upstairs to her room.

And with that, too, I understood my own self a little better. I still love Sheldon, but I can't say I like him very much anymore. The pain of betrayal is just too deep. Do I want to spend the rest of my life hurting like this? And do I want to spend the rest of my life with the man who caused the pain?

I can still divorce Sheldon and start a new life. It's not too late. I do have biblical grounds, after all. Infidelity. I could leave Sheldon and not even God could blame me.

A jarring chord from the organ draws me back to the service. I reach for the hymnal, and we all stand to sing. I glance again at Sheldon, this stranger beside me. He stands there with a hymnal open in one palm, but his lips don't move in song. He used to love to sing the old hymns. Now he has no voice.

A person grows lonely when her loved ones change into people she doesn't even recognize. And, for crying out loud, if the love of your own family isn't certain, what are you supposed to lean on?

9

Digger
Monday, July 15, 1968

"HEY, MAC! WHERE ya been?"

I jump off the big rock and run across the yard when I see Mac come around the side of the house.

He shrugs and says, "Around. Where've *you* been?"

"Right here, mostly."

"Oh."

"Whatcha been doing? You got black stuff all over you."

"Me and Austin been down in the town poking around at the damage from the fire."

"What fire?"

His eyes bug out. He looks at me like he's looking at a ghost. "Don'tcha know about the fire?"

I shake my head.

"Jumpin' Jiminy, Digger! The whole town just about burnt down. Well, most everything down on Sutton Street, anyway."

"It did?"

"Yup. Yesterday. Didn't you see the smoke or hear everybody shouting? Just about everyone was down there with buckets trying to put out the flames."

I shake my head again.

"Where *were* you yesterday?"

"I was here.' Cept for in the morning, when we were at church."

"Well, you must be blind or deaf or maybe even dead because everybody in town knows there was a fire."

He starts looking mad. I can't help it if I didn't know about any fire. I'm thinking he might be lying.

"How'd it happen?" I ask.

"Sparks from the train, they think. Nearly burnt the whole street before they finally got it put out."

"Oh yeah?"

"Yeah. And you didn't know about it?"

Now I'm sure he's mad at me, and I'm mad at him because one of us is lying and it ain't me. "No," I say again, "I'm telling you, I don't know anything about any fire."

His hands are the color of charcoal. He stuffs them in the pockets of his overalls. "Well, you missed it, then."

"Yeah, I guess I did."

"I can show you the burned down street if you want."

"You want to walk from here to town?"

"Ain't that far. I do it all the time. Austin says it's only a couple of miles."

"Who's Austin?"

"He's my brother. And he ought to know."

I stick my hands in my own pockets and feel the pack of gum the lady at the ice cream store gave me. I haven't even opened it. I tug it out now and figure I might as well offer Mac a piece.

I show him the pack. "Want some?"

"What is it?"

"Wrigley's chewing gum. Spearmint."

"Sure," he says.

I open the pack and pull out a stick. "Here."

He reaches out for it. I let go of the gum, and it falls to the ground. "Sorry," I say. He's saying it's all right while I'm already bending down to pick it up.

"Here you go."

Mac's holding out his hand and I give him the gum, but it just ends up falling to the ground again. Mac and I look at each other.

"What's the matter with you?" I ask. "Can't you hold on to it?"

Now he really looks mad. "This some kind of magic trick or something?"

"No, it isn't. Honest. I'm trying to give you the piece of gum."

"Well, it isn't funny."

"I'm not trying to be funny. I'm just trying to give you the piece of gum. Hey—"

But Mac has already turned and stomped away. I run to catch up with him. I want to go to town; I do, to see whether he's telling the truth about Sutton Street getting burned down. But by the time I get around the corner of the house, Mac is gone.

I'm not sure Mac and me are going to be very good friends, the way things are going.

10

Linda
Monday, July 15, 1968

AT LEAST THIS house is in a clearing, so I can catch some rays. Too bad the batteries in my radio gave out, or I could lie here and listen to some rock. What I wouldn't give for an hour of the Grateful Dead, Pink Floyd, Jimi Hendrix. I'd even listen to Sonny and Cher right now, if it'd make me forget where I am. But then again, the radio stations around here probably don't play anything but hillbilly music, so that's not going to do me any good.

About the only thing that's the same down here as back home is the sun. It feels nice and warm on my oiled skin. I lie here with my eyes shut, pretending I'm not here, but there. Back home with my friends. With Brian. What I wouldn't give to have had a chance with Brian.

Yeah, so dream on. He's probably hooked up with Carla Herbicek by now. She always did have a thing for him, and now her toughest competition's been exiled to Possum Holler, and she's probably already wearing his class ring on a chain around her neck. I hate my life.

So today's Dad's first day at the car lot, and while I'd rather be a salesman's daughter than a pastor's daughter, the fact is I'm nothing but the daughter of a hypocrite. I hope he hates the new job. It would serve him right.

After lunch, Aunt Donna came by to take Mom shopping at the A&P. "Want to come, Linda?" she asked. She was all cheerful, like she's offering to take me somewhere exciting. Shopping at the A&P? Like, what, I'm supposed to want to go see what's new in frozens or something?

"No, thanks, Aunt Donna," I said. "I think I'll stay here and work on my tan."

Digger wanted to go though. He said he wanted to see Sutton Avenue all burned down. Mom and Aunt Donna looked at each other like Digger's crazy or something, and Aunt Donna said, "There wasn't a fire downtown, Digger." And Mom added, "Where'd you hear that?" And Digger said Mac told him about it this morning. And Mom said, "Who's Mac?" because she didn't hear Digger talking to Gloria Reynolds about him, so she doesn't know yet about Digger's imaginary friend. So Digger said, "He's a kid who lives around here," and even though Mom looked a little skeptical she said, "Well, he was just pulling your leg," and Digger said, "Yeah, I thought so." The thing is, though, I'm beginning to wonder whether Digger isn't maybe a little bit crazy for real, what with making up this Mac guy and talking about him like he's really there.

Uncle Steve's supposed to give Dad a couple of Chevys. Criminy! Dad has to pay for one, but Uncle Steve's giving him the other one, a used car, just giving it to him to drive around because he says it's advertising for Birchfield Chevrolet. Uncle Steve must be making a heap of money off that dump of a car lot to be able to afford to give Dad a car. And their house—sheesh. Big as a mansion and everything brand new. They had the place built—designed it themselves, for crying out loud. I could tell Mom was jealous when we walked in the front door on Saturday after that little tour of the town. I know exactly what she was thinking: I could have lived in a nice place like this if I hadn't married a loser. Sad thing is, she's right. We'll never live in a place like that. Never. At least Mom won't. I will, though. I'm not marrying a loser. No way.

So Dad said I can have the old station wagon to drive because even though he has to drive a Chevy it's all right if I drive a Pontiac. So whoop-de-do. The ugliest car on God's green earth, and I have to be seen behind the wheel. Not that it matters around here. Who cares who sees me? It'll get me to work anyway, when I start working at the ice cream parlor. Yeah, so I took the job. Called old Gloria this morning and told her I'd do it. She started hooting and hollering again like she'd just won the sweepstakes from Publishers Clearing House. Like hiring me was the best thing that ever happened to her. She said she's glad to have the help, but I should take a week to "get settled" and then start working next Saturday night. I'm not exactly thrilled about the job, but I might as well earn some money. Maybe then, at the end of the year, I can buy that one-way ticket out of here.

I should have told Mom to bring back some soft drinks. I'm working up a thirst here and—oh great, the sun's gone behind a cloud.

I open my eyes to see how big the cloud is when I see that the shadow on my face isn't from a cloud but from some guy who's standing right at the edge of the blanket I'm lying on. He's just standing there like he's frozen, and he's got this shocked look on his face like he's just stumbled across a dead body in the road or something. I scream, and he jumps about a foot. When I'm done ripping my throat up, and he's made no move to attack me, I feel brave enough to yell at him, "Who are you and what do you want?"

By now, he's got his eyes scrunched up into little tight slits, and his face is burning red, and he's kind of hopping from one foot to the other.

"What do you want?" I scream again.

"I don't want anything! Honest!"

"Well, who are you and why are you here?"

He's still got his eyes closed when he says, "Why are you lying out here in your undergarments?"

"My undergarments?" I sit up. I look at the guy with his eyes screwed up, two little prunes in the middle of his face like he wants to look at me but he's afraid to look at me all at the same time. Is he for real? "Look," I say, "first of all, what kind of a word is undergarments? I mean, that went out with the last century, didn't it? And second of all, don't you know a bathing suit when you see one?"

"Well," he blurts out, "that's not like any bathing suit I've ever seen!"

"You've never seen a bikini before?"

"No, ma'am! Never!"

"Figures," I say, "living like you do out here in the backwoods. Women probably swim in bloomers around here. Heck, probably swim fully dressed, for all I know. You can open your eyes now. I've got the blanket wrapped around me. And don't call me ma'am like you think I'm an old lady or something."

He opens one eye, sees I'm telling the truth about the blanket, opens the other eye. What an idiot.

He's not bad looking, though. In fact, he's really cute. He's about my age or a year or two older. Tall, blond and—from what I can tell with all those clothes he's wearing—he's built pretty well. Intense blue eyes, now that I can see them. The bluest eyes I've ever seen. He's wearing a white button-up shirt and overalls. Huge clodhopper boots on his feet, and an old cloth cap on his head. I can't imagine why he's dressed like that in this heat.

"So what do you want?" I ask again, more quietly this time.

"Nothing. Like I said."

"Well, what are you doing here, then?"

He looks at me like he can't understand what I'm saying. Then he says, "I live here."

"Here?"

"Yes."

"In this house?" I point to our house.

"Yeah," he says.

"Oh sure," I say. "And I'm Lady Bird Johnson."

"Who?"

This is getting weirder by the minute. "You know. Lady Bird Johnson? The First Lady?"

He looks confused. I go on. "The wife of the president? Or maybe the news hasn't reached this backwater yet. Of course, I forgot. Johnson's only been in office five years. Not enough time for the news to reach these hills."

He takes a step backward, like any minute he's going to haul tail out of here.

"So what's your name?" I ask. I've decided I don't want him to leave quite yet. This may be my only chance to set my eyes on a good-looking guy for the next year.

"Austin," he says slowly like he doesn't really want to tell me. "Austin Buchanan."

"Well, Austin Buchanan, I'm Linda Crane."

He nods and tips his cap. Tips his cap! "Glad to meet you," he says, though he doesn't sound glad at all, he just sounds kind of scared.

"Sure. Now, listen, this is private property, so why don't you tell me what you want? You a Fuller Brush man or something?"

"A what?"

"You selling brushes?"

"No." He holds up his palms. "I'm not selling anything. I just got off work, and I'm coming home. I'm a little—um, surprised to see you here."

"Yeah, well, I'm *more* than a little surprised to see *you* here."

"But I told you, I live here."

I take a deep breath. "Listen, Austin, you seem like a nice guy and all, but one of us is taking one heck of a wild trip, and unfortunately it isn't me."

"A wild trip?"

"Yeah. You know, acid? Speed? But then again, I guess the only stuff you do around here is—what was it Jeff said you guys smoked? Corn silk? Cow patties?"

"I don't know what you're talking about, but I haven't been smoking anything except regular tobacco. All I know is, I live here, and I've just come home to eat my dinner. Now you probably better put some clothes on and clear on out of here before my father sees you and starts shooting."

I can't help laughing at that. "Oh yeah, right. You mountain boys are crazier than I thought. Plus, I'm getting darn hot under this blanket trying to protect your virgin eyes. So you listen to me, Austin Buchanan. I'm going to shut my eyes and count to three, and when I open them, you'd better be gone."

With that, I open the blanket and lay face down, my forehead on my arms. "One!" I hear shuffling, the sound of footsteps. "Two!" A scurrying, then everything's quiet. "Three!"

When I roll back over, he's gone. I'm a little relieved and a little disappointed both. If I weren't here completely alone—if Mom or Dad were in the house—I might have invited him to hang out for a while, strange as he was. Strange, but good looking. No sir, they don't come much better looking than that, even in Pennsylvania.

11

Meg
Tuesday, July 16, 1968

I STAND AT the counter packing a lunch for Sheldon while he sits at the kitchen table, drinking his morning coffee. We used to drink our morning coffee together. We'd talk about the children, talk about the day ahead. He used to put his hand on mine on the tabletop, rub my knuckles gently with his thumb.

Not anymore.

As I work I feel his eyes on my back, and I don't like it. This being alone together in the same room is awkward. Imagine, twenty years of marriage, and now we are strangers. I simply can't get over that.

More and more I think about leaving him. Striking out on my own. Starting a new life. What keeps me here? Fear, I think, plain and simple. Fear of being on my own when I've never been on my own. Can I muster up the courage to leave?

As though he senses my thoughts, I hear Sheldon sigh. Instead of looking at him, I look out the window.

"Meg," he says.

My jaw tightens. "Yes?"

He hesitates a moment, then says, "I just want you to know I miss you. I miss being married to you."

I don't respond. His words have fanned that ever-burning flame of anger that hangs in my chest. I want to strike out, but I do nothing, say nothing. I don't even turn from the window.

Another sigh, like a wave of despair rolling over the room. "Listen, Meg," he says quietly, "I'm not just talking about making love to you, though heaven knows I miss that. But I'm talking about everything. Everything. I simply miss being with you, talking with you, holding your hand. You don't have to say or do anything right now. I just want you to know I still have hope that someday we can get back to where we were."

I finally whirl toward him. "Back to where we were? How can we, Sheldon? How can we ever go back?"

"I think we can, if you'll just forgive me."

My eyes grow wide. "Just forgive you? Just like that, as though nothing ever happened?" I shake my head hard. "How can I ever forgive you?"

He laces his fingers together on the table and squeezes until his knuckles grow white. "I know you're angry, Meg, and I understand—"

"Oh, I'm way beyond angry, Sheldon, and I don't think you understand at all."

The room falls silent. Sheldon's eyes hold more hurt than I have ever seen before. Good. Let him hurt, just as I do.

He takes a deep breath. "Will we go the rest of our lives like this, then? Because this isn't really a marriage, you know."

"No, this isn't a marriage, but I'm not the one who destroyed what we had."

"I know, Meg. I know. I take full blame. And now I'm asking you again to forgive me. In our life together, you've always forgiven me before, for so many things."

"In our life together, you were never unfaithful before. This isn't forgetting to take out the trash or running over my flower garden with the lawn mower, Sheldon."

"No. No," he agrees. "It isn't. But listen, I'm willing to give you as much time as you need."

"Time?" I echo. "Will time change anything?"

"I can only pray so," he says.

For a moment, I almost feel sorry for him. For a moment, I almost want to give in and tell him I forgive him, tell him I want to try. But the hurt is too deep and the anger too overwhelming, and the strange thing, is I know they exist in proportion to how much I love him.

I wish I didn't love him anymore. That would make everything so much easier.

Sheldon rises and carries his empty coffee cup to the sink. Right beside me now, he lifts a hand to my shoulder, and I flinch. He pulls back.

"Meg," he says, "I just don't see how we can live the rest of our lives like this. My fear now is that you will leave me."

I fix my gaze out the window. I say nothing.

12

Sheldon
Tuesday, July 16, 1968

TWELVE O'CLOCK NOON, which means I can finally reach for the brown paper sack that holds my lunch. I lift it out of the bottom desk drawer and spread out the contents on my desk: a bologna sandwich, an apple, a bag of potato chips. I lift one corner of the bread to find a dollop of mayonnaise. Meg knows that if I must eat bologna, I prefer mustard.

But of course, it's part of my punishment. A petty part, but obvious nonetheless. Because of course, she's punishing me. I don't blame her. When one does wrong, one can expect to be chastened. Maybe when she's satisfied that I've been punished enough, she'll come back to me. I'm willing to wait and to take whatever she dishes out. Maybe when she comes back, she'll be empty of her anger, and I'll be empty of my shame.

I have to wonder, though, whether she'll end up leaving. I fear it's a real possibility. Meg has always seen herself as weak and compliant, but that isn't true. Heaven knows, she has always weathered well whatever I brought her way. Another wife might have complained when her husband left the security of the business world for the ministry, but Meg simply turned the corner with me and kept on walking. Never enough money, never a home of our own, the pressures of being a pastor's wife. She and the kids always living under the watchful eye of the congregation—they were somehow expected to be saints in the midst of sinners, as was I. Meg took it all with her chin up and with a serenity that seemed never to waver, even when I knew she wished our life was different. That to me takes strength of character. I took it for granted there was nothing I could do to knock her off course.

Maybe that's the thing. Maybe I started taking her for granted.

I get up and pour another cup of coffee from the pot here in the trailer, sit back down, bite into the sandwich.

Maybe I should call Meg and see how she and the kids are doing, just as I used to call home from the church. Maybe I should get back to some of those familiar routines, however small. I look at the phone on my desk, but before I can lift the handset, the door flies open and Ike Kerlee enters, carrying a McDonald's bag in one hand and a large drink in the other. He tosses the bag on his desk, removes his jacket and sits. "Feeding time," he says. He pulls three cheeseburgers and large fries from the bag and digs in.

He's a large fellow, with wild red hair and a full round face. The spidery veins on his nose tell me he's had a few too many drinks in his time. I don't know yet whether there's an open bottle in one of the drawers of his desk, but if there is I plan to turn a blind eye. It's the chain-smoking that bothers me, the ever-present cloud of nicotine that drives me out of the trailer gulping for air.

One cheek bulging with food, Ike says, "So how goes it, Shel?"

I nod slightly, work to swallow the bologna that suddenly wants to lodge in my throat. Once it goes down, I manage to say, "Fine, Ike. Everything's fine."

"Good deal, Shel." His first cheeseburger disappears, and he picks up the second. "You'll get your stride," he assures me. "Won't be long before you make your first sale."

"Yeah," I say. "That'll be good, won't it?" We've been working together a day and a half, and I'm trying to like him. Really, I am. But he doesn't make it easy. In spite of his attempts at friendliness, I find him loud, crass, and distasteful. On top of that, I simply don't trust him. He is everything I don't want to be.

I glance at the phone. I should have called Meg when Ike first left for McDonald's. Now it's too late. She's probably eating lunch with the kids anyway, and I wouldn't want to interrupt. Even if she's not eating, well … let's face it. I doubt she's waiting for me to call. At this point, I'm hardly a person she's eager to talk to.

Across the trailer, Ike takes a large gulp of his drink and belches loudly. I am ready to chalk up one more point against him when I realize—there is someone I don't want to be and that person isn't Ike Kerlee. I myself am the person I don't want to be.

Ike swings his feet up on the desk and lights a cigarette. I leave the rest of my lunch untouched and head outside. The air is hot and humid and oppressive. There is nowhere for me to go to get away from the person I've become.

13

Meg
Wednesday, July 17, 1968

WHAT'S THE WORLD coming to? Reverend King was shot in April, Bobby Kennedy last month. College kids are too busy protesting the war to go to class. Negroes are too busy setting cities on fire to move ahead peaceably with civil rights work. Hippies are overdosing on Kool-Aid cocktails laced with LSD. And now they tell us on the news tonight another Miami-bound plane has been hijacked to Cuba. You can't even take a flight these days without wondering whether you'll end up in Havana.

I don't like to watch the news. There's nothing good happening anywhere. Of course, the very worst is when they tally up the dead in Vietnam. It's a number I don't want to hear and don't want to think about. Why can't we just pull out of there? This is not our battle to fight. After too many years of needless death, we're no closer to resolving anything than when we first arrived. They say we're supposed to be encouraged by the Paris Peace Talks, but all of that seems meaningless. Just more empty rhetoric.

"Shall we just turn it off?" Sheldon asks.

"Yes, I've heard enough," I say.

Linda goes to the TV and starts flipping channels. "I want to see what else is on."

It's late. We should go to bed. Digger has already been asleep for hours. But Linda settles on a show and returns to the couch. Sheldon settles back in his reading chair here in the living room. He is reading—again—the sermons of Charles Spurgeon. He can't seem to leave his old life behind.

Sheldon has been a used car salesman for three days now. He comes home looking tired and smelling of cigarette smoke. He says Ike Kerlee is a chain smoker, using the butt of a dying cigarette to light up the next one. Sheldon is the only person at the dealership who isn't fortified for the job with large amounts of nicotine.

But he doesn't complain. Not about the cigarettes and not about the job. He really hasn't said much at all. Apparently, he is just going to do what he has to do to keep the family going.

Linda yawns and stretches, her long slender body taking up the length of the couch. She is in her baby-doll pajamas and her flimsy robe that reveal every inch of her long brown limbs. Her blonde hair is loosely rolled in pink sponge curlers, and her naked, pampered feet are capped with crimson toenail polish. She works very hard at sculpting herself into a fleshy work of art. She believes it is her ticket to paradise. Don't all the pretty girls? It will be years before Linda realizes you can ride the beauty train to the end of the line and still not end up in paradise.

I'm surprised she has deigned to be in the same room with her father and me—we of the older, untrustworthy, square generation. We, who understand nothing about youth, as though we were never young ourselves. But then, she isn't in this room to be with us, she is here to watch the television, one of the few items we hauled down with us from Pennsylvania. The reception here is awful—Sheldon and Steve spent Sunday afternoon installing an antenna on the roof, but still the TV's rabbit ears must be rotated, twisted, and turned before something resembling a black-and-white world appears on the screen.

I don't know what Linda's watching. Something with a laugh track, though Linda isn't laughing. I don't suppose you could get her to laugh now if her life depended on it. She is just too angry, and she wants her father and me to know it. Laughter would flaw her perfectly sculpted sullenness. Heaven forbid!

Saturday she'll begin working at the ice cream parlor, thank goodness. She'll start meeting people, which will be good for her. And it will get her out of the house, which will be good for me. There was a time when I liked nothing better than to be with her. And then time passed, and here we are, the three of us—Sheldon, Linda, me—a whole different cast from the people who started this show, as though our understudies stepped in and found themselves unequal to the task.

I shut my eyes, lean my head against the back of the chair, listen to the droning of the television. I feel myself sink, my breathing grows slow and even. I am not asleep, yet not quite awake. I hear the laugh track as well as the turning of the pages as Sheldon reads. I know that I should go to bed, but I cannot seem to rouse myself until I'm aware that Linda has stood and crossed the room to turn off the TV. The sudden quiet awakens me. I open my eyes to see Linda bending down to pick up the TV guide that she has knocked off the top of the set.

I really must get myself upstairs. Wondering what time it is, I haul myself up out of the chair and turn to say goodnight to Sheldon, but before I can say a word, my breath is stolen by the sight of two people standing in the archway between the living room and kitchen. Gasping, I feel my mind cartwheeling, tumbling, trying frantically to make sense of them. I want to tell myself I'm dreaming, but I know I'm not. Two strangers are in our house, and I didn't hear them come in, didn't hear a door open or footsteps across the kitchen floor. Yet there they are. Linda and Sheldon see them too. Sheldon, the only one left seated, slowly rises, and for several silent seconds we square off, the three of us in the living room and the two of them in the hall, like wax figures in a house of horrors. They—a woman and a teenaged boy—seem as puzzled and as frightened as we are, as though we are the ones who should not be here.

Finally, Linda cries, "Austin! What are you doing in our house?"

"Your house?" the woman begins, but Austin interrupts her by hollering at Linda, "Don't you ever wear clothes?"

I am so confused I feel dizzy, but I hear Sheldon ask, "Linda, do you know these people?"

She turns to her father, looking helpless. "Not really, Dad. I saw Austin the other day when he wandered onto our property, but ..."

The woman takes a step forward and lifts her chin defiantly. "This is our property—"

"Careful, Mother," the boy says, putting an arm around her protectively. "They might be dangerous."

"Dangerous!" Linda cries. One hand flies up to touch her hair. "If I were going to break into your house, do you think I'd do it with sponge curlers in my hair?"

Sheldon takes a deep breath. "All right, I'm sure there's some misunderstanding here. Why don't you tell us who you are and what you're looking for."

The woman looks appalled, as though Sheldon has insulted her. She opens her mouth to say something, but in the same instant a man appears beside them, and I hear the boy cry, "Wait, Dad!" and the next thing I know the barrel of a pistol is pointed directly at Sheldon.

Linda and I both scream and drop to the floor, and I hear the sound of the gun going off, and I hear myself crying, "Sheldon, dear God, Sheldon!" and I'm trembling and crazy with fear. This man, whoever he is, is going to keep shooting until he has killed us all. In a split second I think of Digger upstairs and pray to God that somehow he survives, and I think of Carl, whom I will never see again, and I scream with my face to the floor until I realize that the room is quiet and whatever has been happening is over.

I lift my head. The strangers are gone. Linda is crawling toward me across the room, tears rolling down her cheeks. I rise to my knees, and she falls into my arms and, oh, how I've wanted to hold you, but not like this.

Not because of something like this. Together, as though we are one person, we turn to face Sheldon, afraid and trembling at the thought of what we will see. We are still kneeling on the floor, huddled in fear, gasping for air, expecting to see blood—blood everywhere and Sheldon's body slumped over the footstool.

But he is standing by the chair, unharmed. He comes to us, kneels down, puts his arms around us.

"You're all right," I whisper.

"Yes." He sounds amazed.

"You weren't hit?"

"No."

"How can that be?"

Linda pulls back from us and looks at her father, then at the now empty hall. "What just happened, Dad?"

Sheldon shakes his head slowly. "I don't know, sweetheart."

"Where'd they go?" I wonder aloud.

"I don't know that either," Sheldon replies. "But—" He frowns and slowly stands. "Let me just check something."

He walks to the reading chair—no, he walks behind it. I can't imagine what he's doing. I watch silently. He seems to be studying the painting on the wall. Then he reaches up and grabs it by the frame and eases it off the nail where it has been resting for who knows how long. There, behind the painting, is what appears to be a bullet hole, a splintered circle in the wood.

"Jeff said this place is haunted," Linda reminds us quietly.

"We don't believe in ghosts," Sheldon says.

"Maybe *you* don't, but how do you explain what just happened?"

Sheldon takes his eyes off the wall and turns his gaze squarely on us. "I don't have an explanation for this right now. But there's got to be one, and we're going to find out what it is."

14

Sheldon
Wednesday, July 17–Thursday, July 18, 1968

I HANG THE picture back on the nail and with that, the three of us look at each other and wonder what to do next. What does one do when the inexplicable happens? The thought of turning back to the business at hand—the brushing of teeth, turning off lights, going to bed—is laughable. Minutes pass. No one moves or speaks. Our eyes alone shift left and right as we continue to gaze at each other, hoping one or the other will find words to make sense of what we have just seen.

At length, Linda says, "I'm scared, Dad."

"I know," I say. Because I'm afraid too. Terrified, really.

"Maybe we should just get out of here," Meg suggests. "Just leave, you know?"

My wife and daughter have their arms wrapped around each other. I haven't seen them like that for a very long time. They are pale and wide-eyed, and yet it is a beautiful sight. "Where would we go?" I say.

"Steve and Donna's. They'll take us in for the night."

I think about that for a moment. "Let's not do anything rash." As soon as the words are out, I wonder why I've said them. Meg must feel the same because her jaw drops.

"Rash? You just got shot at by a man who suddenly appeared and just as suddenly disappeared, and you don't want to do anything rash?"

I'm trying to decide how to respond when Linda interrupts. "Dad, do you think Digger's all right?"

Digger! I rush to the stairs, taking them two at a time, and pound down the upstairs hall to his room. He sleeps soundly, his cheek pressed heavily against the pillow, his mouth open. I scoop him up in my arms. He frowns and protests mildly. "What, Daddy?"

I kiss his forehead. "It's all right, Digger. We're all going to sleep downstairs tonight."

He doesn't ask why, just leans his head against my shoulder and closes his eyes. By the time I lay him down on the couch in the living room, he's fast asleep again.

Meg covers him with a blanket, touches his cheek, looks up at me. "What now?" she asks.

I sigh heavily. "I think we should stay here."

Linda hugs herself and begins to cry. Meg goes to her and, holding our daughter tightly, looks at me angrily. "We're scared to death, Sheldon, and you want us to stay in this place? This house is haunted, and we may be in danger!"

I want to put my arms around the two of them, but I know it won't do any good. I raise my hands, pat the air. "Please, sit down. Don't be afraid."

I have to marvel at my own words. I don't know why, but I simply know that we must stay.

Meg's anger turns to incredulity, but she eases into the overstuffed chair with Linda. They look like two abandoned children who are lost in the world. Oh, how I want to protect them!

I sit too, in my reading chair, and moisten my lips with my tongue. How can I expect them to understand what I don't understand myself? Quietly, I say, "I'm a man of God, Meg. Like I said, I don't believe in ghosts."

Linda actually snorts out a small, sarcastic laugh. I know what she's thinking. I will ignore it. I reach for my Bible on the side table and open to the book of Psalms.

"So you think you're going to find an answer in there, Sheldon?" Meg asks. "You think your Bible will explain all this?"

I feel a muscle in my jaw tighten. "Well, I know I'm not going to find an answer anywhere else, Meg. It's got to fit somehow. It's got to all make sense."

Linda starts to cry again. "I don't want answers," she wails. "I just want to get out of here!"

"Honey," I say, "please believe me when I say we're going to be all right."

"But Sheldon," Meg argues, "how can you say that? How can you know?"

How, indeed? I don't know how I know, but this one thing is sure: As I carried Digger down the stairs, the fear began to dissipate. By the time I'd laid him on the couch, it had given way to an unexpected calm. I don't understand it, but it's undeniable. The sense harkens back to the day I was called to the ministry. It's the same knowing. I feel as though I am being given a second chance. Is that possible?

"Let's just try to get a little rest," I say. "In the morning, we'll figure out what we need to do."

"But how? How do we even begin to figure out something like this? I mean, is there anybody at all who will be able to explain what happened?"

I have to think about that. "We'll need to be careful whom we talk to."

"Yeah, no kidding!" Linda says. "We start telling people we got shot at by people who weren't even there they'll lock us all up in the loony bin and throw away the key!"

I nod, try to smile. I look at Meg. "I think you should talk with Donna in the morning. She's a native to this place. She might know something."

Meg, looking skeptical, shakes her head. "I think if she knew something, she'd have told us already."

"Maybe." I shrug. "But we have to start somewhere."

The room is quiet. I look around, half wondering whether someone else will suddenly appear or whether things will be quiet for the rest of the night. Still, I'm not afraid, only curious.

"What now, Sheldon?"

"Get some rest."

"What are you going to do?"

"I'm going to stay awake, read the Scriptures."

"If you're going to read, would you mind reading aloud for a little while?"

"Of course."

My heart constricts, and I must swallow the lump in my throat before I begin. I look at the Bible in my lap, at the Psalm I have opened to. "The Lord is my light and my salvation," I read, "whom shall I fear? The Lord is the strength of my life; of whom shall I be afraid ..."

Before I reach the end of the passage, Meg and Linda are dozing in each other's arms. I am still awake when the sun comes up, sitting quietly, pondering, marveling, and still strangely unafraid.

15

Linda
Thursday, July 18, 1968

MOM AND I sit down at Aunt Donna's kitchen table while she pours three cups of coffee. My nerves are so shot, I'm about ready to kill for a cigarette. I haven't had one since we got to this godforsaken place, but you can be sure I'm going to buy some today and smoke the whole pack at once because even now I'm just about to jump right out of my skin.

"What's wrong with you two?" Aunt Donna says. "You both look like death warmed over." After putting the coffee cups in front of us, she sits down and leans her arms on the table, waiting for an answer.

Mom starts to pick up the cup, but her hand is shaking so bad she gives up and puts it back in the saucer. She sighs and looks at Aunt Donna like she expects to be scolded or something. Then she tells her all about what happened last night.

When she finishes, Aunt Donna looks at her a long time. For a second, Aunt Donna's eyes roll over to me. I nod, and she looks back at Mom.

"I know it sounds crazy, Donna, but it's true." Mom tries again to lift the cup to her lips, and this time she makes it, sipping the coffee loudly.

Donna clears her throat. "I've heard of strange things happening in these mountains," she says, "but this takes the cake."

"You do believe me, though, don't you, Donna?"

"Oh, I believe you, honey. I don't want to, but yes, I believe you." She looks out the window to where Digger and Marjorie are playing with hula hoops in the yard. "Does Digger know?"

"He slept through the whole thing," I tell her.

"That's good," she says, nodding.

"Should we talk to Steve?" Mom asks.

Aunt Donna's eyes grow narrow as she thinks about that. "The first thing we need to do is talk to Vernita Ponder," she says.

"Who?" Mom asks.

"Vernita Ponder. One of the oldest residents of Black Mountain. She comes from the line of Loudermilks that can be traced back almost to the first white settlers of this valley."

"You think she'll know something?"

"If anyone does, Vernita will."

Mom puts both hands together like she's praying and touches them to her lips. "Sheldon said not to let it get around town. Do you think we can trust this Anita Ponder not to talk?"

"Vernita," Aunt Donna corrects her. "I've known her all my life, and yes, I believe we can trust her."

"So when should we talk with her?"

"How about right now?"

I picture an ancient hillbilly woman sitting on the front porch of a weather-beaten log cabin. Her face is as shriveled as a sun-dried apple, her white hair is pinned into a bun, and she clenches a corncob pipe between her toothless gums. She's wearing an old cotton dress that's more patches than anything and a pair of dirty boots without laces. She slowly rocks as she smokes the pipe, her glassy eyes staring off at the mountains that she's never once seen the other side of.

Aunt Donna hollers up the stairs to Jeff and tells him to watch after Digger and Marjorie, then she drives Mom and me into the heart of town.

"What are we doing here?" Mom asks.

"Vernita works here," Aunt Donna says as she parallel parks in front of Black Mountain Beauty Shop.

We get out, and Mom stands on the sidewalk, one hand shading her eyes against the sun. "She works where?"

"Here. She's a beautician. She should be in."

A bell jingles over the door as we step inside. A couple of ladies sit beneath hair dryers, reading magazines and puffing on cigarettes. What I wouldn't give to be one of them right now, just sitting there smoking and reading about movie stars like there's not a thing in the world to worry about.

In front of a wall of mirrors are three beautician's chairs, all of them full. Two of the beauticians are young women, each with a bouffant the size of a ski slope. The third beautician—the one at the middle chair wrapping a woman's hair in strips of foil—that must be Vernita Ponder.

Aunt Donna squares her shoulders and walks up to the middle chair. "Excuse me, Vernita," she says.

The old woman stops fussing with the foil and looks sharply up at Aunt Donna. She's a small woman and wouldn't be able to reach the top of her client's head without the three-inch stilettos she's wearing. The shoes are red, picking up the dominant color of her tie-dyed mini-skirt. Her outfit is topped by a white silk blouse and a fringed vest of brown leather. Every one of her fingers, thumbs included, is encircled by a ring. All the rings are silver and a number of them have colored stones. She's also wearing a pair of earrings that look like chandeliers and about a million charm bracelets on each wrist. When she turns around to face Aunt Donna, I see the peace symbol medallion on a slim strip of leather hanging around her neck.

You've got to be kidding me.

She's a corpse dressed up like Joan Baez and people trust her to cut their hair?

I want to burst out laughing, and would, if not for the stern eye the woman has turned on me and Mom. She has cheeks bright with rouge, fierce red lips, and a jet black beehive that is obviously a dye job. She looks plain mean—and crazy.

When Aunt Donna finishes making introductions, the old woman says, "You say they just moved into the old Cisco place?"

"That's right."

She squints at us.

Mom, obviously startled, asks, "Who are the Ciscos?"

Vernita gives us a look that says we're the dumbest people on God's green earth. "Gordon and Evelyn Cisco," she says slowly. "They lived in that house a long time. When he died in '47, she went on living there alone."

"She's the widow," Aunt Donna adds. "The one who died in the house but wasn't found for several days."

Oh, that one.

"Valerie?" The old woman turns to one of the ski slope ladies who's busy taking the rollers out of some chinless lady's hair.

"Yes'um?" Valerie says.

"Finish up Delilah for me, will you?"

"Sure, Vernita. I'm almost finished with Louise here."

Vernita looks again at the three of us and nods toward the back of the shop. "Come with me."

Mom, Aunt Donna, and I follow the heels that are clicking on the linoleum floor. We reach a small round table in the back room and, after Vernita pulls up a couple of extra folding chairs, we all sit down.

"So what it is you want to talk about?" She sounds annoyed. She reaches for something in the ashtray, and when I see what it is, I almost fall off my chair. It's a homemade cigarette held together by a roach clip! That's not tobacco she's smoking, that's weed! Where'd she get marijuana around here?

She almost lights up, thinks better of it, and lets the matchbook drop onto the table. She lays the toke back in the ashtray. I'm disappointed. I'll take it second-hand, if that's the only way I can get it. What I wouldn't give for just one draw on that thing.

Aunt Donna looks at Mom. "Tell her what you told me, Meg. About what happened last night."

Mom tells the story all over again. She sounds even more nervous this time around. I don't blame her. I wouldn't exactly be wanting to tell our crazy story to this beady-eyed little gnome. Vernita Ponder just sits there, her face growing whiter with every passing minute. She begins to look more and more like that corpse, and I begin to think that if she collapses on the floor, I'm going to pretend like I never had that class in CPR.

Mom finishes by saying, "I know it sounds pretty unbelievable but …" And then we sit there in silence, hardly even looking at each other.

Finally, the old woman swallows hard, draws a tissue out of the pocket of her miniskirt and uses it to wipe the beads of perspiration off her forehead. She seems to be trying to collect herself before she finally leans forward and says, "You must not ever tell anyone else what you just told me."

Mom looks shocked. "Why not?"

"You do, Mrs. Crane, and that's the end of Black Mountain."

"What do you mean?"

"People hear a story like this, and we got reporters and news cameras all over the place. We got hippies hiking over the hills and setting up communes in the mountains. We got religious freaks coming to see if there might be statues in the woods that shed real tears or bleed at the palms."

I have no idea what she's talking about. I can tell Mom's trying to stay calm when she says, "Well, we don't want anything like that going on, Mrs. Ponder. We just want to know what happened in our home last night."

The old woman looks at the roach again. I know she's dying to light it, and I wish she would but she doesn't. "The legend is true then," she says slowly. "I've always wondered."

"What legend?"

Vernita Ponder moistens her lips with her tongue and kneads together her silver-studded hands. "These hills are full of stories," she begins. She's talking quietly like she wants to make sure her words can't be heard out on the floor of the shop. "One of the legends has it there's a place in these mountains where all of time is happening at once."

She looks at each one of us like she's wondering whether we understand. Our blank stares tell her that we don't.

"What do you mean, Vernita?" Aunt Donna is the only one brave enough to ask.

"Just what I said. For centuries, people have believed there's a place in this chain of mountains where all of time is going on at once, so that sometimes, something happens such that you can see the goings-on of another time. Not only see it, but, talk to it, I guess you'd say. Can't become a part of it, can't enter the time, but you can talk to the people there."

"Oh right," I blurt out, leaning back heavily in the folding chair. I can't help shaking my head and rolling my eyes. Either this lady's nuts or she's been hitting on something a whole lot stronger than weed this morning.

She looks at me, and I close my mouth. "You don't believe me, missy?"

"Like, how am I supposed to believe that?" I say.

"Linda," Mom starts, but the old lady raises her hand.

"It's all right, Mrs. Crane." She turns back to me and says, "What's your answer, then, for what happened last night? You were there. You saw it yourself. How do you explain it?"

I think a minute, then shake my head. She's got me there. What happened is just as unbelievable as Vernita Ponder's explanation for it.

"So what you're saying, Vernita," Aunt Donna says, "is that what they saw last night were people who used to live in the house?"

"Or will live in the house. Time goes both ways."

I sit up straight then, remembering something. "Did a family by the name of Buchanan ever live there?"

Vernita's beady old eyes shift back to me. "Yes. Back to the turn of the century, or a bit later."

"That was them! They were the ones that tried to shoot Dad!"

"And was there a fire in the town?" Mom asks. "A fire that destroyed much of Sutton Avenue?"

Another slow turn of the old woman's head as she looks back at Mom. "1916," she says.

I think I'm going to faint. Or throw up. Or both. I mean, even when I was on some of my best trips, high on a good batch of speed, I never came up with anything like this. Seeing into another time! Jumping Jehoshaphat!

None of us knows what to say. I mean, what *can* you say? It's not like we're talking about summer fashions here, or a new shade of hair dye. We're talking about something we've never talked about before, something most people will never talk about in their whole entire lives.

Finally, Vernita Ponder says, "I remember that fire like it was yesterday."

"You were here?" I ask.

"Of course. Where else would I be?"

"Then you knew the Buchanans?"

"Not all that good, but I knew who they were. I'd see them around town, of course. Seems Mr. Buchanan come down here for the cure."

"The cure?"

"He had tuberculosis. Back then, folks'd come to these mountains from all over the place, thinking the air would cure them. And it did, too."

Mom asks, "So the Buchanans weren't native to the mountains?"

"Hardly," Vernita Ponder says. "They come down from Chicago and were only here long enough for Palmer Buchanan to take the cure. That was a year, maybe. After that, they went back to Chicago. They did come back summers, though, and stay in one of the inns around here like the other tourists. I heard tell that after they died they sent themselves back down here to be buried. I believe they're in the cemetery over at the Valley View Baptist Church … but I don't know for sure about that. They weren't folks I cared for much." She pauses, then adds, "Except for the youngest boy. He wasn't a bad kid. He made himself useful by running errands for me and some of the other young mothers in town. He was young, but he was always responsible, that Mac."

Mom and I look at each other. "Digger's imaginary friend," I say.

Mom nods. "Maybe not so imaginary."

"Then Digger already knows."

"Knows, but probably doesn't understand. We'll have to tell him—even though I hardly understand myself." She pauses and looks at Vernita Ponder. "So you think the Buchanans were the people we saw in the house last night?"

The old lady nods. "Sounds like, anyway. I wouldn't put it past Palmer Buchanan to pull a gun first and ask questions later. He loved the mountains, but he didn't think much of the hill people."

Mom frowns and her eyebrows scrunch up. "Mrs. Ponder, it's a little hard to … well, accept all this. I mean, you've never actually encountered someone from another time yourself, have you?"

When Vernita Ponder shakes her head, the chandelier earrings send her earlobes flapping. "No," she said. "Always thought I'd like to have that privilege, but never have."

"So, you've always believed the legend might be true?"

"Of course I believed it. And now after hearing you talk, I know it's true. In fact, I've had my suspicions that house was the place, but I just never knew for sure."

"Do many people know about this legend, Mrs. Ponder?"

The old lady shrugs. "Folks don't talk so much about legends anymore. But when I was a girl, plenty of people hoped to find this place where all of time was happening at once. They'd wander the mountains for days, weeks, hoping to come across the place where you can see into time, but no one ever did. Not that I knew of anyway. And now here it is, right here in the town of Black Mountain. Been here all along. Imagine that." She pauses again and looks like she's thinking real hard. "I can only figure it must be like a volcano or something. It lies dormant for a while, years maybe, waiting for the right people. I never heard tell the Ciscos saw into another time when they was there."

"Why do you suppose that is?" Aunt Donna asks.

Vernita Ponder shrugs. "It's like the Brown Mountain lights, I reckon. You heard of them?"

Mom and I both shake our heads.

"Well, over to Brown Mountain strange lights have appeared, going on for centuries now. No one can explain them. Many people have tried, but no one can say for sure what the lights are. But the thing is, not many people have seen them. Only a handful. Some people go back again and again, waiting and hoping just to catch a glimpse, only to be disappointed. Some others might go one time, twice, and there's the lights, dancing over the ridge of Brown Mountain, sure as the stars. Who knows why one person sees them and another don't. Only way I can explain it is to say, it's a gift."

"A gift?" Mom asks.

"A gift," Vernita Ponder repeats.

Mom looks worried. "But is it evil? Is the house evil?"

The wrinkled old face softens for the first time. "Of course not," she says. "That part of the legend is sure. That place is good. It's a good gift."

Then she pushes back her chair and rises. "One more thing," she says, her stoniness returning as she looks from Aunt Donna to Mom to me. "I'm glad to have met you today, and I'm glad to finally know that the legend is true, that there really is a place ..." Her words trail off then, and she starts staring into space like she's the one who's suddenly seeing people from another time or something. But in the next minute she snaps back and says, "But as far as the rest of the town goes, this conversation never happened." And then she clickity-clacks her way back into the shop on her stilettos, letting us know that this discussion we never had is now over.

16

Sheldon
Thursday, July 18, 1968

EVERY GOOD GIFT and every perfect gift is from above, coming down from the Father of lights ... but never have I heard of a gift like this. It's outside the realm not only of my own experience, but of all that I know about God and Scripture.

"Can it really be possible?" I say. I lift a fork laden with roast beef to my lips, lower it without eating. "Who is this Velveta Ponder anyway?"

"Vernita," Meg quietly corrects me. "It's Vernita Ponder. And I already told you. She's an elderly woman who has lived in these mountains all her life. That's why Donna thought we should talk with her."

"She's pretty weird, Dad," Linda throws in. "But you've got to admit, what happened last night was pretty weird too. I mean, how many times do people just appear in your house, shoot at you, and then disappear?"

"And I missed the whole thing!" Digger cries, throwing his elbows onto the table and pushing his fists against his cheeks. "Why didn't you call me? Next time call me. I always miss the good stuff."

"Yeah, well, not really, Digger," Linda says. "You've seen that kid Mac, haven't you? Remember, we told you he's one of those people from that other time."

"Yeah." He's still pouting, but he nods.

"So, where he is it isn't 1968. It's 1916."

"Yeah?"

"Yeah."

"Really?"

"Really."

Digger sits up suddenly, his face full of excitement. "Cool!"

"Now listen," I say, "we don't know that for sure."

"But Sheldon," Meg protests, "what other explanation can there be?"

"I don't know, but I know there must be one. This all-of-time-happening-at-once legend—it's … it's, well, I'm trying to reconcile it with what I know about God."

"But Dad!" Digger says. "You don't know every single little thing about God, do you?"

"Well—"

"Yeah, Dad," Linda interrupts. "And like you're always saying anyway, all things are possible with God. Remember that one?"

I open my mouth to respond, but Meg jumps in first. "I seem to remember you preaching on God being—what was it?—the Alpha and the Omega, right? The beginning and the end. I distinctly remember you saying he sees the end from the beginning. Maybe it has something to do with that."

I am silenced.

No, Digger, I do not know everything about God.

And yes, Linda, with God all things are possible.

And yes again, Meg, God is the Alpha and Omega, the beginning and the end.

But a place in this finite world where all of time is happening at once?

Can it really be possible?

17

Linda
Friday, July 19, 1968

"Your dad tried to shoot my dad," I say.

"Yeah, I know," Austin says. "So, what happened?"

"He missed by about fifty years."

Austin and I are staring at each other, and I'm waiting for him to say something. Instead, he's just standing there completely still, and his face is bunched up like his stomach hurts. "I don't understand what you mean," he finally says. He's speaking slowly like he thinks I have to read his lips or something. "What's going on here? Do you know?"

I nod. "Sit down," I say, pointing with my thumb toward a spot on the porch steps beside me. I have to admit, I've kind of been sitting here hoping he'd show up. You know, like I'd catch him coming home from work again because I've been wanting to talk with him about what's going on around here.

He hardly takes his eyes off me while he climbs the steps. He's acting like if he takes his eyes off me, I'll start swinging at him for his dad trying to shoot my dad. He settles himself on the top step and retrieves a pack of cigarettes from the front pocket of his overalls.

"Hey, can I have one of those?" I ask.

I don't like the way his eyes pop open in surprise. "You smoke?" he asks.

"Whenever I can get my hands on a cigarette, I do."

"I don't know many girls who smoke."

"That's because your generation was full of prudes."

"What do you mean? We're the same age, aren't we?"

"Listen, are you going to let me have a smoke or not?"

"Well." He looks at the pack of cigarettes. "All right." Then, sounding rather proud, he says, "Most of the folks around here roll their own tobacco, but Dad has these sent down from Chicago."

"Nice. So hand one over."

He places one in my hand, but it goes right through my skin and lands on the porch.

"What the—" Austin swears and leans away from me like I'm a ghost or something.

I try to touch the cigarette, but my finger goes right through it. "I should have known," I say quietly. I feel something like awe as I run my finger through the cigarette again and again.

When I look at Austin, his face is white, and there are beads of sweat breaking out all over his forehead. He's trying to say something, but he's having trouble getting the words out. "Should ... should have known what?" he finally manages to ask.

"That I wouldn't be able to touch it."

"Why not?"

"Well," I have to stop and think a minute. "I'm not really sure."

Austin stares at me for a good long while. "You're talking in circles," he says angrily. "Listen, get to the point. I want to know what's going on around here."

"Okay," I say. "Okay, here's the point. It's time."

"Time for what?"

"No. Not time for something, just time. We're living in a place where all of time is going on at once."

Now he's looking at me like I'm wacko, with his eyes bugging out and his mouth hanging open. "What are you saying?" he asks.

"Do you know a woman in town named Vernita Ponder?"

"No."

"Well, I guess if she'd told you, she would have told me she told you, but she said she never spoke with you, so I guess it's obvious she didn't tell you."

Austin stands up abruptly. "That's crazy talk," he says. "I don't know what's going on here, but I don't like it. Maybe you'd better leave before—"

"Sit down, Austin," I say. When he doesn't make a move, I add, "Please. Please sit down, all right? I don't really understand it myself, but I'll try to explain."

To my surprise, Austin doesn't argue with me. He just sits down again. He waves the unlit cigarette in his hand. "You mind?" he asks.

"No, go ahead."

His fingers tremble slightly as he strikes a match. He inhales deeply, looks at me and waits.

I lean back against the step and settle in. This might take awhile, and I want to be comfortable. I look up at the sky and take a deep breath. "There's a legend in these mountains," I begin ...

18

Digger
Saturday, July 20, 1968

I'M SITTING AT the kitchen table eating a peanut butter and jelly sandwich, when I hear a weird noise outside. I run out the back door and see Mac sitting on top of the rock, playing a harmonica.

"Hey Mac! You know what?"

He stops blowing on the harmonica. He wipes the spit off his mouth with the back of his sleeve. "What?"

"My sister told me where you're at it's 1916."

"That's right."

"Well, did you know where I'm at it's 1968?"

He nods a little. "That's what Austin told me. He said your sister told him."

He starts playing the harmonica again.

"Well, don't ya believe it?"

He stops blowing again. "Sure, I believe it. Why not? Your sister a liar or something?"

"No," I say. Then, "Well, maybe sometimes. But I don't think she's lying about this because my mom says so, too."

"Yeah? So?"

"So, it seems kind of strange, doesn't it? Us living at different times but talking to each other?"

He shrugs. "Lots of things seem kind of strange. My Grandma Lowry, my mom's mom—she used to talk all the time to the Archangel Michael. No one else could see him, but Grandma'd talk to him like he was sitting right there at the kitchen table."

"Yeah? What'd they talk about?"

"I don't know. I never listened much."

"She still talk to him?"

"Naw."

"How come?"

"She died."

"Oh."

He plays the harmonica for a minute, and then he stops. He looks around like he's looking for something.

I say, "We're not supposed to tell anybody, you know."

"About what?" he asks.

"About us living at different times."

He shrugs. "So who would care? No one cared about Grandma talking to the angel. They just said she was queer in the head."

"So you're not gonna tell anyone?"

"Naw."

"Me neither. But I can tell you about the future, if you want. Want me to?"

"Naw, not really."

I listen to him play a little bit. If he's trying to play a song, I don't know what it is. I think he could use a lot of practice.

"You want to play Cowboys and Indians, then?"

"Sure!" He stuffs the harmonica in his shirt pocket, leaps up and jumps off the rock. "Geronimo!" he yells.

I guess that makes me the cowboy, then, if he's the Indian.

19

Meg
Saturday, July 20, 1968

WE HAVE TO drive into town to the post office to get our mail, but I'd go a hundred times a day if every time I went I found a letter from Carl waiting for me. This is the first one we've received from him since we arrived in Black Mountain. It was hard to do, but I waited until I got back home to open it. Opening his letters is a moment to savor.

"Dear Mom, Dad, Linda, and Digger, I am fine."

He always starts that way. "I am fine." He has no idea how I grab at those words the way a drowning person grabs at a rope. Or maybe he does. Maybe that's why he always says it first, before anything else.

I settle back in the rocking chair to read. It's not a long letter. Words of thanks for the box of baked goods I mailed off right before we left Abington. He shared the cookies and pound cake with his buddies in his hut and no one complained about them being a little stale. The chow they serve in the mess is awful and while he might feel full he's never satisfied, and he can't wait to get back to a home-cooked meal. He's working like a dog, he says, especially when it comes to the daily report. The report, reviewed each evening by both the Executive Officer and the Commanding Officer, tells where every man in the battalion is at all times. This includes a breakdown, by pay grade, rate, company, etc., and when and where the detachments are and which men are in the detachments (name, rate, service number, and company), emergency leaves, R & R, TADs, men on security watch, mess detail, trash crew, laundry detail, the rear echelon, men in school (back in the States), etc. And the numbers are always changing, every day, and each one requires a diary entry, and sometimes it's enough to drive him crazy. But he likes the guys he works with in the office, and on the whole the place isn't too bad, and at least he's getting used to the nighttime mortar attacks. They don't happen every night, just sometimes. When the siren goes off, most of the men run out of the huts and jump into the mortar pits naked so it'd be pretty funny— all of them running around in their birthday suits—if only there weren't incoming artillery to worry about.

He ends his letter, ironically, by saying, "Don't worry," and I wonder, how can I not worry when my firstborn is in a war zone? Thank God he's not on the front lines, but even so, like Carl himself said in his last letter, "This place is no picnic." No, it's no picnic when young men who have barely even started living are shipped home in body bags.

I lean my head against the back of the chair and shut my eyes. I don't want to think dreadful thoughts. Please, God, let Carl come home safely.

When I open my eyes, I notice a half-eaten sandwich on the table. Digger's lunch, the peanut butter and jelly I made him before I headed down to the post office.

"Linda?"

"What?"

She's in the living room, watching something on TV while she paints her fingernails a fiery red. I can see her from where I'm sitting in the kitchen.

"Where's Digger?"

"I don't know." She shrugs. "Out back, I think."

"You were supposed to be watching him."

"Yeah, well, I'm not my brother's keeper."

"You are when I'm not home."

She shrugs again.

I feel a momentary wave of panic ripple through my stomach. I should have looked for Digger the moment I got back from the post office, but I was too anxious to read Carl's letter. Moving to the kitchen window, I look out at the empty yard.

"Linda?"

"What?"

"Did Digger say anything to you?"

"About what?"

"About where he was going?"

"No."

My panic turns to anger. "Listen, Linda, I've told you time and time again that when I'm not home—"

But I'm interrupted when the front door crashes open, and Digger runs through the front hall to the kitchen. "Hi, Ma!" he says. He is dirty and sweaty, and I feel his sweet warmth as he throws his arms around my waist. I squeeze him in return, then ruffle his unruly blond hair. "Where have you been?" I ask.

"Outside playing with Mac," he answers.

"Oh!" I nod. I'm hardly used to any of this. "Mac. He's your friend from …"

"Yeah," Digger says. "He's the kid who lives in 1916."

An odd sensation ripples through my chest. "And does he know you live in 1968?"

Digger nods. "Yeah, he knows."

"And doesn't he think it's … strange?"

"No." He shakes his head. "I offered to tell him about the future, but he wanted to play Cowboys and Indians instead."

"Really?"

I have to think about that for a moment. Would I want to know the future? Will I ever meet anyone to ask? In a place like this, that may very well be possible.

"Yup, so that's what we've been doing, but he had to go. I'm hungry. What can I have to eat?"

"Well," I say, pointing at the table, "you didn't finish your sandwich."

"Oh yeah!" He jumps into the chair and tears into the sandwich with his usual gusto.

I shake my head and begin to work on the dirty dishes in the sink. Only a little while ago we lived in Abington, Carl was with us, Sheldon was still a pastor, and time was fixed. All we had of time was the present moment.

Now everything has changed, including the fact that time has expanded, or maybe constricted, or somehow melted from something solid to something fluid. It was orderly once, broken down into increments of minutes, hours, days, years, but now all those barriers are gone, and I don't know how to measure it anymore, don't even know whether it *can* be measured or whether, in this one strange place, there are moments when time ceases to exist, becoming a calendar of blank pages.

It can be hard to make sense of things when your life isn't determined by the orderly movement of time.

20

Linda
Saturday, July 20, 1968

THE MINUTE I opened the door to Pop's Ice Cream Parlor I was almost sorry I took the job. But here I am, tying on my apron and waiting for Gloria Reynolds to tell me what to do. She's all smiles, that Gloria Reynolds, welcoming me to this hole-in-the-wall like I've just landed the best job on the planet. You can spare me your enthusiasm, lady. I'm just doing this so I can buy that ticket out of here.

"Well, let me go over the menu—" she begins, but she's interrupted when some girl comes flying in the front door.

"Sorry I'm late, Gloria!" the girl hollers. "I was helping Grandpa with—"

"Cool your jets, Gail," Gloria interrupts her. "It's only just now five o'clock. According to my schedule, you're right on time. Now, I'd like to introduce you to our newest employee."

The girl comes behind the counter and starts to tie an apron around her waist. All the while she's looking at me and smiling.

Gloria waves a hand at me and says, "Gail, this is Linda Crane."

"No way!" Gail exclaims, and she looks so excited, I think she's going to go spastic on me. "I can't believe it. My mom's named Linda too!"

"Oh yeah?" I say, and I can hardly keep from rolling my eyes. She thinks this is some huge coincidence or something? Like what, she just scored some extra points because she now knows two of the million billion Lindas in the world?

"And Linda, this is Gail Leland. You two will be working evening shifts together."

"Well, Linda, I'm glad to meet you," Gail says.

"Yeah, same here."

"I was about to show her the ropes, before we start to get busy," Gloria says.

The ropes include how to make sundaes, malteds, milkshakes, and banana splits and ring them up on the cash register. That's about all the place offers, except for coffee, hot chocolate, soda, and candy. Once I learn where everything is, the job should be a cinch.

"Well, girls, I'll be in the back room," Gloria says when she finishes filling me in. "Holler if you need anything."

I look at Gail, and she looks at me. She smiles. She's a pretty girl with long brown hair and big brown eyes and skin that doesn't have one single pimple anywhere. Not even a blackhead. Her nose might be a tad too long but it's nothing that's going to scare any boys away. I think I'm going to like her, but I might as well not let on yet.

"You're not from around here," I say. The missing Southern accent gave her away.

"No." She shakes her head. "Toledo."

"So what are you doing here?"

A couple of kids come in looking for tootie-fruity ice cream cones. I can't believe we have a flavor called tootie-fruity. Gail serves them the cones, rings them up, and then says, "My dad was sick a long time and then he died last year. After that it was just my mom and me, so she decided she wanted to live with Grandpa who lived over near Chicago. He said okay, but he'd been thinking about retiring here in Black Mountain. Mom said great, why don't we all go down? So here we are." She shrugs.

"Oh." And then I add, because I know it's expected, "I'm sorry about your dad."

"Thanks."

"So, you like it here?"

"You kidding? I love it here."

Well, after Toledo, maybe that's no surprise.

She says, "So you just moved here too, right?"

"Yeah, from Pennsylvania."

"Cool. So, what do you think so far about Black Mountain?"

I have to think for a minute about how to answer since I don't want to burst her bubble or anything. "Well," I finally say. "It's different. From Pennsylvania, I mean."

"Yeah." She laughs. "I guess so." She's puttering around as we talk, wiping down the counter, checking the supplies, filling up the canisters of toppings. I feel like I should be doing something, but I don't know what.

Finally, four old men come into the shop, and Gail greets them like they're a bunch of long-lost relatives. She calls them by name and introduces me to them, and you'd think we were having a party or something instead of just serving ice cream to a bunch of old geezers. I smile at them and say it's nice to meet them even though I'd much rather be meeting guys about a hundred years younger. They say they'll have the usual, and I guess Gail knows what that is because they take a seat and she goes to work digging out scoops of ice cream from the freezer.

"They'll want coffee too, so you can pour that," she tells me.

I'm glad for something to do. I pour coffee into Styrofoam cups and carry them on a tray out to the geezers. They're at a couple of tables that have checker boards painted on the top so people can play while they're sitting there eating their ice cream.

"Why, thank you, pretty miss," one says, and then they all say something like that, and they're all looking at me with their beady little eyes, and I want to tell them to keep their comments and their eyes to themselves, but I just smile and walk back behind the counter. Bunch of perverts, is what they are.

"Hey Gail," one of them calls, "Bim coming tonight?"

Gail lifts her head up out of the freezer. "He'll be here in a bit." She finishes scooping up four dishes of various flavors and carries them out to the men, who are setting up the checkers games. When she comes back she says to me, "They're regulars here on Friday and Saturday nights."

Boy howdy, aren't we lucky. Something I can look forward to all week.

We start getting busy then, with the bell over the door tinkling like wind chimes in a gale, and after a while Gloria comes out and mans the cash register while Gail and I are freezing our hands off digging up scoops of ice cream for just about everybody in town it seems. There's little kids everywhere and moms and dads and young couples out on dates and several more old geezers and I think my arm is going to fall off before they're all satisfied.

I'm digging up some sort of black cherry walnut concoction when Gail says, "Well, it's about time you got here, Grandpa. The others have been at it for an hour over there."

I look up from the freezer and see yet another old geezer across the counter. This one takes the cake for ugly, though, like he's been dead five years and he doesn't know it and no one's bothered to tell him. His eyes and cheeks are sunken in, and there's a sack of skin under his jaw that looks like a turkey wattle, only worse because it's got tiny gray whiskers sticking out all over it. I mean, this guy's got hairs sticking out all over the place—his ears, his nose, his chin. And his eyebrows look like a wig factory blew up in his face. Sheesh! Why doesn't somebody just bury him and get it over with?

"Linda, this is my grandpa," Gail says proudly. "You can call him Bim. Everybody does." The next thing I know the old guy's got his old eyes fixed on me and they're starting to water up like he's crying or something, and I almost start to wonder if he *is* crying, except I know old people's eyes are always watering for some reason.

"Gramps, this is Linda. She's new in town. She's going to be working with me. Isn't that great?"

The old man nods his head a little. He works his mouth for a minute like he has to gather up some spit to wet his whistle before he can talk. Finally he says, real quietly, "Linda." Just that. Just my name. Like he doesn't have the strength to say anything else. Holy cow, somebody call the undertaker, will you?

"Hi," I say. But that's it. I'm not going to be caught dead calling anybody Bim.

The old guy turns his head when someone calls, "Hey Bim, where you been? I've just been sitting here waiting to beat you at a game."

"Go on and have a seat, Gramps," Gail says. "I'll bring you some coffee in just a minute."

The old man turns his eyes back to me. Now that he's turned off the waterworks, I can see that his eyes are a deep blue, so much so that I'd say once, when he was young, they were probably his best feature. But that was before the rest of him shriveled up into this walking prune. He goes on staring at me, and I want to tell him to take a picture, it lasts longer, but I can't say anything because he's giving me the creeps. Another pervert. In my first two hours working at Pop's Ice Cream Parlor, I've met a dozen old geezers, a bunch of middle-aged losers, about a zillion little kids, and a few high school kids who have already paired up, but not one single unclaimed good-looking guy. Not one single hunk like—well, like Austin Buchanan. Yeah, somebody like Austin Buchanan. I wish Austin could walk in that door, but it's 1968 here and on this end of the timeline he's probably been dust for at least a good decade. Maybe even longer than that. Yeah, probably even longer than that.

21

Sheldon
Monday, July 22, 1968

I HAND THE ignition key to a local named Ruben Poteat so he can take the '57 pickup for a test drive. Steve said last year they let a fellow named Ernest Fortune take a brand new Camaro for a spin, and he drove it all the way to California. The highway patrol was alerted in a dozen states, but before he could be spotted and arrested for grand theft auto, Ernest totaled the Camaro and killed himself somewhere along the Pacific Coast Highway.

I just hope we see the pickup truck again. Ruben Poteat is another matter. I'd feel just fine if he took his business elsewhere. I'm not sure I trust him. But then, he probably doesn't trust me either. I am, after all, a used car salesman.

Ruben honks the horn and waves and pulls out of the lot with tires squealing. Great. Just what I need. Some guy who thinks he's a Nascar racer taking one of my better models on the road.

Well, for now, I'd best get back to my desk. Plenty of paperwork waiting to be done. The Setterquists—nice young couple—want to know what kind of deal I can give them on that '65 Chevelle. It's in good shape, mid-size but roomy, not too many miles on the odometer. They're going to need something larger than that Volkswagen Beetle they have now, once the baby comes.

Inside the trailer a cloud of tobacco smoke wafts like morning fog, drifting outward and bumping up against the walls of faux oak paneling. I have the windows open and a fan that blows straight across my desk, but the fan doesn't do much to spare me the stench. It just means my papers have to be anchored with paperweights. I can't imagine how bad it's going to be in here, come winter.

Ike Kerlee has his feet up on his desk and his hands behind his head. "That Ruben," he says with an admiring smile, "he really knows how to burn rubber, don't he?"

I grunt my assent and turn away. Today marks one week on this job, and I am miserable. I had a calling once, and now it's gone. I destroyed it with my own two hands.

Sitting at my desk, I take inventory of the tools of my new trade: loan application forms; pens that advertise Birchfield Chevrolet; pencils and erasers and scrap paper; an adding machine; extra rolls of adding machine paper.

I hate numbers. The only numbers in my old job were chapter and verse. And of course, the deficit in the church budget—though I managed never to worry too much about that. I floated on the assurance of the Lord's provision.

But that was then, in the other life. Now it's through numbers that I will feed my family.

I look out the window and see Steve in the distance, wandering around the new car lot with a couple of prospective buyers. Funny thing about Steve is that he has no idea about the strange happenings up at the house. Oddly enough, it was Donna who said we shouldn't tell him. "I know Steve better than any of you," she'd said. "You tell him what Vernita said, not only the whole of Black Mountain knows, but the whole world knows."

Meg and I agreed to keep the secret, knowing that was best for now. One thing we wondered, though, was whether there would be any more "sightings." Or maybe we've seen all we're going to see. That Vernita Ponder said the thing seems to go dormant and nothing happens for a long time. Maybe the shooting was a small eruption and the volcano has gone back to sleep.

Certainly that would be all right. I have more than I can handle right here in 1968. With Meg and Linda both angry at me and the memory of Charlene plaguing me—well, the mystery of how to do right by women is enough. The mystery of seeing into time can be solved by the next occupants of the house, far as I'm concerned.

Charlene. Every memory of her leaves me feeling kicked in the gut. Still, I can't help wondering what she's doing now. She returned to Des Moines, I know. But what she's doing, what her plans are—that's a blank. We all agreed there would be no contact ever again, not between me and Charlene. Even Charlene agreed. She wept when she said it, but she took her leave and that was that. Though I can't help feeling that somehow even that was left incomplete. Something, I sense, was left undone. But it's too late now to make things right.

A squeal of tires signals Ruben's return. Ike Kerlee drops his feet to the floor and laughs. He crushes out his cigarette in one of the ashtrays on his desk and lights up another. The front door of the trailer flies open and Ruben Poteat, dripping sweat and looking windblown, steps inside. "You got anything that can do zero to sixty in thirty seconds or less?" he asks.

I long for the days when the numbers were chapter and verse.

22

Meg
Wednesday, July 24, 1968

I DECIDED TO play some music on the old widow's phonograph, so I looked through her albums and chose the collection of Brahms. *Piano Concerto No. 1* is playing now. I pause in my dishwashing to listen. There has always been something uncommonly soothing about this piece, as though just below the notes someone is speaking words of comfort. I believe I could stand here for hours, just gazing out the window and listening.

"Beautiful, isn't it?"

I turn abruptly from the sink to see who's behind me. A woman sits in one of the rocking chairs by the fireplace, holding a teacup in her hands. "I'm sorry," she says quietly. "I didn't mean to startle you."

I'm aware of my heart pounding in my chest. Yes, she startled me, to say the least. "It's all right," I say. "I'm just not used to—" I finish the sentence by shaking my head.

"To people suddenly appearing?"

"Yes."

"It *is* rather strange, isn't it?" But she doesn't *look* like she thinks it's strange. She looks as though, to her, this is perfectly normal.

I take a moment to catch my breath and let my heart settle. Then I ask, "You know about the house then?"

She smiles placidly. "Yes, I know about it."

She is a strikingly beautiful Negro woman, with well-defined features, intelligent eyes, and skin the color of creamed coffee. She wears her shoulder-length hair in a myriad of braids, very different from the Afro that's so popular now. But then, she doesn't live in the now, does she?

"What year is it," I ask, "where you are?"

She looks at me with a face of unchanging serenity. "2005."

I gasp, feeling myself once more awash with wonder. "2005," I whisper. "Why, it's the twenty-first century!"

"And where you are?" she asks.

"1968."

She nods. "I'd offer you some tea but ..." Her voice trails off and she smiles again, somewhat apologetically.

"I know," I say. "My daughter told me. I wouldn't be able to hold the cup."

"No. But you can sit down." She gestures toward the other rocking chair. I put a hand on it and find it solid. Of course it is; it has been here since we moved in.

"The chairs are here in both times," I say as I sit.

"Yes. Much of what is in the house today was there in your time."

"But the things you brought to the house, like the tea cups—they're outside of my time, and beyond my reach."

She nods again. "That's right."

"You are outside of my time, and yet I can see you and talk to you."

"Yes. It's amazing, isn't it?"

"Yes. But—well, it's amazing and frightening at the same time."

"No need to be afraid," she says.

"You sound as though you're used to this."

"No, I'm not used to it. But I've been told what to expect. And, anyway, it's a gift, something good. It's nothing to be afraid of."

"That's what Vernita Ponder said. Do you know her?"

"The name is familiar, but I'm not sure I ever met her."

"But of course not. She wouldn't be alive in your time; it's so far in the future. But then, how is it that you know about the house?"

"The elderly woman I work for in Asheville, Mrs. See—she told me."

"Mrs. See?" I cock my head at the strange name. "Is that S-E-E?"

"Hmmm," she says as she sips her tea. She turns her glance toward the empty fireplace and sits quietly a moment.

"Do many people know about this place then, in your time?"

"Oh no. No, very few."

"But Mrs. See knows?"

"Yes."

"But how? How does she know?"

She thinks a moment. "I'm not sure I can tell you that. At least, not yet."

I frown at her answer. I want to know everything, to know the reason behind what's happening here. That this woman knows something I don't know—that she cannot or will not tell me—is annoying. At the same time, I sense that I need to trust her, and that she will somehow be my ally in all this. "So you live in the house now?" I ask. "Your now, I mean?"

She moves her head from side to side, her long braids rubbing the shoulders of her dress. It is a floral dress, sleeveless, and without a waist. A sort of casual summer gown that falls all the way to the sandals on her feet. She looks freer, more comfortable in those clothes than I imagine I do in this housedress and patent leather slippers.

"No, I work here for Mr. Valdez. I work part-time here and part-time for Mrs. See. In fact, it was Mrs. See who told me about the position. She said she knew of a man in Black Mountain who needed help, and she sent me here to speak with Mr. Valdez. When I showed up, Mr. Valdez was rather surprised, saying he hadn't even advertised for the job yet. When I mentioned that Mrs. See had sent me, he seemed to understand, and he hired me right away."

I cock my head a moment in thought. Finally I say, "I'm afraid I don't completely understand."

She chuckles and shrugs. "Never mind," she says. "It's not important. You asked whether I live here and the point is, no, I don't. I work here. I care for the house and for the child, Nicholas. Mr. Valdez is at work right now and the boy is napping upstairs."

"And where's the child's mother?" I ask.

"Oh. Well, Mrs. Valdez is in Iraq and—"

"Iraq?" I interrupt. "My heavens! What's she doing there?"

For the first time, the woman looks uncomfortable. "Well, there's a war on and—"

"And she's a nurse?"

"No. No, she's not a nurse. She's a soldier."

"A soldier?"

"Yes. In the Army National Guard."

"A woman soldier? What kind of world …?"

My voice trails off as I leave the question dangling. The woman smiles. "It's not so different, really, from the world of your time. After all, women served in the military in your time, too."

"Yes," I say. "I suppose some do. But in your time they're drafting mothers?"

"Oh no." She shakes her head. "There's no draft. It's all voluntary. Men and women both serve because they want to."

"I see," I say weakly, trying to understand. A woman has gone to war voluntarily and left her child behind?

She takes a last sip of tea and settles the cup and saucer on the hearth. The record finishes, and the house falls quiet. I should turn off the phonograph and put the arm back on the rest, but I don't want to leave the company of this woman.

After a moment, she says, "By the way, I'm Celeste. Celeste Mosley."

"Celeste," I repeat. "That's a beautiful name. Well, I'm happy to meet you, Celeste. I'm Meg Crane."

She offers another kindly smile. "You're new to Black Mountain, aren't you?"

"Yes. We just moved here from Pennsylvania. We lived outside of Philadelphia. And you?"

"I grew up here. But after I graduated from the University of North Carolina, over in Asheville, I moved to Dallas. I had a degree in business, and I was ready to make my fortune."

"Oh?" I try to hide my astonishment, but I'm afraid I fail. The future is simply too full of surprises. A woman soldier in a place like Iraq and a Negro housekeeper with a college degree. "So, what happened?" I ask.

"Well, I succeeded." She pauses as though to give me time to let that sink in. "Eventually, I became an executive with a big-name company, and I was spending all my time making money and let me tell you, I was spending lots of money too. But I had no time left to enjoy the things I was spending money on. So when I turned forty, I asked myself, Celeste, what are you doing? What are you doing with your life? And I didn't have a good answer. So I came back here to where I started." Once more, she shines upon me that gentle smile of hers. "And now, I just spend time. That's all. I came back here so I can just spend time."

Her words hang suspended in the air, hovering over us like a protecting hand. We both seem to rest in them. Several quiet moments pass in which she allows me to join her in simply spending time. The clock on the mantle keeps rhythm with the swaying of our chairs. The seconds fall away, expended in being.

But then, suddenly, Celeste herself breaks into the circle of quiet. Holding up her left hand, she announces joyfully, "I also got engaged." The diamond on her finger sparkles in the light. "I'm finally getting married for the first time," she continues. "I had to come back to Black Mountain to find a man like Cleve. Forty-two years old and, come next spring, I'll be a bride. Imagine that."

"Congratulations," I say. "I'm happy for you."

I want to hear more of her story, but a child's wail reaches us from somewhere upstairs. My thoughts fly to Digger, but no, this is a far younger child, a toddler.

"Nicholas is awake," Celeste says. "I'd best go check on him." She stands and steps across the kitchen, but then turns back and says, "Well, I'll be seeing you, I trust." And then she walks into the dining room and quite literally disappears.

23

Linda
Sunday, July 28, 1968

DAD'S PLEASED AS punch I came to church with them this morning. As if I care one whit about church. I didn't come because I wanted to hear some bald-headed old man babbling on up there in the pulpit, and I sure didn't come for the funeral dirge hymn singing. I came because of the cemetery. I want to see if the Buchanans are buried here, like Vernita Ponder said.

Man, it's hot. People are fanning themselves with their bulletins, and the preacher is droning on like he thinks we care about what he has to say, and if he doesn't wrap this up in another minute, I think I'm going to kill someone. I mean, sheesh mister, stifle it. Can't you see you're boring us to death out here? We're sitting in these pews committing the sin of murder in our hearts, and you have no idea how close you are to seeing your Savior face to face in about another ten seconds.

I lean over and whisper to Mom, "I've got to get some air. I'll meet you guys outside after the service."

She gives me a look that says she's not happy, but I'm not exactly happy myself right now, so I'm just going to do what I came here to do. I get up and squeeze past Digger—who wants to go too but Mom grabs his arm. Sorry, kid. Better luck next time.

Outside it's cooler, but not much. Just walking from the church steps to the cemetery I'm breaking a sweat. Criminy, this is a pretty good-sized cemetery too. It could take me all day to find these people. If they're even here. Vernita said she thought they were, so I might as well take a look around.

As a rule, I'm not exactly fond of cemeteries. They kind of freak me out, especially when I think of what's down there under the ground. Like, I'm walking over the bones of a bunch of people who used to be walking on top of the ground just like I am now. And they're down there with their skin all rotting away and the worms feasting on their eyeballs and all that. Reminds me of that song Carl used to always sing whenever we drove by a funeral procession. *When a hearse goes by, never laugh, for you may be the next to die* ... Man, oh man, I hated that song when we were kids. I still do.

So let's see. What've we got here? Besides the Hatfields and McCoys, that is. Frady. Watford. Milling. Buck. Gupton. Cisco. Cisco? That sounds familiar. Gordon Cisco and his beloved wife Evelyn Mae. Oh yeah! She's the old biddy who died in our house. Yup, 1959. That's her. Good grief.

I wonder what time it is. I wonder if that preacher's done or if he's still flapping his jaw. I might as well skip some of these smaller stones and just check out the bigger ones. I mean, if the Buchanans had money like Vernita Ponder said, they probably went for something pretty flashy, you know?

Oh man, these sandals aren't the best choice for hiking around a graveyard. I might as well take them off. Grass is cool under my feet, anyway.

Now this one looks like it might be ... Nope. Otis Emerson Pritchard. Nice headstone you got there, Otis. Angel with a trumpet and everything. Pretty fancy. You must have been some sort of bigwig around here or something. Yeah, so, way to go. Rest in peace.

Let's see. Badgett. Adams. Clegg. Federspiel. Federspiel? Well, whatever. But, gee whiz, I'll be here forever. I could ... hey, wait a minute. That old stone there with the little lamb on top and the name Malcolm

Buchanan. Malcolm Buchanan! That's Mac! That's—but hold on here. This stone says he died in 1919. Wow, I can't believe it. He was still a kid when he died. I wonder what happened.

"Linda!"

I turn and see Mom making her way through the headstones, walking toward me. She's alone. Dad and Digger are probably eating donuts in the church basement.

"Mom, look!" I point at the little lamb headstone. "It's Mac!"

In another moment, she reaches me and stands there reading the stone. "Oh, dear," she says.

"He died in 1919."

"Yes, I see that." She lifts a fist to her chest, like her heart hurts or something. I know she's thinking about Digger. Or maybe she's thinking about Mac, or Mac's mother. I don't know. She's always feeling bad about something.

"What do you think happened?" I asked.

She shakes her head. "I don't know. Life was harder back then. So many diseases, and they didn't have the medicines we have now." She keeps on looking at the stone, and then after another minute she says, "Oh, you know what? I think the Spanish flu was still going on that year. Killed thousands of people around the world. My great uncle Benton died of the flu, along with two of his children."

"Oh yeah?"

"Yes. So maybe it was that. Maybe Mac died during the flu epidemic."

"Yeah. Probably."

She sighs so heavily, I think she's going to deflate. Then she says, "Listen, Linda, let's not tell Digger, all right? About Mac's death."

What can I do but shrug? "Sure. I won't tell him."

"I just don't think he'd understand."

"Like any of us can understand any of this, Mom. I mean, how often do you talk to people who are living in different times?"

Mom nods, then points to the stone next to Mac's. "Look. Did you see this?" she asks. "It's Mac's parents. Amelia and Palmer."

The stone is not so big after all. Just a regular stone, with their names, birth dates, and death dates. So here they are, buried here in this cemetery, just like Vernita Ponder said.

"Wow," I say, "Palmer Buchanan died in 1929, but Amelia didn't die till 1948. She was a widow for a long time. And Palmer outlived Mac by ten years."

"It was probably the tuberculosis that killed him."

"Yeah, I guess so."

But I don't care what killed Palmer Buchanan. I'm already looking around again. I'm looking for Austin, for a headstone that says Austin Buchanan. But there isn't one. Not here by the rest of the family, anyway.

"Austin isn't here," I say.

"No?"

I shake my head. "I wonder where he is?"

"Well …" Mom thinks a minute. Finally, she says, "No telling. He may have lived the rest of his life in Chicago and was buried up there. Or who knows, Linda? I mean, there was a war, the First World War, Austin might have—well, you know."

"You think Austin might have died in that war?"

"It's possible. So many young men did. Too many."

I'm thinking she said that because she's always worrying about Carl dying over in 'Nam. But maybe she's right. I know about that First World War, how ugly it was. All wars are ugly. No wonder the peaceniks sit around singing, *How many deaths will it takes till he knows that too many people have died?* Yeah, so according to Bob Dylan, the answer, my friend, is blowing in the wind. Like that's really going to help. It only sounds good when you're stoned.

"So where would he be, Mom? I mean, if he died in the war, where would Austin be?"

"Well, lots of our soldiers were buried in France," she says. "It was just impossible to bring them all home."

I haven't seen Austin in more than a week. All of a sudden, I'm scared. I mean, this is really blowing my mind. I've got to see him again. I only hope it's not too late. I hope he hasn't already gone to war.

24

Digger
Tuesday, July 30, 1968

I WISH AUNT Donna and them would hurry up and get here. I been ready to go swimming all morning. First time to go to the swimming pool—oh boy! I wish Dad could come but he and Uncle Steve are working at the car place. But Dad promised he'd go swimming with me soon as he can. I'm supposed to try out the diving board and tell him how bouncy it is. I bet it'll be great for cannon balls!

"Hey, Digger, where you going swimming?"

It's Mac! I've been watching down the drive for Aunt Donna's car, and I looked away for just a minute and now here he is, standing right in front of the porch. He plops down on the step beside me like he's tired out.

"How'd you know I was going swimming?" I ask.

"Those are swimming trunks you're wearing, aren't they? And you got a towel around your neck."

"Oh yeah."

"So where you going swimming?"

"At the pool."

"There's a pool around here?"

"Yeah, over that way somewhere." He looks to where I'm pointing then looks back at me.

"Austin and me, we go to the lake when we want to swim."

"Oh yeah? Where's that?"

He shrugs. "I don't know. Somewhere around here." He pulls his shirt off and uses it to wipe his face. "Boy, I'm hot and tuckered. I wish I could go swimming with you."

"Yeah, me too. Guess you can't, though."

"No, guess not."

"Whatcha been doing?"

"This kid I know from school named Jeb, he and I've been down putting pennies on the train track."

"Wow, they must be smashed flat as pancakes!"

"Flatter than that, even. Smashed clear into the tracks. They're never coming off. After that, we wished we'd used the money for ice cream."

"My sister works at the ice cream shop. She brings some home nearly every day."

"Yeah? You're lucky."

"Yeah."

He throws his shirt on the porch floor and leans his chin in his hands. "You know what Jeb told me?" he asks.

"No. What?"

"He said there's gold out there."

"Where?"

"Out there. In the mountains. He said people come through here all the time looking for gold. They dig these mines, see, and go down underground and pull out all the gold. They get rich, too."

"No fooling?"

"That's what Jeb said. He said his own uncle found enough gold to build himself a mansion over in Asheville."

"Wow!"

"Yeah. Someday when I'm bigger, I'm going to come back here and look for gold."

"Come back here from where?"

"You know—Chicago. That's where we really live."

"You do? Then what are you doing here?"

"We came down because Dad had the consumption."

"What's that?"

"You know, where you cough all the time. He had to be in that sanitarium for the longest time. We couldn't even see him for months. But he's better now, so the doctor let him come home. Dad wants to stay here for a little while because he says it's good for his lungs. But then we're going back to Chicago."

"For good?"

"I think so. But Dad says we'll come down here for vacation. He likes it here. Me too. It's a whole lot better place to explore than Chicago."

"Yeah, I guess so. Think you'll find any gold?"

"Sure. You just have to know where to look."

"Do you know where to look?"

"Not yet, but I'm sure going to find out."

"Think there'll be any gold left by the time you're older?"

He nods. "Not many people know about it. Jeb swore me to secrecy. But I know I can tell you because you're not even born yet."

"Yeah I am!"

"Not in 1916, you're not."

"Oh yeah. Well, when you find the gold, will you leave some there so I can find it after I *am* born?"

He shrugs. "Can't make any promises. Depends on how much there is."

"I hope there's lots."

"Yeah, me too."

I hear a horn honk and finally Aunt Donna's car is coming up the drive. Jeff and Marjorie are waving their arms out the window at me. I wave back at them and say, "Well, Mac, I'm going swimming. I'll see you later." But when I look over to where he is, he's already gone.

25

Sheldon
Friday, August 2, 1968

IN THE ROOM above me, Meg's footsteps tap lightly across the bare floor. I listen for another moment; now it's quiet. She has probably gone to bed. I sit here in the living room, looking at the Asheville paper. Looking, but not reading. I'm already too filled up to take in any more. And the shameful thing is, most of what fills me is my own sorrow. So much so, there is little room for anything else.

I'm certain I know now what sin is. It's a wall. It's one huge wall that keeps you from everything good in life.

It's almost midnight now. Linda should be home soon. I don't like to think of her out so late, but we are, at any rate, not in the big city anymore. Surely we are safe enough here in Black Mountain. Steve even tells me not to bother reading the Black Mountain News as nothing ever happens.

I'll leave the light on, so she can see when she comes in. I'd better go to bed myself, before it gets any later. I'm not used to working on Saturdays, having to get up early. Lots to do tomorrow, getting ready for the upcoming End-of-Summer Blow-out Sale. Reduced prices on every car in the lot. It almost sounds like something I should be excited about. If only I could muster up a little bit of enthusiasm for the job. Maybe it would help if I thought in exclamation points like the newspaper ads Steve has submitted to the Asheville Tribune ... *Huge End-of-Summer Blow-out Sale! Reduced prices on every car in the lot! You won't find a better deal anywhere! Come check us out and ...*

Nope. It's no use.

I toss aside the newspaper and head for the stairs, stepping lightly in my stocking feet. There is a nightlight on in the upstairs hall for Digger, in case he needs to find his way to the bathroom during the night, but also because he's not yet comfortable falling asleep in the dark. He is beginning to seem so grown up, I almost forget what a little guy he still is.

I stop at the door of my room and reach inside for the light switch, but before I find it, the light suddenly goes on and I discover I am not alone. A young man sits at the desk with his face only inches from a television screen.

He turns his head, and when he sees me, he stands abruptly as though coming to attention. We stare at each other for what must be only seconds, though it seems like a very long time. I know what Meg has told me about the house, and yet, I am trying to understand how it can be that this fellow is here. Finally, he says, "Don't be afraid."

Oddly enough, I am not afraid, only puzzled. I am made even more so by his announcement not to be afraid. It seems a strange way to greet a person, even a person who shouldn't be there.

"I suppose I should be surprised to find you here," I say in response. "But I understand that there's—something—about the house ..."

I'm not quite sure what to say, or whether an explanation is needed, though before I can go on the man jumps in and says, "I'm very pleased to be meeting you."

I take a small step forward. "You seem to have been expecting me."

"Not really, no. I was only hoping—"

"Do you know me, then?"

"Only in a manner of speaking. You see, I've heard of you."

"In what year do you live?" I ask, stepping closer.

"2005. And for you it's ..."

"1968."

"Yes." He says that as though he already knows and is simply agreeing. "I would shake your hand," he goes on, "but I'm afraid I can't."

"Why's that?"

"You don't know?"

"No, I suppose I don't."

He reaches out his hand to me, and though his flesh looks perfectly solid, when I try to clasp it, it somehow isn't there.

"We're not allowed to touch," he explains.

"Not allowed?"

"So it seems. Or not able. I don't fully understand."

"Neither do I."

"Well." He points to the wing chair beside the desk. "Would you like to sit a moment?"

I am being invited to sit in my own chair. "Thank you," I say. We both sit down. "My name is Sheldon Crane."

"Yes, I know."

"Oh? But then, I suppose you would. Since you are—in the future. But I'm afraid I don't know who you are."

"My apologies," he says quickly. "I should have introduced myself earlier. My name is Gavan Valdez."

Gavan Valdez. I am amused. The name seems the result of an odd coupling between an Irish lass and a Spanish gentleman. And yet he is so fair, he doesn't appear to have anything of Spain in him.

"Valdez," I say. "That's some kind of Spanish name, isn't it?"

"Hispanic, yes."

"You don't look Spanish."

"My mother married a man from Costa Rica when I was four. He adopted me."

"I see. And now you own this house?"

"Yes." He is distracted momentarily by the television screen. Something has happened to the reception and there are spirals, like those Slinky toys, rolling from side to side. He touches what looks like a typewriter keyboard on the desk in front of the TV, and the picture returns. But there is no sound.

"What kind of television is that?" I ask.

"Oh." He smiles. "It's not a television. It's a computer."

I'm baffled. A computer? "But computers fill whole rooms."

"Not anymore they don't." He looks amused as he says that.

I ask, "Why do you have a computer in your home?"

"Most people do today. They're called PCs. Personal computers."

"And everyone has one?"

"Not everyone. But most people. The way most people had TVs in their homes in 1968."

I am awed by this. "We have gone far then, haven't we?"

"In some ways, yes."

"But what do you do with—this thing? This computer?"

"Well, before you came upstairs, I was—well, I was kind of using it the way people used to use typewriters. It's called Word Processing. You type on the keyboard. See, it's laid out just like a typewriter, but it has more keys. Function keys. The words go into the computer and when you're finished, you can print it off here." He pats a boxy thing on the desk beside the computer. "I was just working on a lesson plan for the fall semester. I teach at Ridgecrest College. It's just up the road from here, about five miles."

I nod. I'm familiar with the college, but I'm intrigued with the machine. "So it's a modern typewriter," I conclude.

"Yes, but it can do so much more than that. I mean, it can give you all sorts of information. Anything you want to know."

"Do you mean, you can ask it a question and it'll tell you the answer?"

"Something like that."

"But how does it work?"

"Well, I'm not sure I can—"

He is interrupted by a tap on the door. Before I can say, "Come in," the door opens a crack and Linda pokes her head in the room.

"Dad," she says. "You still up?"

"Linda." I rise from the chair. "I didn't hear you come home."

"What are you doing? I thought I heard you talking to someone." She's all the way inside my room now.

"I'm—"

But Gavan Valdez and his machine are gone. He must have disappeared the moment Linda tapped on the door.

"I'm just getting ready for bed."

"Oh." That seems to satisfy her.

"You must be pretty tired yourself."

She shrugs. "I want to ask you something."

"Sure." Can she see that I am delighted? I am thrilled that she wants to speak to me.

"I want to call Monica and see how the guys are doing back home. I know it's long distance and all, but I thought now that I'm working, I can pay for it. I can call tomorrow when the rates are cheaper."

I wave my hand. "You go ahead and talk to Monica all you want, honey," I offer. "And you don't have to pay for it."

"Really?"

"Yes. You let me worry about the bills."

"You sure?"

"Of course. I should have told you to go ahead and call sooner."

She looks at me like she's not sure who I am. Finally she shrugs again. "Well, okay. Thanks, Dad."

I'm hoping she'll kiss me goodnight like she used to do when she was a little girl, but that is too much to hope for. She smiles at me briefly, though, before she leaves. At least that's something. Tomorrow she may be as grumpy as ever, but for the moment, in the warmth of that frail smile, I count myself blessed.

26

Linda
Sunday, August 4, 1968

SO THERE'S BEEN a double murder over in Asheville, and whoever did it is on the loose. Yeah, well, that's just great. Here I am, home alone, reading the Sunday paper while the rest of the family is off to church, and for all I know there could be some creep with a hatchet wandering around outside the house right now. I mean, Black Mountain is what—ten miles from Asheville? He could have made it this far in one night even if he's on foot. *Elderly couple slain in their home*, it says here. *The perpetrator should be considered armed and dangerous.* And Dad thinks we're safer down here than we were in Abington. Oh sure. See if he still thinks as much if he comes home and finds me hacked to death—

"So what's the news?"

I drop the paper and scream. This is it! The ax murderer is in the house, and I'm going to die! I'm—

"Hey, Linda, calm down! What's the matter?"

"Austin! Oh, it's you!"

"Sorry. I didn't mean to scare you."

I'm still trying to catch my breath when I say, "I just about had a heart attack, you jerk. How can you sneak up on me like that?"

"I didn't sneak up on you. I was just sitting here and then suddenly, there you were."

"Oh. It's ..." I don't know how to continue.

"A little hard to get used to?"

"Yeah. You could say that. So, what are you doing?"

He's in the chair Dad usually sits in. He waves a magazine and lets it fall to his lap. "Reading. Like you."

"Oh. Is it Sunday there?"

"Yes. Sunday morning."

"You alone?"

"For the moment. The family's at church."

"And you didn't go with them?"

He looks disgusted. "Churches are just tools in the hands of the capitalists."

Well, I'm stumped. Where in the world did he get that? I'm not fond of churches myself, but this is a whole new take on things. "What in the world are you talking about?" I ask.

"You know, the rich want the poor to believe in heaven so they'll be resigned to their lot on earth. They can spend their whole lives breaking their backs and never having enough to eat, but that's all right, so long as they get their heavenly reward in the end. If the poor are resigned and don't go after their due, then there's even more for the rich. The rich can keep getting richer, and the poor won't do anything about it."

"Hold on a minute, Austin. Just listen to you, talking that way when your own family's rich."

"Who told you that?"

"Vernita Ponder."

"Her again?"

I shrug, nod. "She said your family's not from around here, but that you came down from Chicago or someplace because your dad had TB."

"That's right."

"And she said you were rich."

"Yeah, well, my family may be well-off, but I'm not. I don't believe in being rich."

"You don't?"

"No, I don't. You know what the rich do? They spend their lives dancing on the misery of a million people."

Holy cow! Give this guy a soapbox, will you? I mean, is he practicing for the annual convention of American Commies or something? For a moment, I'm speechless. Then I say, "You have some pretty fancy ideas."

He shakes his head. "Nothing fancy about it. I just don't like social injustice. I don't like the fact that capitalism breeds inequality. I think it's dead wrong. And I intend to do something about it."

"Oh yeah? Like what?"

He waves the magazine again. "I'm going to join the American Socialist Party and work to change the system. It's the only way. We can't make any progress as a nation as long as we continue as a capitalist country."

For a minute, we just sit and stare at each other. Finally I say, "I'm not sure I'm following you."

"Well," he says, "how come you're not at church with your family this morning?"

"Because I think it's a bunch of baloney."

"So, see there?"

"What?"

"You've got the right idea. Of course, it's a bunch of baloney. Having faith in some unseen God is just foolishness, and all the church does is pander to people's ignorance. It *keeps* them ignorant instead of allowing them to progress."

"Well, whatever you say, Austin. I just think religion's totally irrelevant. Bunch of hypocrites, like my dad."

"Your dad?"

"Yeah. He was a pastor, you know. Up in Pennsylvania. He—well, you could say he had a fall from grace. So here we are. You know what I just found out from Gail at work, though? Billy Graham lives in the next town up the road. Can you beat it? My dad falls out of the pulpit and here we land practically in Billy Graham's backyard. How's that for crazy?"

He's looking at me with a puzzled expression. "Who's Billy Graham?" he asks.

"Who's Billy—" And then I remember. "Oh yeah. Never mind. I keep forgetting you're in another time."

He smiles a little. "I keep forgetting about it myself. So," he nods toward the newspaper in my lap, "what's the news?"

I suppose I could tell him about the double murder, but I don't really want to think about that kind of stuff too much. "Most of it's just a huge bore," I say. "It's an election year. You know, vote for this person, vote for that person, blah blah blah. Like it really matters who makes it into the White House."

"You think it doesn't matter?" he asks, looking steamed. "It makes all the difference in the world, who gets into the White House! Listen, it's an election year here too and ..." Suddenly he stops and looks at me like he's seeing me for the first time. "Say, Linda. You know who wins, don't you? You know who wins the election in 1916. Who is it?"

Jumping Jehoshaphat! Like I know who's running for president in 1916. He's asking the girl who got a D in history two years in a row and that by the skin of my teeth.

"I don't think I can tell you," I say. There, that's one way not to look stupid.

"Why not?" He looks offended.

"Well, it just wouldn't be right."

He starts to say something, stops himself. Then he smiles. "Maybe you're right. I'll find out soon enough anyhow. If Wilson's reelected, I just hope he'll keep us out of the war."

"The war?"

"The war in Europe."

Now I remember. Criminy! How could I forget? *Lots of young men were buried in France*, Mom said. "The First World War," I say aloud.

"What'd you say?" Austin asks.

"The First World War," I repeat breathlessly.

"What do you mean by that?"

I look at Austin and feel frightened. More than a week has passed since Mom and I were in the graveyard, and I had almost forgotten about our talk of war and of Austin's not coming back. "Listen, Austin," I say, "if the United States does get involved in the war, you won't go, will you? I mean, you'll burn your draft card like the other guys are doing, won't you?"

"Burn my draft card? Who's burning their draft cards?"

"Oh yeah," I sigh. "I forgot. That's today. That's Vietnam."

"Vietnam?"

"Oh, man, I'm getting confused. But I mean if there's a war, you'll try to get out of going, won't you?"

He looks at me a long moment. "I don't believe in war," he says. "War is something socialism will do away with."

"It is?"

He leans forward in his chair. "Don't you understand, Linda? In this country, right now, we're in a class war. Because of capitalism, we've got the rich and we've got the poor. The poor are struggling under the burden of injustice, though some of them, some of them are trying to lift themselves up, trying to find some sort of equality, but all the while the rich are fighting to keep them down. The whole system's built on greed, you know. But, you see, once we can get rid of private ownership, and once we overthrow capitalism and replace it with socialism, once the class war is won—and I mean, won all over the world, not just here but everywhere—then everyone will be free. There won't be any more exploitation or misery or inequality or war. We'll all be cooperating with each other instead of competing. We'll be working together, helping each other, living in peace. Can you imagine it, Linda? Can you see it?"

Right now, the only thing I can imagine is Austin Buchanan wearing a tie-dyed T-shirt and a beaded headband while he's sitting around with a bunch of peaceniks smoking weed and swaying along to the tune of "All You Need Is Love." It may be 1916 where he is, but it might as well be 1968, far as I can see. I mean, what is he? The original flower child or something?

If he weren't so doggone cute, I'd laugh right in his face. Maybe I'll laugh in his face anyway. How can anyone listen to this and not crack up? I mean, the world's on its way to hell in a hand basket, and he's sitting there talking about peace and justice and thinking things are only going to get better? I may not understand half of what he's talking about, but I *do* know how some things turn out between 1916 and 1968, and it's not exactly pretty.

"Listen, Austin," I say, "I hate to be the one to have to break it to you but—"

Well, good grief! How typical! Isn't that just like a guy? The minute you're ready to open your mouth and challenge them, they disappear as if they suddenly decided they got something more important to do than listen to a word you have to say.

27

Sheldon
Thursday, August 8, 1968

MEALTIMES CAN BE awkward. Like right now. The four of us sit around the dining room table, quietly downing our pork chops and mashed potatoes. Forks and knives tap out a dull thud on the cheap plastic plates. I search my mind for something to say, anything to break the silence. Finally, I remember. "Looks like I'll be closing another sale tomorrow," I announce, trying to sound enthusiastic. "All I need is the signature on the paperwork."

Meg gazes at me down the length of the table and manages the semblance of a smile. "That's good news, Sheldon," she says.

Linda offers what sounds like a grunt of approval, though I can't be sure.

Digger, his mouth bulging with food, grins at me and says, "Way to go, Dad! Pretty soon we're going to be rich!"

"Well …" I pause and clear my throat. "I don't know about rich, son. But—"

"Hey," Digger cries, "I forgot to tell you guys! Last time I saw Mac he said there's gold in these mountains and when he's bigger he's going to go looking for it!"

"Gold?" Meg echoes. "Are you sure?"

"Sure I'm sure! Mac told me some guy found enough gold around here to build himself a mansion over in Asheville."

"Oh sure," Linda says, rolling her eyes. "That's crazy. There's no gold around here."

"There is too! Mac said so!"

"Well, what does Mac know? He's just a kid."

"He knows plenty. Probably more than you know—"

I sense this is a good time for me to step in. "Well, Digger, there's been some mining done in these mountains, but mostly for gemstones, I think. And mica. And who knows, but there may be some fool's gold out there, but I haven't heard of gold being found around here."

"But Mac told me he knew for sure people had found gold."

"Well, he may think so, but—"

"Listen, Digger, I'm going to ask Austin next time I see him," Linda says. "I bet he'll say his little brother's a big fat liar—"

"Mac's not a liar!"

"All right, you two," Meg says. "That's enough. I'm sure there's some way to find out whether there's gold in these mountains, but let's drop it for now."

We turn back to our plates. The quiet returns. But after a moment, Meg speaks again. "So Linda, how often do you see Austin?"

Almost at once, Linda goes on the defensive. If she were a cat, her claws would be unsheathed. "I can't help it when he shows up, Mom! I mean, I'm just sitting there or something, and next thing I know, there he is. It's not like we're dating or anything, and besides you don't have to worry because he can't even touch me, you know—"

"Linda," Meg breaks in quietly. "I'm not accusing you of anything. I'm just asking if you happen to see him often."

Linda's eyes narrow and her mouth becomes a small line as she slices a bite-sized piece of meat off the chop. If it were possible, I would say she is rather sweet on this young man who lives in 1916. If so, surely it is a rather star-crossed affair, one whose end is inevitable disappointment.

Finally she shrugs and says, "I've only seen him a few times. The last time was Sunday. I haven't seen him since then. It's kind of creepy, never knowing when he might show up. The whole thing's kind of freaking me out but …"

She doesn't finish. I say, "Listen, maybe I'm wrong not to move us out of this house——"

"No," Linda says firmly. "No, I think we should stay here."

"Me too, Dad!" Digger agrees. "This is the coolest place I've ever lived."

"But," I say, "something is happening we don't understand. And you have to admit, it *is*, as you say, kind of creepy. People coming and going that don't even live in our own time. Is everyone all right with that?"

Silence. Befitting a strange question, I suppose.

Then Digger says with a shrug, "Sure. Why not, Dad?"

And Linda says, "It's all right with me as long as Austin doesn't show up when I'm in the shower or something."

"Well—" I begin, but Meg interrupts and says, "I think they may come only when we need them."

All eyes turn to her. Linda says, "Yeah? Why do you think that, Mom?"

"I don't know, Linda. It's just how it seems."

"Have you seen someone?" I ask Meg.

She nods. "A woman. Her name is Celeste. She works here in the house in 2005."

"Wow!" Digger cries, his eyes saucers. "You've seen someone who lives that far in the future?"

Meg nods again and Linda whispers, "Far out! Why didn't you tell us?"

Meg thinks about that. "I don't know, really. I've only seen her once. She's … she's very nice. She works for the man who owns the house at that time."

"Gavan Valdez," I say.

"What's that, Sheldon?"

"She must work for Gavan Valdez. He owns the house in 2005."

"How do you know that, Dad?" Linda asks. "You've seen him or something?"

"Yes, I've met him … once."

"Well," Meg says. "We all seem to have our … special someone, don't we?"

"I don't know," I say. "At least that's how it seems."

"What's the guy like," Linda asks, "who owns the house in the future?"

"Well, he's a young man, a college professor."

"Is he married?"

"I don't know."

"He is," Meg says. "But it's very strange. His wife is—" she stops and looks around. She seems reluctant to finish the sentence. "She's a soldier in the war."

"She is?" Linda asks.

"What war?" I ask.

"The one in 2005."

Silence again. Then Linda says, "Criminy, they're drafting women now? Or I mean, then—in the future? I think I'm glad I live now."

"Who are we fighting?" I ask.

"I can't remember—Iraq, I think Celeste said. She didn't tell me much."

"Man oh man, Austin would freak out if he knew."

"Why's that, Linda?"

"I don't know, Mom, I mean—he's a nice guy, but he's kind of weird. He's got this idea that if we can just get rid of capitalism there won't be any more wars. But good grief!" She laughs lightly and starts to count off on her fingers. "What he doesn't know is there's World War One, World War Two, Korea, and now Vietnam and *now* we know in 2005 there's *another* one. Sheesh, it would absolutely blow Austin's mind."

I ask, "Is the boy a communist of some sort?"

"I think he said he wants to be a socialist. Like he thinks if he can join this party he can change the world. You know, no more poor people, no more war. Just peace and harmony and everybody's happy."

"Well, that's not so strange, I suppose. A lot of people believed the same thing, back around the turn of the century," I say. "If I'm remembering my history right, socialism was pretty popular then, much more so than now."

"Yeah well, I was about to tell him that if he thinks America is on the road to happiness, he has another think coming. I was going to tell him the whole world's so screwed up by 1968, it's never going to get straightened out, but then he just up and disappeared on me."

I think about that a moment. "Maybe," I say, "you weren't supposed to tell him."

"But why not? He might as well know."

"It may be best for him not to know. It may be—" I make a line of my mouth and pause again. "It may be there are some things we're not supposed to tell them. And there are some things we're not supposed to be told."

"Why do you think that, Sheldon?"

I look at Meg and shake my head. "I don't know. It's just a feeling. Like your feeling about these people coming when we need them."

"Like there are rules to this game?" she asks quietly.

"Yes," I say. "Something like that."

"Oh sure," Linda spits out. "And who's supposed to have made the rules?"

I feel myself frowning. "God?" I say. It isn't an answer; it's a question.

Meg looks at me but says nothing.

Linda rolls her eyes.

Digger helps himself to more mashed potatoes.

Silence comes back and settles over the room.

28

Meg
Thursday, August 8, 1968

I'M WASHING THE supper dishes when Sheldon comes in and asks if he can help dry. I don't really want him to, but he has already picked up the dishtowel and begun to wipe the plates, so what can I do?

It's not yet dark outside, and won't be dark for another hour or more. Linda has gone off to work, and Digger is playing in the yard. I can see him out the window above the sink. He's such a happy child. I hope that never changes. I hope his joy follows him into adolescence and adulthood.

Sheldon speaks, his words seeping vaguely into my thoughts like smoke curling under a door. "I'm sorry," I say. "What was that?"

"I said, I wonder why it's happening, this whole thing with the house. Our being able to see into other times. Why do you suppose it's happening?"

I shake my head. "I don't have any idea. Maybe that's not for us to know."

He doesn't respond. He spends a full minute wiping the same plate before putting it away in the cupboard. Finally, he says, "There must be a reason."

Digger jumps off the big rock in the yard, his arms spread wide like he is trying to soar. My heart swells just watching him. "Maybe we're privileged in some way to be able to see into time," I say, "but, I don't know, Sheldon, I guess I'm more concerned with 1968 than with any other time."

He stops wiping a glass and smiles at me gently. "Of course you are," he says. "This is our time. This is where we live our lives."

I nod and turn back to the soapy water in the sink. "I find I don't really want to know what happens in the future."

"No, I guess I don't either. But I don't think that's what it's all about."

I think of the tombstones in the cemetery, and how I know that Mac will die in 1919. If I were to see his mother, the woman we saw in the hall the night of the shooting, what would I say to her? Would I tell her to hold her son close? To use every measure possible to protect him from illness? But I can't change what has happened, what for her *will* happen; what's done is done. Mac will die as a child. And I can't warn that mother to keep him from harm. I hope and pray I never see her again.

Shuddering, I blurt out, "I just want Carl to come home."

Sheldon lays a slightly damp hand on my shoulder. I don't pull away. "I want that too, Meg," he says quietly. "We have to keep believing he will."

"But these people we see who live in the future—Celeste and that man you've seen—they know. They know whether he will come home or not."

"Maybe they don't. Why should they? They don't necessarily know everything about us, simply because they live in the future."

"I don't want them to tell me what happens."

"I don't think that's their job. And somehow I think they know that, just as we know it."

I take a deep breath, and sigh heavily. "It's all so strange."

Sheldon laughs lightly. "Yes. Yes, it is. Who would believe it, if we told them?" He lifts his hand from my shoulder and goes back to drying the dishes.

We are quiet for a moment. Then I say, "I left Carl's letter—the one that came today—by your reading chair. Did you see it?"

"Yes. He sounds good. He sees it as a kind of adventure, doesn't he?"

"Because he's young," I say, "and he thinks he's invincible. Even with people dying all around him, he thinks it has nothing to do with him, as though he's exempt simply because he can't fathom his own death."

"But that's human nature, isn't it? Let's just be glad he's a clerk and not out leading point in the jungle somewhere."

"I suppose. Though I find it hard to be thankful for anything concerning this war. Sometimes I think it's never going to end. Maybe the war in 2005 is just a continuation of this war somehow. Maybe even Digger will go—"

"It will end," Sheldon says firmly. "And Carl will come home. What was it Nixon said yesterday about his top priority if he's elected president? He wants to bring an honorable end to the war in Vietnam, right? I think he means it. I think he wants to work for peace."

Sheldon's statement strikes me as naïve. "I'm not so sure," I retort. "A man will say anything when he wants to be president."

"Well, I suppose," Sheldon relents. Though my gaze is beyond the window, I know he is studying me. "What else is bothering you?" he finally asks.

There *is* something else on my mind at the moment. Taking a breath, I confess, "It's Linda—"

"Oh." He gives me an understanding smile. "I know her attitude can be hard to take but—"

"No, it isn't that. It's something else. You see, she's spooked by that crime spree over in Asheville. There's been another murder—well, you've read about it, I'm sure. First it was that elderly couple, and now a young woman's been killed the same way." I look down at the pot in my hands and shake my head. "It's awful to think about, somebody breaking into your home and doing that. The police don't have a clue. Anyway, Linda's afraid because she has to drive home from the ice cream parlor late at night, and she's alone—"

"I wish she'd told me," Sheldon interrupts. "I'll wait up for her, of course. I'll call down there and let her know I'll be watching for her. After tonight, I'll even drive her to work and pick her up if she wants."

"Well, I think she wants to be independent and drive herself. But, yes, it would be good to let her know you'll watch for her. We *are* so isolated up here on the mountainside, away from the town."

"I don't think we need to worry."

"Yes, well, you never think we need to worry."

He looks vaguely hurt. He says quietly, "I always pray for God's protection over us."

I think about that a moment. "Do you really, Sheldon?"

"Of course."

I don't want to be comforted by that but, strangely, I am. I wish I too could pray for God's protection, but I've never been good at prayer. I've never even been very good at believing that God would intervene, even if I asked him to.

"I hope he answers your prayer then, Sheldon."

Sheldon nods. He smiles, but his eyes are sad.

We go back to washing the dishes.

29

Linda
Thursday, August 8, 1968

"Hey, Linda, phone's for you!"

I can't imagine who's calling me or why, but Gloria's hollering at me, so I'd better get back there and see who it is. I finish scooping up a chocolate cone, then step back into the office and pick up the receiver from the cluttered desk.

"Hello?"

"Honey, it's Dad."

"Yeah?"

Gloria gives me a questioning look like she's wondering whether something's happened. I shrug.

"Mom tells me you're concerned about driving home alone—"

"Well—"

"So I just wanted to let you know I'll be watching for you. I'll walk you in from the car."

I want to tell him he doesn't have to, but I might as well admit I want him to. I mean, I don't want to be the next person making the headlines.

"Sure, okay," I say. "So, thanks, Dad."

When I hang up, Gloria asks, "Everything all right at home?"

"Sure. No problem." I'm sure not going to tell her the old man's going to be waiting up for me like I'm some sort of sissy or something. If Gloria wants to get axed to death, that's her business, but I'm not going to let it happen to me.

Gail didn't even know about the murders in Asheville. "You don't read the papers?" I asked.

"Naw. It's too depressing. There's never any good news anywhere."

I hardly ever read the papers myself, but I'm not going to let on.

Gail's out there now, serving up the coffee for the perverts. Good timing on the phone call, Dad. At least I was back in the office when the old men came in. I wonder what they're doing here. It's not even Saturday night. Guess we lucked out; get the honor of their company on a Thursday. Yeah, I'm sure they've got nothing better to do than sit around here drinking coffee and playing checkers. What a way to end a life.

And there's Bim too, the dead man walking. Sheesh, what a face. He won't even need to wear a mask come Halloween. That guy's a walking zombie. If I was Gail, I'd be embarrassed to say I was related to anything like that.

But Gail's cool. I like her. I mean, yeah, I guess you could say we're friends. Hey, wow, I made a friend in Black Mountain. Will wonders never cease? She's a far cry from Monica and the old gang up home, though. I mean, I can just see Gail and me smoking weed together out in the woods somewhere. No way, not Miss Goody Two-shoes. She's never smoked so much as a cigarette in her life. Told me so herself. "I'm not messing with any of that stuff, not even tobacco," she said.

"What are you, some kind of saint?" I asked.

"Naw, I just don't want to go down that road."

"Yeah? Well, you don't know what you're missing."

I should know. I'm missing it something fierce. What I wouldn't give for one small joint, just one chance to get high. Monica offered to mail me some grass. I almost said all right, but Mom's the one who drives to the post office to pick up the mail. How could I hide it from her? It'd be my head on a platter if she figured it out.

Back behind the counter, I'm waiting on a couple of kids who can't decide what they want when some middle-aged woman walks in the front door.

"Hi, Mom," Gail says.

So, what's this? A family reunion? Grandpa Bim is here, and now her mom.

"You want some ice cream?" Gail asks. She's smiling. She seems really happy to see her mom. They are one weird family.

"No thanks, sweetie," her mom's saying. "You forgot your pill, so I thought I'd bring it to you."

Criminy! Gail's on the pill? I can't believe it! I never would have thought—

"It's an antibiotic." Gail's looking at me like she read my mind or something. She lays an index finger against her temple. "I've got a sinus infection."

"Oh." Man, I was going to say, there's no way that girl's on the pill. "I didn't think you looked so hot. You sure you should be here?"

"Yeah, I'm okay. I'm past the contagious stage. Hey, you met my mom?"

No, I guess I haven't had the pleasure. So what's her name? She's Bim's daughter, right? So I guess that makes her … what? … Bimbo? A ha ha ha …

"Oh well, Mom, this is Linda. And Linda, this is my mom, Linda. You're both Lindas, remember!"

Oh yeah, now I remember. That grand coincidence. Gail's laughing like she's some sort of stand-up comedian, and she's just made the funniest joke in the world.

Her mother laughs too and says hello to me. Looking at her now, I notice she's got one giant ugly scar just above her right eyebrow. She's trying to cover it up with bangs, but it's not working so hot. You can see the scar, all red and bumpy, between the strands of hair.

"Glad to meet you, Linda," she says. "Gail's told me so much about you. Welcome to Black Mountain."

"Oh, um, yeah. Thanks."

Gail's drinking down her pill with a bottle of Orange Nehi. When she finishes, she says to her mom, "Why don't you sit with Gramps a while and have a malted or something?"

"No thanks, honey. Looks like Gramps is in the middle of a pretty intense game of checkers there, and I've got to get home and get the laundry out of the dryer."

Wow, the life these people live down here. What's Abington got—what's the whole of Philadelphia got—compared to excitement like that? I can't imagine why these hills aren't overrun with people just flocking in to join the fun.

Gail's mom leaves, and the two kids who can't decide what they want finally settle on a couple of root beer floats. After I fix them and ring up the sale, I ask Gail, "So, how'd your mom get that scar on her head?" Yeah, I know it's tacky. I shouldn't be asking about a scar, but I can't help it.

Gail doesn't seem offended, though. "Uncle Lyle hit her with an iron poker when they were kids. Not hard enough to kill her but hard enough to leave a scar."

I can't believe it! "You mean her own brother did that to her?"

"Yeah. Nasty, huh?"

"So how old was he?"

"Old enough to know better."

"Sheesh! Nice guy. So where's this uncle now?"

"Leavenworth."

I start cracking up. Now she *is* joking. "Yeah, that's good!"

"No," she says. "Really. He's in Leavenworth."

I stop laughing. Her family's getting weirder by the minute, but it's kind of cool. I've never known anyone who had someone in their family in prison.

"So what'd he do?" I ask.

"What *didn't* he do?" she says. "He has a criminal record as long as your arm."

"Oh yeah?"

"The last thing he did was kill a U.S. Marshal. That landed him in Leavenworth."

"Wow." I look over at Bim who's playing checkers with another of the perverts. Bim may be ugly as sin, but he looks too harmless to have a son in Leavenworth. I don't know what else to say, so I just say "Wow" again.

"But we're not close to him," Gail adds. As if she needs to explain.

"Um, I guess not. Is he ever getting out?"

"Yeah," she says quietly. "Soon as they're done frying him in the chair."

Double wow! Death row. I never would have guessed, coming from someone like Gail. All of a sudden she looks different somehow; like, a little more real or something, now that I know she's got an uncle on death row. Sheesh. People sure are full of surprises.

30

Sheldon
Sunday, August 18, 1968

A SOFT RAIN falls outside the window. I can hear the raindrops and wind rustling the leaves of the trees behind the house. The windowpane is streaked with dozens of tiny slithering droplets. What I see in the glass, though, is not the outside world, which is dark now, but my own wraith-like reflection and the reflection of Gavan Valdez sitting behind me in the wing chair. He appeared a few moments ago, jotting notes in the margin of a thick book on his lap. He says he is reading about the everlastingness of God, the one who had no beginning and will have no end.

"You are a theology professor," I say.

"That's right."

I turn from the window and look at him. He has a face I feel I've seen before, beyond the one time I met him earlier, but I cannot place it. He smiles kindly. I am comfortable with him, as though I've known him a very long while. "What do you think, then?" I ask. "About this—about our being able to see each other. Do you think it has something to do with God?"

He closes the book and leans forward in the chair. "I think it has everything to do with God," he replies.

I pace the room a moment, then sit down on the edge of the bed facing him. "How can we understand what's happening?"

"I'm not sure we can. Not fully, anyway."

"But do you have any idea?"

"Well—" He frowns, and two deep lines appear between his brows. "There are varying theories among theologians about God and time, you know."

I nod, though it's not a subject I studied while at seminary.

"Some theologians claim God exists within time, much as we do, and that as such, he experiences events in sequence, also as we do. Others claim God exists outside of time, that he exists but he doesn't exist *at* any particular time. Or perhaps, he exists at all times. So that, instead of experiencing events in sequence, he somehow experiences all things at once." He pauses and looks at me a moment. Then adds, "It's complicated, of course."

"Of course," I agree. "But what do *you* think?"

He nods. "Personally, I think he exists outside of time. I think he exists in an Eternal Now."

"An Eternal Now," I repeat. The room is quiet as the thought settles over us. "So that, to God, you and I don't actually exist at different times, but we both exist in this Eternal Now?"

"So it would seem."

"And this place, this house somehow, for whatever reason, is itself caught up in an Eternal Now?"

"I can think of no other way to explain it. Though, as I say, no one can know for sure. Who, after all, can understand the depths of God?"

I stand and walk back to the window. My hands rest together at the small of my back. The Eternal Now.

"But why?" I ask. "Why is this happening?"

"Consider it a gift," Gavan says.

"Oh!" I say, turning to him in surprise. "Then you've heard that too? That this is a gift? Who—"

"I'm not sure I can tell you that," he interrupts. "But yes, I've been told it's a gift."

There is so much I want to ask this young man who lives in my future. But in the next moment, he rises from the chair. I look at him questioningly.

"My son is crying," he explains as he moves across the room. "Another bad dream, I suppose. I'd better go tend to him."

Now I hear it, the child crying. "Of course," I say, "But …"

At the doorway Gavan stops and looks back, allowing me time to finish.

"But, you'll come back, won't you?" I ask.

"I'm always here," he says. "I'll see you again soon."

And then he leaves the room, and only my now remains. I'm alone again and filled with wonder.

31

Meg
Monday, August 19, 1968

I WALK INTO the kitchen and find Celeste dozing in one of the rocking chairs, her feet propped up on the hearth. I can't help but to gaze upon her face and wonder at the serenity so evident there. It's the middle of the day, and she's napping. I think of how she told me she came back to these mountains so she could stop spending money and just spend time. I myself have never had any money to spend, but neither do I think I've spent time, not the way Celeste does. I have not spent it, I've wasted it. I think I'm beginning to realize that now. I have wasted my time.

A phone rings. But it's not the phone on the kitchen wall. The ringing seems to be coming from near the fireplace. It's—why, it seems to be Celeste's shoe! How very odd. In 2005, people are like Maxwell Smart, Secret Agent 86. They can take the sole off their shoe and answer the phone!

Celeste goes on sleeping, undisturbed. I would put a hand on her shoulder to waken her, but I know that I can't do that. "Celeste," I say. She begins to stir. "Celeste, your shoe is ringing."

"What?" She looks up at me with puzzled eyes. She yawns and blinks. The phone goes on ringing. Suddenly, Celeste bursts out laughing. "Oh! Oh honey," she says as she pulls her feet from the hearth. "That's not my shoe. That's my cell phone!"

There is an odd silver device sitting on the stones. It had been hidden behind Celeste's feet. She picks it up, opens it the way you open a powder compact, pushes a button and says, "Hello?"

What's a cell phone? I wonder. How can Celeste be talking to someone on that little device that doesn't have a cord and isn't connected to anything?

"Yes, Mrs. See," she's saying. She laughs; she seems to be enjoying herself. "No, no, it's no problem. I can pick some up on my way to your place … Uh huh. No, don't worry about that. I'll see you around five … Uh huh. All right. You get some rest now."

She says good-bye and folds the device back together. She looks at me. "That was Mrs. See, the woman I work for in Asheville."

"But what's that thing?" I ask, pointing at the silver compact.

"Oh. It's a cellular phone. It's—well, never mind about that now. You'll know about them in another couple of decades or so."

"Phones don't need cords anymore?"

"Well, some models of landlines still have cords, but cell phones don't. They're made to be taken anywhere."

"It's a strange world," I say.

"That it is," Celeste agrees. Then she adds, "I'm glad to see you again."

I smile. I'm glad to see her again too, and tell her so. "It's nice to have some company up here," I say.

"Hmmm," she says. "You must get lonely sometimes, being new to town."

I haven't really thought about loneliness, not until this minute. But I suppose she's right; at times I do feel lonely. I sit down in the second rocking chair in front of the hearth.

She asks, "Do you miss Pennsylvania?"

I have to think a moment. "No," I finally say. "I guess I don't. I wouldn't want to be there anymore." I look at her. I realize suddenly she may know more about me than I think. "Do you know why we moved here?"

She smiles placidly, and her face fills with compassion. "I'm afraid so," she says quietly.

"Well," I say, "at least that keeps me from having to explain. But tell me, is it common knowledge? Does everyone in Black Mountain in 2005 know why we moved down here?"

"Oh no," she assures me. "I doubt anyone in Black Mountain in 2005 knows why you moved down here."

"But you do."

"Yes."

"May I ask how you happen to know?"

She's silent a moment, then says, "I'm not sure you'd understand if I told you."

I nod. I feel she is at some advantage, being in the future. But that is neither her choice nor her fault. "Maybe someday I'll understand."

"Yes," she says. "I think you will."

We rock quietly for a time. It's pleasant simply to be in her company. I feel remarkably at ease. I say, "Are you busy making wedding plans?"

"Oh my, yes. I guess that's why I was so fast asleep a minute ago. I was up half the night looking at wedding magazines." A smile fills her face. Her teeth are white and even, lovely as ivory against her pale brown skin. For a moment, I envy her joy. But I'm afraid for her too, wondering how long this happiness will last.

"I wish I could meet this young man," I say.

She laughs softly. "At the moment, Cleve is older than you are."

"Really?"

She nods, laughs again.

"Well," I continue, "I wish you all the happiness in the world."

"Thank you." After a moment, she adds, "Though I know what you're thinking. You're thinking every bride believes she's going to be happy, and it seldom works out that way."

"Hmm, yes." I find myself nodding. "Although I think it's possible to be happy. I think some couples are."

"Yes," she agrees. "I know some couples who are happy. Cleve's not perfect, but then, neither am I. I guess you could say we're both imperfect but perfectly suited for each other. I think so, anyway. He's such a good man, Cleve is."

"Sheldon is ... well, he's a good man too, certainly. And we were happy together for a long time. But then ..."

"But then, he went and had an affair," she finishes for me.

I nod, but I can't speak for the sudden tightness in my throat. I thought I was done with tears but apparently not. I brush them away and sniff, trying to compose myself.

"I'm sorry," Celeste says quietly. "I know he betrayed your trust."

"Yes, he did," I manage to say. "That changed everything. It effectively brought our marriage to an end."

She cocks her head. "And yet you're still together."

"For now," I say.

"Are you thinking of leaving?"

"I think of it every day. I just don't know ..."

"Don't know what?"

"What to do, where to go. How to support myself and the children."

"I see." She folds her hands and raises them to her chin. She looks deep in thought. Then, "Did he break it off with the other woman?"

"Yes."

"And is he sorry?"

"He says he is."

"Then why don't you forgive him and move on?"

I turn my gaze from her. How to answer? "I can't," I finally say. "I just can't forgive him."

"You're still too angry."

I nod slowly and look at her again. "Yes. Angry and hurt. Nothing will ever be the same again."

"No," she agrees. "I suppose it won't."

I take a deep breath. My tears are gone. I say, "Sometimes I want to ask you to find me in the future and find out what I chose. You know, did I leave him. and did I do the right thing?"

She smiles at that. "I'm afraid I can't tell you much about the future. It's simply ... not allowed."

"So there *are* some rules to all of this?"

"In a manner of speaking, yes."

"Are the rules meant to keep us from changing the course of events?"

"No, it's not that. The events themselves can't be changed, as such."

"You mean, the future's set, the way Calvin always said it was?"

"Well, I don't know about all that. I only know there's a limit to what can be revealed between us. If I were to start to tell you something you're not supposed to know, you or I—one of us—would simply disappear."

"I don't understand."

"And I don't either, really. But listen, honey, you don't need to look into the future to know what's the right thing to do."

I sigh at that. "You think I should forgive him, don't you."

"I don't think you'll ever be happy until you do."

I look at my hands in my lap and shake my head. "I don't know, Celeste. I'm not sure I can forgive him and mean it."

"All right then," she says. "You don't have to forgive him today, honey. Nor tomorrow. Nor even the day after that. I hope you will eventually, but for right now, maybe what you need is time. Lord knows it takes time for anger to die down and for wounds to heal. My suggestion to you would be to move on down here to Black Mountain and rest yourself awhile."

I frown at her. "I don't understand. I *have* moved to Black Mountain."

Celeste stops rocking and leans forward in the chair. "Honey," she says, "your body's here, but your mind's in Pennsylvania, wrestling with the things of the past. Come on down here and just let yourself rest." She relaxes back into the chair and begins to rock again gently, as though to show me what it is I ought to do. In another moment, she closes her eyes and hums a tune. I recognize it as a hymn we sometimes sang when Sheldon was a pastor. *There is a balm in Gilead, to make the wounded whole* ...

I too lean back in my chair and, shutting my eyes, I simply listen. *There is a balm in Gilead, to heal the sin-sick soul* ...

I listen until she fades away, and the room is quiet. I open my eyes. I walk to the front porch and look out over the sloping front lawn, the towering trees, the distant hills. I am here in Black Mountain, North Carolina. Come and rest awhile, she said. It is an invitation to spend time. It is, quite possibly, the loveliest invitation I have ever received.

32

Linda
Wednesday, August 21, 1968

WHEN I SEE Austin walking up the drive, I get the same feeling I used to get when I saw Brian walking down the hall at school. It's like, the best thing in the world just happened, and I wouldn't want to be anyone else, or be any*where* else, or be doing any*thing* else. I just want to be right here with him, wherever he is.

He sits down on the porch steps beside me. "You spend a lot of time here on these steps, don't you?" he says.

"Yeah," I say, "I guess I do."

"You been waiting for me?"

"I guess I was," I admit.

"Well, that's good, because I was hoping you'd be here."

"You were?"

"Yeah."

We just sit there for a minute saying nothing, but it doesn't feel weird or awkward. It just feels kind of nice. "Where've you been?" I ask.

"At work."

I realize then that his cheeks are flushed, and his face is shiny with sweat, and his overalls are dirty and dusty. His longish hair, which he usually combs straight back, is hanging down around his ears.

"I've been meaning to ask you about that," I say. "If your family's rich, why do you work?"

"To experience the life and hardships of the working class," he says, and he sounds like he's shooting back an answer to the Baltimore Catechism or something. Like it's something he's worked hard to memorize, and he can't wait to recite it.

All I can think of is, oh yeah, we're back to that mess about the poor working class. Austin seems like a different person when he's talking like that, and I'd rather he just be the nice hunky guy instead of the intellectual socialist wannabe. "Um," I say, "so where do you work?"

"The Swannanoa Furniture Manufacturing Company. It's down by the river between here and Asheville. We make furniture."

Yeah, I gathered that much on my own. "So, you walk all that way?"

"Naw. A guy named Chester Randolf picks me up and drops me off at the bottom of the drive. He got me the job there. We work the same shift."

"So, you like it?"

He laughs a little at that, and gives me a look that says I've got to be kidding. "No, I don't *like* it." He's mimicking me, and I don't like *that*. I'm not going to say anything, though. He goes on, "It's grueling and it's demeaning, and it's one more place for the bourgeois to take advantage of the working poor."

"Oh. Okay." I can't even remember what bourgeois means, but I suppose he's talking about the rich. Gee whiz, Brian never talked like that. He just talked about getting high on weed and drag racing at night in front of the school. Things I could understand.

"It's just all wrong," Austin goes on. "Long hours and little pay, and there's not a man or a woman there who's considered by the bourgeois owners to be a real human being. They're just cogs in a wheel, they're just part of the machine that does nothing for *them* but does everything to make the rich guy richer."

"Uh huh." I kind of scrunch up my eyes and try to look like I'm thinking hard on that one. "Is that how that Chester guy feels about it too?"

Austin's quiet a minute. Finally, he admits, "He's never said one way or another. But I'm sure he doesn't want to be there."

"How do you know if he's never said?"

"No one in their right mind would want to be working in a factory. No one with any education, anyway. That's the problem; Chester's got no education. He told me himself he dropped out of school in the third grade. That's why he's doing what he does. Because he can't do anything else."

"So maybe he likes making furniture. Maybe he's proud of his work. Why don't you ask him?"

"I don't need to ask him."

"Why not?"

Austin looks at me and says, "Listen, you ever heard of Eugene Debs?"

I shake my head. "I don't know. Maybe in history class or somewhere."

For a second, Austin looks cross. "Everyone should know who Eugene Debs is. Someday everyone *will* know who he is. Like George Washington. No, better than that, because Debs is going to change the country. Maybe the whole world."

"So he's what, some kind of politician or something?"

"He's only the leader of the whole Social Democratic Party," Austin shoots back. "He's run three times for president on the Socialist ticket. Next time, he's going to win."

Yeah, well, I don't remember learning about any President Debs, but I guess I'm not supposed to spill the beans about stuff like that.

Suddenly, Austin looks at me hard and says, "Listen, I know you know things about the future that I don't know, and I don't blame you for that. But 1968 isn't the end of history. I mean, you don't know *every*thing. You don't know what's going to happen *after* 1968."

I shrug and just kind of sniff, like of course I don't know what's going to happen after 1968 and what's your point? Criminy, he's all of a sudden got some sort of chip on his shoulder. I just look at him and say, "So?"

"So no matter what you might tell me about the next fifty years, I'm not going to stop believing in my dream, and my dream is that we're going to end up living in a socialist society where everybody's equal and everybody's taken care of. It's going to come sometime, whether it's before 1968 or whether it's after."

I shrug. "Well, that's okay, Austin. I mean, it's a free country, right? You can believe whatever you want to believe."

"It's a free country, yeah, but not in the right way. Until everyone is equal, we're free in the wrong way. We're free only for the few. The few rich and the few powerful, and that's it. Everybody else is in bondage to the system."

"They are?"

"Yes."

"Well, my family's sure not rich, but I've never felt like I was in bondage to any system."

"That's because you just don't know."

"I don't?"

"You're just going along with it because you don't know there can be a better way."

"I am?"

"Listen, Linda, there's a new day coming. I don't know when it's going to come, but I'm going to help bring it in. That's what I'm here for. That's why I'm alive. I can feel it in my bones."

His talk about a new day coming sounds familiar. That's what all the hippies are talking about, isn't it? I mean, this is the dawning of the Age of Aquarius, right? "Oh, well, you know," I say, "there are plenty of people today who talk about a new day dawning, stuff like that."

"There are?"

"Sure. I mean peace and harmony. Brotherhood of man. People say it's coming. So, yeah, I guess you could say people are still working on it. People want it, that's for sure." I give him one nice big, peace-loving smile.

"Yeah?" he says, smiling back at me. "That's good. That's good. That means we're still moving forward."

"Sure, I guess so." I might have just won myself a few points with Austin, even though I don't believe a word of it.

"You know what it's going to be like to live in a classless society, Linda?"

"No. I guess I don't."

He smiles serenely, closes his eyes, lifts his face a bit higher. "Paradise," he whispers.

I'm not going to say as much, but he looks like he's just hit the sawdust trail at a Billy Graham Crusade. I mean, I should know. I'm the daughter of a Baptist preacher who gave an altar call practically every Sunday at church. So I don't know—I guess whatever your idea of Paradise is, that's cool.

"Okay," I say, "so that would be, the world's going to be perfect someday, right?"

"Yes." He opens his eyes. "Once we get rid of capitalism and we're living in a classless system. Think of it, Linda. No more war, no more poverty, crime, hatred, hunger. No more illness—"

"No more illness?" Okay, here's where I draw the line. Seems a big stretch to me, saying no one's going to get sick anymore just because there's been an overhaul in the government.

"Well, yeah, eventually."

"And how do you figure that?"

"Knowledge," he says. "Progress. Education. We can master science; we can learn how to keep people from getting sick."

I think about how far we've come in the way of medicine since 1916. Sure, we got antibiotics now, and we got the polio vaccine; I know that much. But I can hardly believe we're going to get smart enough to keep people from getting either a cold or cancer. I mean, like what? We're going to start producing perfect bodies or something? Blame it on my upbringing, but I just can't see things getting that good. Everything's too much of a mess and, to me, people are basically rotten. I don't know about the Fall and all that stuff, but it sure seems to me the world's way too bad to ever be as good as Austin thinks it's going to be.

"I'm not sure I can see it, Austin," I admit. "I mean, the world's a pretty bad place, you know? Bad things happen all the time, and I don't know if we can change that. Dad says it's because of the Fall."

"The Fall?" he says. "Well, your dad's a preacher, right?"

"Yeah. Used to be, anyway."

"So, all right, he has to believe that. But listen, forget about the Fall. Forget about evil. It doesn't exist."

"It doesn't?"

"No. Not really. But ignorance does. It's ignorance that causes the problems. That's why we have to get rid of ignorance. We need to keep moving forward, gaining knowledge all the time. That's the only thing that's going to save us."

Baloney. And I'm not just saying that because I'm fifty years ahead of him, and not just because I've got Baptist roots, but because I've got eyes, and I can see where the world's headed, and it isn't toward any sort of Paradise on earth, that's for sure. Just the opposite, far as I can see. Bottom line: I don't think we can be saved. I think people are going to go on being rotten till we wipe each other out—probably in some sort of atomic war or something. But what, like Austin's going to believe me if I tell him about flying across the ocean to drop atomic bombs? He probably can't think any bigger than Molotov cocktails, and far as he's concerned airplanes are nothing more than oversized kites. And I'm going to try to tell him we dropped a bomb out of a plane that wiped out an entire Japanese city in a matter of minutes? Right. Let his 1916 mind chew on that one for a while. Yeah, sure. Say Austin, we got this little thing called nuclear power now. So while you're back there in time worrying about things like chopping enough wood to keep your feet warm in the winter, over here we're ducking under tables in air raid drills in case Russia decides to drop the big one on us. Think about it, will you? If I said the words "air raid shelter" and "nuclear fallout," you wouldn't have a clue what I was talking about. So welcome to the world of progress.

I'm not going to try to tell Austin any of that stuff, wouldn't do it even if the Great Rule-maker let me. One, Austin wouldn't believe me. Two, I like him too much to disappoint him.

"Well, I'll say this much for you, Austin. You've got big plans for the human race."

He nods, and he actually looks kind of proud. "It's not just me, Linda. Lots of people believe it. Lots of people are working for it. I'm just sorry I won't live long enough to see it, but maybe it's enough to have a part in bringing it about. We're building a kingdom here on earth better than anything heaven has to offer. I mean if there were a heaven, that is."

"But there isn't."

"No. We can't be hoping for some sort of eternal life that's going to make up for this one. That's why we have to work to change the world. All we have is now."

I have to think about that for a while. Something's bugging me, something I don't understand, and I've got to figure out how to get it into words. Finally, I say, "Okay, I think I'm following you, Austin, but I'm wondering about one thing. If you're right—and I'm not saying you're not—but if you're right, and all we have is now, would that be your now or mine?"

Austin looks at me like I'm asking him a trick question—even though I'm not really—and then he changes the subject. I guess he doesn't know the answer.

33

Sheldon
Sunday, August 25, 1968

"If I'm not being too intrusive, do you mind if I ask you what you're doing with that machine?"

"Why, hello, Sheldon. I didn't notice you. Have you been here long?"

"No, only a moment."

Gavan looks from me back to the screen of—what did he say it was? A PC? A personal computer. He had been staring at it intently until I interrupted him. "It's—well, I'm reading a letter. It's from my wife, Melissa."

"A letter?" I lean forward in the wing chair and try to see the words on the screen, but then I realize that if it is indeed a letter, it's not addressed to me and not mine to read. I look away, settling my eyes on Gavan's face again.

"It's called an email," Gavan explains. "That is, electronic mail."

"But how did you get the letter into that, um … computer?"

Gavan is frowning in thought. "I didn't put the letter in there. Melissa sent it to me from the computer where she is. It comes to me through cable modem."

"I'm afraid I don't understand."

"Hmmm. You see, the message is sent from one computer to another, something like—well, say, the way a telegram was once sent from one telegraph machine to another. Melissa types the message into her computer, then sends it to mine where I'm able to call it up and read it."

The gap between our eras is somewhat too great for me. I can see why people must move forward moment by moment, taking in small bits of life at a time.

"Your wife," I say. "She's a soldier, right?"

"Yes, with the National Guard. Her unit has been deployed."

This to me, too, seems inconceivable. The woman has gone off to war while the man is here on the home front. With the child. And this, not forty years from now. What lies in those individual moments ahead that would bring about this kind of change?

"How is it," I ask, "that it's the women now who go to war?"

He chuckles at that. "It's not as though our troops are made up entirely of women. They're still far in the minority as far as the military goes. And they aren't drafted. Well, men aren't drafted anymore, either. We have a volunteer military, at least for the present. Both men and women volunteer."

"So the women who go to war, they *want* to go?"

"I suppose you could put it that way, though it isn't that they want to go to *war*. What they want is to be in the military, whether our country is at war or not."

"And so they become soldiers, just like men?"

"Well, for the most part, yes."

"Women? Wives and mothers?"

"Yes."

"They go to war and—get killed?"

Gavan nods solemnly. "Sometimes."

I am stupefied. I try to imagine Linda marching off to war, and I can't. She won't, of course. Not Linda. Though, perhaps, her daughter might if this is indeed what the future holds. "And we as a country—we allow this?"

"We can't *not* allow it. That's what gender equality is all about."

"I'm not sure I like the idea," I say.

"You're not alone in that," Gavan assures me. "But women have many more choices today than they did even in your time."

"I guess they must. But how do you—well, I'm not sure I could let my wife go to war."

Gavan gives me an understanding smile. But then, just as quickly, he shrugs and says, "Melissa was a member of the National Guard when I married her. It wasn't something she surprised me with later. Being a soldier was part of who she was."

"But wouldn't you rather the tables were turned? That is, that you were there and she were here?"

"You have to understand," he replies gently, "it was her choice to go."

"Does that make it right?"

"For her, I think it must."

He seems unsure, and perhaps uncomfortable, as though I am questioning him as a husband, as a man. I'm not, really. I simply want to understand. But I'll let it drop, turn the conversation to a slightly different vein. "At any rate, we've got ourselves into another war, haven't we?"

"I'm afraid so."

I think about Vietnam, of how little has been gained, how we likely shouldn't be there. "Is it a necessary war, this one we're fighting in your time?"

"I believe it is, yes. Though certainly not everyone thinks so. Many are dead-set against it. So, unfortunately, it's a divisive issue in our country right now."

"Something like Vietnam, then."

"It's similar, as far as our being unable to agree about it. Really, the last war that saw us unified was the Second World War. You know, Victory bonds, scrap metal drives, everyone pulling together—that sort of thing. Now Americans are too busy arguing with each other to present any sort of united front to the enemy. So," he smiles morosely and shrugs, "war within, war without. It can get rather ugly on the editorial pages."

"The world seems a strange place in 2005."

"Yes. But then, the world was a strange place in 1968."

When I think of my own era, of the cultural upheaval and drug-induced sorrows, I have to agree. Every generation is immersed in its own fashion of peculiarity.

"But, Gavan?"

"Yes, Sheldon?"

"I'm sorry, but I have to ask. Aren't you afraid? You and your wife have a child together. Aren't you afraid of losing her?"

"Yes. Of course I am. I pray she'll come home."

"How do you live with it, then?"

He presses his hands together and lifts them to his mouth in thought. Finally he says, "I know that God is with her. Or, if she is killed, I know she will be with God. Either way, God is there. That's how I live with it. Otherwise, I couldn't."

God is with her, or she is with God.

I nod thoughtfully. He turns back to his machine and goes on reading.

34

Linda
Monday, September 2, 1968

So THIS IS Gail's house, this brick rambler that looks about as interesting as peanut butter on white bread. I guess it's a step up from a single-wide, but not by much. Compared to this place, I live in Elvis's Graceland. But then again, plenty of the houses around here are about as classy as this one. Or worse. Unless you live in Uncle Steve's neighborhood, where the wealthier folks hang out together in big new homes.

Well, anyway, I'm glad she's coming with me to Uncle Steve's party. That way she and I can find something to do, and I won't have to go around being friendly to a bunch of people I don't know and pretend like I'm having a good time just so Aunt Donna doesn't feel bad. Like I really want to spend Labor Day with Uncle Steve's family and a bunch of their weird friends, but then again there's nothing else to do, is there?

I ring the doorbell and then I see Gail bouncing down the front hall. She swings the front door wide open, greeting me with that million-kilowatt smile. "Hey, Linda! Come on in," she says. She's dropped her northern lingo in favor of the local greeting, yelling "Hey!" at everyone she sees. I'd better be careful, or I'm going to end up mutating into some sort of southern hick myself.

"You ready?" I ask.

"Almost."

Not that I'm in any sort of hurry to get to this particular party. I'd just as soon Gail and I skipped out and drove right past Uncle Steve's and on over to Asheville to spend the day there shopping. But Mom would have a fit, and it wouldn't be worth the wrath of Meg Crane. So we'll put in an appearance, help ourselves to the food, and maybe do something fun later. Though I still haven't figured out what's fun to do around here. The only thing I really enjoy is seeing Austin, and that doesn't happen very often, and it's not like I can call him up and ask him to come over or anything. He just shows up out of nowhere, hangs around a while and disappears. All we can do is talk. I can't even hold his hand. Yeah, Mom and Dad would get a kick out of that, I guess. Better than any chastity belt—this falling for someone who lives in another time.

I'm following Gail into the room off the hall, not knowing where she's going or why we don't just head out to the station wagon I've got parked halfway up the sidewalk out front. I never was good at parallel parking, and I didn't realize I was on the sidewalk till I got out, but I figured I'd only be a minute. We enter what I guess is a living room but it doesn't have carpeting, just a bare floor, and it looks like it's been furnished with stuff you'd see piled next to a Salvation Army dumpster. Well, I guess not many people live in luxury when you're a widow trying to keep your family together. I have to feel sorry for Gail's mom, her husband dying on her and all that. And now she has to work. She's even working *today,* on a holiday, because the stores are having their big sales and Mrs. Leland works in ladies lingerie over at Harris Dry Goods. What a life.

"Hey, Gramps," Gail says, and then I notice the old guy sitting in the ugliest flea-bitten overstuffed chair I've ever set eyes on. He looks like he's sinking down into it, like all the springs are gone or something, and there's nothing to hold him up except maybe his own two stocking feet anchored on the matching footstool. If he lifted up his feet, he'd disappear.

"I'm going with Linda now," Gail is saying, and the old man is looking at me like he's not sure whether I'm taking his granddaughter away for good or if he can trust me to bring her back. "I just have to get the cake in the kitchen." She turns to me then and explains, "I made a cake. I didn't want to go empty-handed."

"That's nice," I say, though *I'm* going empty-handed to my own uncle's Labor Day party, and she's going to make me look like a dork, but maybe the food Mom's taking will count for me too. Whatever. I wish she'd just grab the cake and get going because I don't like being in the same room with a dead person, especially one who's got his eyes on you and won't look away. Old people always give me the creeps, especially when they're men.

"I'll be right back," Gail says.

And even though I want to follow her, I don't move because it seems like what I'm supposed to do to be polite is stay here and talk to her grandfather—which is just about the last thing on the face of this earth I want to do. He's sitting there sinking into that pothole of a chair, and he's looking at me like he's waiting for me to say something, and finally, I decide I'd better because saying something, anything, has got to be better than standing here in this embarrassing silence. "So, how you doing?" I ask. I don't want to call him Bim or Grandpa Leland, so I don't call him anything at all.

He goes on staring at me like maybe I wasn't talking in English or something, but finally he says, "Not bad, for an old man."

I laugh because I think he's maybe trying to make a joke, but when I see he's not even smiling I shut up. I feel my mouth going dry and my stomach turning slightly, and I wish Gail would hurry up with that cake. What in the world could be taking her so long? She still baking the thing or what?

"And how are you?" the old guy says, and then he adds, "Linda," and it gives me the willies to hear him say my name. Plus, when he presses his lips together, a drop of saliva on his lower lip sticks to his upper lip and forms a small column of spittle that expands like a rubber band while he's talking.

I tell him I'm fine even though his beady eyes are freaking me out. He nods his head just slightly, and he looks like he's trying to figure something out, though I can't imagine what, though if he's like the other old men at the ice cream parlor he's probably just wishing he was eighteen again. Yeah, well, sorry. Your life's over, and you missed your chance.

"You liking Black Mountain?" he asks in his gravelly voice. The column of spittle disconnects from the upper lip and collapses.

"Yeah, sure," I say, but I'm thinking if Gail doesn't make an appearance in about one second I'm going to hightail it out of here quicker than you can say Jim Beam. But not before I've wrung Gail's neck for leaving me here with the old man.

"You living up at the old Cisco place?"

"Yeah. Why? You know the place?"

Now his jaw works a while like his mouth has misfired or something and he has to get his motor started again before he can get the words out. Finally, he says, "No. I haven't been there." He shakes his head and says again, "I've never been there. Never." And I wonder why he's trying so hard to convince me he's never been there because I don't care if he has or not.

Just then, Gail calls from the kitchen, "Sorry to be taking so long. I'm trying to find the cake tin."

Forget the cake tin, I want to say. Forget the *cake*. Let's just get out of here. "Can I help you?" I holler, hoping she'll pick up on the desperation in my voice.

But she just hollers back, "No, here it is. I'll be right there."

I look at the old man again, and he's still looking at me. But now he's got this expression on his face like, I don't know what—like he's afraid or something, or like he really wants to say something but he doesn't know how to say it, or maybe he wants to cry out for help because the chair really is sucking him up like a Venus Fly trap capturing a fly, and he's afraid he'll never get out again. But then Gail finally appears carrying a plastic cake tin and looking as cheerful as ever, having no idea her old gramps and I have been in here having the equivalent of a conversational nightmare.

"Bye, Gramps." She bends down and kisses his scruffy old cheek, and it may be my imagination, but I can smell his rancid breath like I'm the one kissing him. "I hate to leave you here alone. I wish you could come with us."

Over my dead body! But thankfully the old man waves his hand and says, "I'm fine, dear. You go on and have a good time."

I've never been so glad to leave a house in all my life, not since that time I had dinner at Monica's and her great uncle, the one from Sausalito, spent the whole meal coughing up phlegm and spitting into his napkin. I hope God goes ahead and kills me before I ever get old. I'd rather die young than spend the last years of my life giving myself the creeps.

35

Digger
Tuesday, September 3, 1968

DAD'S SITTING AT his desk all hunched over with his forehead on his hands. "Dad?" I ask.

He looks up surprised, like maybe I woke him up or something. "Well, hi, Digger. Come on in."

"Whatcha doing?"

"Just paying some bills, going over the budget. Nothing fun, I'm afraid."

I walk over to the desk where he's got big piles of paper everywhere.

He's smiling at me, but he doesn't look happy. He just kind of looks like his stomach hurts. "You getting ready for bed?" he asks.

"Yeah."

"Big day tomorrow, huh?"

I nod. First day of school. I wish summer would just keep going forever. "Linda's mad about having to drive me to the bus stop every day."

"She'll get over it."

"Next year she won't have to 'cause she'll be gone to college. Then she won't be around to bug me anymore."

Dad's smiling again. "I think you'll probably miss her when she's gone."

"No way! I'll be the only kid left at home. I'll be able to do whatever I want without anybody yelling at me."

Now Dad's trying to look mean, but I know he's just pretending. "Well, not exactly, Digger. You'll still have to put up with your mother and me."

"Yeah, well, that's okay. You guys are nice."

He puts his hand on my head and messes up my hair, the way he always does when I say something that makes him happy. "I'm glad you think so, son."

I look back at the papers on his desk. "Hey, Dad?"

"Yes, Digger?"

"I've saved up ninety-five cents from my allowance. You can have it if it'll help."

Dad doesn't say anything for a long time, just sits there looking at me with his lips all pressed tight together. Then he says, "Thanks, Digger. But you keep it. We'll be fine."

I shrug. "Okay, if you're sure."

"Yes, I'm sure."

He smiles at me, and I smile back. Dad looks at his watch and says, "Well, guess you'd better hop on into bed. Mom tucking you in?"

"Yeah. She said to holler when I was ready."

"Did you brush your teeth?"

"Yeah."

"Let me see."

I smile real big so he can see all my teeth. Then I remember. "Say, Dad, look. This one's pretty loose."

I take his finger and put it on the tooth down on the bottom that's starting to wiggle. Dad's eyebrows fly up, and he looks surprised and happy, like I've done something really good.

"Hey!" he says. "Won't be long before the tooth fairy comes. That is if you're not too big for the tooth fairy now."

And miss out on a nickel? No way! I shake my head real hard. "Nope. Soon as it comes out, I'm putting it right under my pillow."

"Good boy," Dad says. "Now, you're not too big for a goodnight hug and kiss, are you?"

He opens his arms, and I fall into them the way I like to do, because he always catches me. He pulls me up on his lap for a minute and wiggles back and forth like we're doing a little dance, and then he kisses my cheek and I smell the last of that aftershave he always wears. It smells good. It smells like Dad.

"Goodnight, Dad," I say.

"Sweet dreams, Digger."

I go out to the hall and holler for Mom to come tuck me in.

36

Meg
Saturday, September 7, 1968

"So how are the kids doing in school?" Donna asks.

We're sitting in the kitchen, she and I, in the rocking chairs by the hearth. Digger and Marjorie are playing out back. Steve and Sheldon are at work. Linda, thankfully, has found a friend in Gail Leland and is spending the afternoon with her. In the evening, they'll go to work together at the ice cream parlor.

"Well, you know Digger," I say. "He does fine wherever he is. He says he likes his teacher and the other kids in the class. So far, so good—as far as the third grade goes. But Linda ..." I shrug and look past Donna's shoulder to the open kitchen door. I can hear the kids laughing in the yard. It is a lovely sound. "Linda doesn't tell me much, you know."

Donna glances up toward the ceiling and nods her understanding. "Ditto with Jeff, now that he's almost sixteen. He's in his own little world, never wanting to tell us anything."

We exchange a knowing smile, one that seals our sorority as mothers of teenagers. "My sense is that it's going better than Linda thought it would," I say. "At least, she grunted something that sounded like a yes when I asked if she liked the teachers. She did tell me in actual words that she's joined the yearbook staff. That probably means some kids on the staff are worth getting to know, in her humble opinion. Probably the editor is a tall, dark, and handsome senior."

Donna laughs, "Now that you mention it, I believe the editor this year is Rodney Sugarman. He's not dark, but he *is* tall and handsome. I believe he's also captain of the track team. One of those all-around good kids, involved in a little bit of everything at school."

"Well, that explains Linda's sudden interest in the yearbook then."

Outside, Marjorie wails, giving off a scream of obvious frustration. Donna sighs, pushes herself up from the rocker, and goes to the door, with me close behind.

"What's going on, kids?" she yells through the screen.

Marjorie is stamping her foot on the ground and glaring at Digger. "He won't wear the clover necklace I made!"

I laugh quietly to myself, but holler over Donna's shoulder, "Digger, be nice and wear the necklace."

"Ah, Mom! That's girl stuff!"

"No one's going to see you other than Marjorie. Just wear the necklace."

Marjorie, looking triumphant, slips the necklace over Digger's head. He scowls, but in another moment raises his hands and, giving a playful whoop, starts to chase his cousin around the yard. She squeals in delight as she runs away, but she can't outrun Digger, and in another moment they're tumbling together in the grass and laughing again.

"Digger's a good sport," Donna remarks.

"Yes, he's a good little guy." I'm proud of my son, and I feel my mother-love swelling against my ribs.

I offer Donna some coffee, but she says no thanks, and so we sit again. "I've got a hundred things to do around the house," she says, "but they're just going to have to wait. I'd much rather just sit here and talk with you."

"I'm glad you're here," I say. "You don't come over nearly enough."

She nods. "Life has a way of interfering with those things we really want to do, doesn't it?"

"Yes, I guess it does. There's just never enough time for everything."

"No," she agrees quietly. Then she says, "Yesterday, I saw Vernita Ponder when I went into town to have my hair done."

"Oh?"

"She pulled me into the back room and asked whether we'd told anyone about the house. She's very concerned that word not get around."

"She doesn't need to worry. I'm certainly not going to tell anyone, and neither are Sheldon and the kids."

"You don't think Digger will slip up, maybe say something at school?"

"No, I don't think so. And if he did, who'd believe him? He's a kid. Kids make up all sorts of stories that no one believes."

"Yeah, I guess you've got a point."

"So what about you? You still haven't told anyone, have you?"

"Heavens, no."

"And you haven't told Steve?"

"No," she says again, emphatically. "Maybe someday I'll tell him, but not yet."

We sit quietly awhile. We listen to the children play. Then she says, "If I sit here long enough, do you think I'll see Celeste?"

"I have no idea. Why?"

"In a way, I envy you. I'd like to see someone from another time, the way all of you do."

I've told her about Celeste, and the little I know about Mac and Austin and Gavan Valdez. But I don't know what to say now, how to answer her envy.

She asks, "Why do you suppose it's happening?"

That seems to be the big question, doesn't it? Sheldon asked me that very thing not long ago. As though I would have the answer! "I have no idea," I confess, telling her what I told Sheldon. "Maybe there's no reason for it. Maybe it's just something that *is*, the way—well, the way the mountains are. They're there, and we live among them."

She looks thoughtful. She lets her head rest against the padded rocker and pushes herself with the ball of one foot. "I don't know, Meg. I always think things happen for a reason."

I take a deep breath and lift my shoulders in a shrug. "Maybe. But I certainly don't know what that reason would be."

"Perhaps you just don't know *yet*. But maybe someday you'll know."

"Maybe."

She stops rocking suddenly and gives me a puzzled smile. "For someone who's experiencing something as—well, as *unusual* as seeing into other times, you certainly don't seem overly *impressed*."

I have to think about that. What exactly do I feel? "It's kind of odd, Donna," I admit. "I feel like I'm just, I don't know, waiting for something. I simply feel as though I'm waiting and watching for something. I don't know what."

"Hmm." She shakes her head. "I can't imagine."

She looks dreamily toward the empty hearth, and I follow her gaze to the kettle dangling there. She doesn't see it, I know, because she's lost in thought, but I can't help wondering whether someone, in an earlier time, is using that kettle right now to boil water over a fire, to make herself a cup of tea. Perhaps that someone is tired and would simply like to rest awhile. Perhaps she is, as Celeste says of the mountain people, simply spending time.

In another moment, Donna turns back to me and says, "If it's already made, I think I will have that cup of coffee."

I pour us both a cup. We go on talking quietly, moving away from speculation about the house and on to other things, inconsequential things. We slip easily from one train of thought to another. The minutes pass. I enjoy listening to the refined lilting of her voice and to the children's laughter that rises up occasionally in the yard. It is a time of isolated loveliness, full of serenity. I am almost happy to be here in this house in Black Mountain.

At length, the afternoon edges toward dinnertime, and Donna rises to go. She calls Marjorie in from play. The child is warm and flushed and happy. Several chains of clover circle her neck.

"You're good at that," I tell her, "making those clover necklaces."

She beams. "Yeah, and I think Digger likes his. At least he didn't take it off."

He is still in the backyard, working hard to poke a stick into the ground so that it stands upright like a flagpole. He seems oblivious to the clover chain around his neck; he has probably forgotten it's there.

At the front door, Donna kisses the air close to my cheek, calls me "Hon'" in that sweet southern way of hers, says she'll come back soon for another visit. I smile. I did not know her before—not really anyway. I think she and I will become good friends now that I'm here.

I go to the kitchen and begin to prepare dinner: a hamburger casserole, fresh corn on the cob, a green salad, cherry cobbler. Sheldon will like that, especially the cobbler. I pause in my work and lift my head. Funny that I should think of Sheldon and what he might like, just as I used to do, once upon a time.

Well, never mind. Maybe old habits die hard.

Tonight, there will be only the three of us, with Linda over at Gail's. Someday, all five of us will sit around the table again, when Carl comes home from 'Nam.

I put the casserole in the oven and turn to look out the window over the sink. The stick Digger had been diligently working into the earth is still upright, though tilting slightly toward the ground. Digger isn't there.

I step out the back door and call his name. But he doesn't answer. After a moment, I call again. There's only silence. I've told him time and time again not to go into the woods. "Digger!" I holler. "Where are you?"

Perhaps he has simply gone around to the front yard. Maybe he wandered over there to play with his trucks in the driveway. And yet, if he's in the yard anywhere, he should have heard me calling for him.

Suddenly, I'm frozen with fear. I'm certain something has happened to Digger, but I don't know what. I—but I mustn't panic. No, I can't allow myself to panic. He must he nearby somewhere. He must be.

"Digger!"

37

Linda
Saturday, September 7, 1968

GOOD GOSH ALMIGHTY, what was I thinking? When Gail invited me to have supper at her house, I should have just said no right off the bat. I mean, I *wasn't* thinking, that's the problem. I didn't think what it might be like to sit across the table from a dead man while we're both trying to eat. Really, this trying to chew when you forgot to Polident your uppers ... not a pretty sight. Gail never told me her grandfather wears dentures, but when he opens his mouth and his upper gums are all naked and pink because his top teeth are still down with his bottom teeth, it's kind of obvious. He keeps pushing his upper plate back into place with his thumb. Gail and her mom pretend not to notice, but that's probably because they're used to it. Well, I'm not, and if I have to spend much more time watching that shriveled old goat pushing his spaghetti-coated teeth back into place, I'm pretty sure I'm going to barf.

"So you say you've joined the yearbook staff, right, Linda?" Gail's mom looks at me and smiles. The huge scar on her forehead is about as appetizing as the old man's false teeth, but at least it isn't glossy with saliva and tomato paste.

"Yeah," I say. "I've got to take an elective, so I figured that'd be better than most everything else they were offering."

"And it doesn't hurt that Rodney is the editor," Gail adds.

"Oh yes," Mrs. Leland says. "He's a nice boy."

"Nice?" Gail echoes. "Mom, he's absolutely dreamy. Right, Linda?"

"Um, sure, he's all right." When I say that, I notice the old man's watery eyes roll toward me.

"What I wouldn't give to have a date with him," Gail goes on. "Just one date and I'd be in hog heaven."

Well, yeah, he's not the best-looking boy I've ever seen—not near as good-looking as Austin—but what I wouldn't give to have him sitting across the table from me right now instead of the old man. At least his teeth don't fall out when he eats.

"So what are you going to do on the yearbook?" the old man asks.

Which means if I'm going to be polite, I've got to look at him when I answer. "Oh, I don't know." I shrug. "Take pictures, maybe."

I drop my eyes to my plate and work on twirling some spaghetti on my fork, but I'm pretty sure I'm going to throw up any minute now.

"Well, I think you'll have fun," Mrs. Leland says. "And I'm glad you two girls have a couple of classes together. That makes it nice."

"Yeah," Gail says. "Linda and I can study for algebra and biology tests together. Won't that be great, Linda?"

I nod and try to sound at least a little enthusiastic when I say, "Yeah, great."

"Oh say, Gail," Mrs. Leland says, "did I tell you Abner and his wife are celebrating their fiftieth wedding anniversary next weekend and we're invited to the reception at the church? That's what you told me, isn't it, Dad?"

The old man nods. His thumb is in his mouth again so he can't speak.

"No way!" Gail cries. "Fifty years? Really? Hey, Linda, maybe you'd like to come to the reception with us?"

I look at her like I can't believe what she's saying. I'd rather eat roadkill than go to the anniversary reception of one of the perverts. Yeah, I finally remember the names of all the old men and even know which is which. Abner is the one whose stomach hangs down over his belt. Otis has the glass eye that doesn't move. Luther is the one with the hairy knuckles and the nose that was permanently flattened when he drank too much and fell face down on the sidewalk. And Buford is the one missing the top half of his right ear. He claims a bear bit it off, but I don't believe him. More likely his wife did it, and probably for no other reason than his name is Buford. Yeah, not one good strong name among them, just a bunch of hillbilly names.

And then there's Bim. I don't even know what his real name is and, on my life, I have no desire to know. It can't be anything good, like Austin. But then, Austin's from Chicago where people are normal and have some self-respect and don't name their kids after comic strip characters.

Bim's looking at me now like he's waiting for me to say *of course I'll go to the old folks' anniversary party*. I'm thinking about being stuck in a church basement with a bunch of beat-up old geezers and their wives when the phone rings and Mrs. Leland excuses herself to walk across the kitchen to pick up the extension on the wall. After she says hello, I hear her say, "Oh yes, Mrs. Crane, she's still here. In fact, we haven't quite finished our supper yet, but that's all right, I'll put her on. Here she comes."

I'm already standing up and making my way across the kitchen because I'm eager to get away from the old man's eyes. I take the receiver from Mrs. Leland, who smiles her pleasant smile at me before she goes on back to the table.

"Yeah, Mom?" I say. "What's up?"

"I'm sorry to interrupt," she says, "but I want you to come home."

My first feeling is relief, but then I realize there must be a reason she wants me home, so I ask her what it is.

"Digger's missing," she says, and she sounds like she's about to cry.

I turn my back to the three people at the table who are now staring at me and say, "What do you mean, missing?"

"I mean, he was playing in the backyard, and now I can't find him. I've already called your father. He and Uncle Steve are on the way here."

"So what do you want me to do?"

"I want you to come home—"

"Well, you know, Mom, I've got to go to work tonight. And anyway, he's probably just playing up in the woods, and he can't hear you calling him. He'll probably be home soon."

"Maybe you're right, but I don't know." Now I know for sure she's crying because I hear her sniffing on the other end of the line.

"All right, Mom. Gail can tell Gloria I can't make it in, and I'll be home in just a few minutes."

Even as I'm hanging up the phone, I'm placing my money on the bet that Digger will be home before I even make it out to the car. Dumb kid's probably just collecting animal droppings in the woods and lost track of time. I'll get home and find Mom yelling at him and blubbering all over him at the same time. Yeah, and for once he'll probably be in big-time trouble with Mom and Dad both. The perfect little angel is not so perfect.

"Everything all right, Linda?" Mrs. Leland asks.

"Yeah." I shrug. "But I gotta go. Digger's wandered off, and I guess I got to go help find him."

When I say that, the old man's eyes get as big as his dinner plate, and I think they're going to fall right out of his head. "You got to be careful in these mountains," he says. "Maybe you ought to call the …"

But I don't hear the rest of it because I'm already halfway down the front hall, thanking my lucky stars for giving me the perfect excuse to escape the old man's flapping gums.

38

Sheldon
Saturday, September 7, 1968

"DIGGER!"

I pause to listen. No answer.

"Digger! Where are you, buddy?"

My voice breaks on the last word, but there's no one around to hear. I've been scouring the woods for the last hour, going up the side of the mountain while Steve works his way down. He's following the road from our house; I'm following a footpath that's overgrown and barely visible. I must keep my bearings, or I'll be lost too. Certainly, I must be back at the house before nightfall, and that's only a short time away. But I can't come off this mountain without my son.

"Digger! Where are you?"

My fear threatens to evolve into full-fledged panic. I can't let it. I have to keep a level head.

Dear God, please help me find my son. Please keep him safe and bring him back to me.

I want to say the words out loud, but they dissolve like ashes in my mouth. If I say the words aloud, it means this is really happening, and Digger is really missing.

Listen! A rustling of leaves. I turn quickly, my heart pounding. Digger?

A squirrel scurries across the path. I watch it disappear into the underbrush. The world seems far too big for me; I'm not sure I can bear it.

Where in this wide world is my little boy? He has to be somewhere. People don't just disappear. Maybe when I walk back down the mountain, I'll find him at home. Maybe Steve has already found him and brought him back.

Digger, you know not to leave the yard. You know that. And you have so rarely disobeyed. On the little things, yes, but not on the big things—the life-threatening things. Why did you wander off this time? What would cause you to so blatantly disobey and wander off?

Oh dear God, Digger, please be home when I get there.

I stand in the middle of the woods watching and listening. How far should I go? All the way to the top? If I go to the top, will you be there?

I push the thought of bears from my mind. And poisonous snakes. The woods are a dangerous place for a little boy. When we find you, son, you will be getting the punishment of your life. Believe me, Digger, this will be one lesson you will never forget. If you've never seen me angry before, you will see me angry now. I swear to you, son, as soon as I see you I will … I will … oh dear God, I will grab you up in my arms and hold you, and I'm not sure I'll be able ever to let you go.

I look up past the tops of the trees. A ghostly moon hangs pale and transparent in the sky.

"Digger!"

39

Meg
Saturday, September 7, 1968

I HEAR FOOTSTEPS on the front porch, and my heart leaps up with hope. In the next moment, though, the hope gives way again to fear. It's Steve, but he's alone. He lets himself in and shakes his head at me. "I looked everywhere," he says, "and there's no sign of him."

"No sign?" I repeat. My voice is weak. "Nothing?"

Linda grabs my hand. "Don't worry, Mom," she says. "Maybe Dad's found him. He'll be back soon."

I turn away from Steve and let Linda lead me out to the backyard where, arms around each other, we wait for Sheldon to return. If Linda weren't holding me up I'm not sure I'd have the strength to stand.

Did I know what fear was before tonight? I thought I did when Carl went off to 'Nam. That was fear, yes, but now I know that fear has no limits, that it plunges to depths I never would have imagined.

Steve joins us outside and sits in the folding lawn chair. He takes a pack of cigarettes and a lighter out of his shirt pocket. He lip-tugs a cigarette from the cellophane wrapper, his fingers tremble slightly as he lights up. Squinting against the smoke, he inhales deeply, lets it out. He looks off toward the woods. Like Linda and me, he is now helpless to do anything but wait for Sheldon to return.

Dusk has fallen and the moon, round and luminous, is starting to appear. The stars will follow soon, and then darkness. And then I don't know how I will keep from losing my mind.

"If Sheldon comes back without him," Steve is saying, "we'll call the sheriff. I'll call. I maybe should have done that right away, maybe shouldn't have waited. But I was sure he'd be right around here somewhere. I mean, a little kid like that can't go far, can he? But listen, don't worry, the sheriff and I go way back. John's a good man, very capable. He and his men will find Digger. They'll organize search parties and send men out into these mountains so fast your …"

Once he starts talking, he can't seem to stop. But I can't take in this steady stream of sound. There's no room for it. The fear takes up every inch of space inside of me.

Oh God, where is my son? What have you done with my son?

"Mom. Mom." Linda is squeezing my arm.

"What it is, Linda?" Our voices sound small and distant, like I am only half conscious.

"What's that light up there?"

She has disentangled one arm from me and is pointing upward. I follow her finger to the darkening sky. I can't think. I'm groggy and dizzy with dread. "A star," I say. "Venus, maybe." Why is she talking to me about anything other than Digger?

"I don't think so," she says. "I've seen Venus before and that's not Venus. That's the biggest star I've ever seen."

I take a deep breath. I do not care about the stars, the sky, the earth, or anything *on* the earth other than my son. Don't speak to me about anything but my son.

"Meg." Steve stands abruptly. "I just saw a light in the woods. It must be Sheldon's flashlight. He's on his way back down."

I see it now too, a thin beam bouncing off the trees.

"Sheldon!" Steve hollers. "Did you find him? Did you find Digger?"

Sheldon doesn't answer. Several excruciating moments pass as the light comes closer. I'm trembling. I forget to breathe.

When Sheldon emerges from the woods, Steve asks again, "Did you find him, Shel?"

But still Sheldon doesn't respond. He doesn't even shake his head. He doesn't need to. He's alone, and that's our answer.

Digger is gone, night has fallen, and I know as sure as I'm standing here that life is never going to be the same again.

40

Sheldon
Saturday, September 7, 1968

"LET'S START WITH the simplest and most likely scenario," the sheriff says. "Have you called the boy's friends? Because chances are he's gone off to another house in town just looking for someone to play with."

Friends? It never occurred to us to call anyone other than Steve. Digger didn't have any friends. Except Mac. But how do we explain Mac without falling under suspicion ourselves? A single mention of seeing into time and we'd be condemned as lunatics, capable of doing who-knows-what to our own son.

Before I manage to say anything, Meg speaks up. "We only just moved here this summer," she says. "He hasn't had a chance to make friends yet, outside of his cousin Marjorie. He was just starting to get to know the kids at school, but he was only there for three days before ..."

Sheriff Fields nods as he shifts position on the edge of the overstuffed chair. A deputy stands beside him, scribbling in a small notebook pulled from his breast pocket. The stub of a pencil scratches at the paper the moment anyone begins to speak.

Both speech and scratching stop in the wake of Meg's unspoken words. We all know what she had meant to say but couldn't. *Before Digger disappeared.*

The sheriff clears his throat. "I see," he says. "So he hasn't ever visited at the homes of any of the kids from school?"

I shake my head. An ache is forming at the base of my skull; it tightens when I take a deep breath. "No," I say. "Not that we know of, anyway."

"All right. And you don't believe he's come into contact with any kid or group of kids who might have talked him into doing something he shouldn't be doing?"

I shake my head again, harder this time. "No. No, we're certain of that."

We are sitting in the living room, Meg and I on the couch, Steve in the wing chair. Sheriff John Fields and his deputy arrived a few minutes ago. They wear their authority like a second badge pinned to their uniforms. Their imposing presence here both comforts me and fills me with dread.

Just as I finish answering the sheriff's question, Linda returns from upstairs with last year's school picture of Digger. She hands it to the sheriff, who studies it a moment before handing it to the deputy. Instead of sitting, Linda moves to the archway between the living room and kitchen and simply stands there, as though she wants to be on the periphery of things.

"Tell me about today, then," the sheriff goes on. "Anything out of the ordinary happen to him today?"

"Out of the ordinary?" Meg echoes.

"He have a fight with anyone, get in trouble for anything? Were you punishing him for anything?"

My eyes wander over to Linda, who is listening with a fist to her mouth.

I hear Meg say, "No, he wasn't being punished. Nothing happened at all. Donna and Marjorie came over and the kids were playing in the yard, they were getting along all right, having a good time."

"Linda," I say quietly, "do you know anything?"

Her eyes widen. She shakes her head. "No, I don't know anything."

"Did you fight with Digger today?"

"Fight with him? I wasn't even around very much. Gail and I went shopping over in Asheville, and then we went to her house to do homework, and then I was eating supper with them when Mom called to say Digger disappeared."

"All right," Sheriff Fields says. "What about school then? He had any trouble with the teachers?"

"None at all." Meg says. "He says he likes his teachers, and he's happy at school. We certainly haven't gotten any reports from the school that he's been in trouble."

The sheriff gazes at both of us for a long moment. The house becomes so quiet I can hear the blood pounding in my ears. Finally, Sheriff Fields asks, "Has your son ever run away before?"

Meg gasps. Color creeps up her neck and fans out over her cheeks. I feel my own jaw tighten. By now the ache has climbed to my brow and has fastened itself there like a vise.

"Digger's never run away," she tells the sheriff. "He's a good boy."

The sheriff's eyes shift from Meg to me. He's waiting for me to respond as well. The deputy's pencil is poised to write.

"There's no question about him running away," I say firmly. "He didn't. He had no reason to."

"So the boy was happy here at home?"

"Of course!" Meg's hands clench into fists in her lap. I long to put my hand over hers to comfort her, but I don't dare.

The sheriff looks at me, and I nod my agreement. Digger was perhaps the one happy person in this house.

"Listen, John," Steve interjects. He leans forward in the chair where he's been sitting quietly till now. "I know my nephew. We're not dealing with a runaway here."

The sheriff takes a deep breath. "I know how you all feel. I have a boy myself, right about your son's age. I know this isn't easy, but there are certain things I have to ask." He pauses long enough to cough and clear his throat again. "What was your son wearing when he disappeared?"

Meg puts a hand to her forehead. "Um, a striped shirt—"

"What color?"

"White and green. A white and green shirt and brown shorts. Blue sneakers."

"Socks?"

"Yes, white socks. And a clover chain necklace."

"A clover chain necklace?" Two deep lines form between the sheriff's brows.

"His cousin Marjorie made it for him."

"I see."

I know what the sheriff is thinking. Why would Meg mention such a necklace? It won't last long.

As though she hears the unspoken question, Meg says, "Maybe you'll find the necklace somewhere. That way you'll know he was there."

The sheriff nods. "Any identifying marks? Scars? Birthmarks?"

I think a minute. I almost mention Digger's loose tooth, but that won't last long either. It was almost ready to fall out. My heart clenches with the fear that it will never go under his pillow to be exchanged for a nickel.

Meg is slowly shaking her head. "No, no scars to speak of. And no birthmarks."

We sit quietly a moment, waiting for the deputy's pencil to catch up. A lift of the young man's brows tells us he's almost there.

But I'm unwilling to wait any longer. "I searched the mountain behind our house," I tell the sheriff, "and Steve walked the road to the bottom of the mountain. We turned up nothing. How soon can you send your men out?"

Sheriff Fields looks apologetic, but his voice is firm. "We can't do anything for twenty-four to seventy-two hours," he says.

I am stunned. "B-but why not?" I stutter.

"I'm afraid that's the way the law works, Mr. Crane. Problem is, at this point, we have nothing to go on. We don't even know yet whether we have a crime or a missing person."

"What do you mean, Sheriff?"

"Well, he could be missing because he's gotten himself lost out in the woods somewhere. Now I don't like to think of these things, but he may have gotten himself caught in a bear trap. He may have been captured by a bear or some other wild animal. If it's a scenario like that, we're not talking crime. On the other hand, Digger may have been abducted. Someone may have taken him."

"But," Meg cries, "that's the whole point, isn't it? Wherever he is, surely he needs our help now!"

"Yes, ma'am," Sheriff Fields agrees politely. "And that's why I'd encourage you to call around. Call anyone in town who might know anything at all of his whereabouts. But like I said, the soonest I can put out an APB is twenty-four hours. Without a scrap of evidence, there's nothing I can do before that. Right now we can't rule out the possibility the boy will come home on his own."

The thought of waiting is like a kick in the gut, knocking the breath out of me. Finally I manage to ask, "What kind of evidence are you looking for?"

"Signs of a struggle. Any clue that a stranger might have taken him. Anything at all."

Megs says, "He was in the backyard, and then he was gone. There weren't any signs of a struggle. I didn't even hear Digger scream. How could anyone have taken Digger without me hearing them?"

The sheriff sighs heavily, as though he's wearied by our questions. "That's why I'm thinking the boy wandered off somewhere. And the most likely scenario is that he'll wander back home. Still, we can't rule out abduction. It's unlikely but still possible that someone kidnapped your son."

"But why? Why would anyone kidnap our son?"

"Could be a couple of reasons." The sheriff looks down at his hands. I have a feeling I don't want to hear what he's about to say. "It may be someone looking for money, wanting you to pay a ransom to get the boy back."

"A ransom?" I ask. "Why would they choose us?" I wave a hand at the room as though to say, *We obviously don't have any money.* "Don't kidnappers usually take the children of wealthy parents?"

"Sometimes. Not always. There may be a misperception as to how much money you have."

"All right," I say slowly. "If that's the case, how soon can we expect a ransom note?"

"Well now, I can't say exactly, but it'd be soon. A day, maybe two. But if we're looking at kidnappers here, money isn't the only reason children are taken. There are some unsavory characters out there who might steal a child for their own satisfaction."

Steve sits up straight. "Are you talking about child molesters, John?"

"Unfortunately, yes, I am, Steve."

"Don't tell me we have any of their kind here in Black Mountain."

"I'm not saying we do, but I'm not saying we don't either. Very often the molesters are the people in your own midst, your own neighbors, people you might work with."

"That may be, John, but I've known the folks around here for twenty years, and I'm telling you not one of them is any kind of pervert."

"I hear you, Steve, but listen, there's new folks moving in and out of Black Mountain all the time these days. You can never be sure who's coming in."

"So you're saying our son—" I begin, but the sheriff interrupts me.

"I'm not saying anything yet, Mr. Crane. I'm just laying out the possibilities, starting with the most likely scenario and moving on to worst case."

Steve asks, "When was the last time we had a kidnapping around here?"

Sheriff Fields nods. "Been a long time, I'll grant you that. It never has happened on my watch. Not a single kidnapping in the past five years, and none I remember hearing of in the decade before that. In fact, I believe— if I'm remembering right—the last kidnapping was more than twenty years ago when a kid was taken by his own father in the midst of a custody battle. He was found living in the lap of luxury on a Floridian estate and didn't want to come back to Black Mountain after that." The sheriff looks at his deputy for confirmation. The deputy complies with a quick thrust of his chin.

"That's right," the deputy says. "He never did come back up here. Can't blame him, neither."

"So chances are slim," Steve says, "that Digger has been kidnapped."

"Chances are slim, yes, but it's a possibility we've got to consider. We've got to view this thing from every angle, and right now, we can't dismiss any scenario out of hand, even that of running away. We've had plenty of those, kids running off thinking they'll find a better life somewhere else. Well, we usually find them first, hanging out at a bus station in one of the surrounding towns, trying to drum up enough change for a ticket. They don't get far."

"But most of those are probably older kids," Steve says. "They're not eight years old, are they?"

"You're right there, Steve," the sheriff agrees. "They're mostly a little older, mostly teens. They've had time to decide they don't want to spend their lives in a little mountain town."

"So what about getting lost in the mountains?" I ask. "That happen often?"

"It does happen on occasion," the sheriff admits, "but generally those kids make their own way out or else we eventually find them. Not very many missing children stay missing for long around here."

I suppose I should take comfort in that, but I don't. "Okay," I say, "but our son is out there somewhere, lost, maybe hurt, and you say you can't go looking for him?"

"Not for twenty-four to seventy-two hours," he repeats.

My head is pounding now. Meg is crying quietly into a handkerchief that I didn't know she had. Steve must have handed it to her. Linda is still standing in the archway, hand still over her mouth.

"Sheriff Fields?" I say.

"Yes, Mr. Crane?"

I lift a hand to my head in a useless bid to stop the pounding. "Where do you think our son is?"

The sheriff sniffs, rubs his hands together, and says, "We might do better for me to ask that of you, sir. Where do *you* think your son is?"

I look at him, mouth agape, my mind knocked senseless by the absurdity of his question. Finally, I manage to mutter, "If we had any idea at all, Sheriff Fields, we wouldn't be here. We'd be there with our son bringing him home."

The deputy's pencil stops scratching. The room falls silent.

I think my skull and heart both will burst wide open for the pain.

41

Meg
Sunday, September 8, 1968

No sleep last night, and now at 5:30 in the morning—while it is yet dark—the yard is full of men from the town, some of whom we know, many of whom we don't. They have half a dozen dogs with them, all bloodhounds. The men have volunteered to form teams and search for Digger. If the law won't do it, they told us, then they will. Steve spearheaded the whole effort. He told one man who told someone else who told someone else until a couple dozen men showed up in a caravan of cars and pickup trucks.

Their wives came with armloads of food. We are feeding the men before they head out. We will be here when they come back. We have everything from sandwiches to potato salad to donuts to huge thermoses filled with hot coffee. I am in the kitchen, helping distribute the food. Donna is here too. And Linda. We avoid eye contact as much as possible. If our eyes meet, we will break down. We must go through the motions as though our hearts are stone.

The men are mingling in small groups while eating from paper plates. They look solemn as they talk together, nodding, strategizing. The dogs are leashed in the beds of the pick-up trucks, anxious to go. Donna is spreading mayonnaise on slices of white bread while I pour endless cups of coffee. Linda is scooping out potato salad. A number of women are chopping vegetables for the stew we'll serve the men later in the day, when they return from the search. Digger's third-grade teacher, Miss Purcell, is here making a chocolate cake. When she asked what Digger's favorite dessert is, I handed her a box mix and she got to work, saying, "I'll have it ready for when he comes home."

The mayor of Black Mountain, a man everybody simply calls Big Joe, seems to be the one in charge. Even now, he's waving an arm, calling the men together. They gather round him in a circle, still chewing, still sipping coffee from Styrofoam cups. They listen intently, nod, exchange glances. Their voices carry in from the yard, muffled voices that speak of places unknown to me, places where they will search for my son. A small seed of gratitude takes root in my heart. While the police must wait for the proper number of hours to pass, these men give up their day to search for a missing child most of them have never met.

Through the window, I see Sheldon break away from the group. He steps into the kitchen and gently lays a hand on my shoulder. "We need some of Digger's clothes," he says.

"His clothes?"

"Yes, not clean clothes. We need pants, socks, underwear, anything with Digger's scent on it. For the dogs. You haven't done the wash since yesterday, have you?"

I shake my head and say, "I'll bring you something."

He nods his thanks and returns to the men. I go upstairs to Digger's room where I find what I'm looking for on the floor of his closet. I am on my knees, gathering shirts and underwear, when I surprise even myself by clutching the dirty clothes to my chest.

Oh, Digger. How can this be happening?

I wonder whether he'll ever wear these clothes again. The tears come as my arms ache to hold not his clothes but *him*.

But I can't stay here. The men are waiting. It's time for them to go.

I carry the clothes out to the backyard. Someone has brought one of the hounds around. It's explained that this dog will go with a group up into our own mountain behind the house. Other groups will spread out, covering areas around the perimeter of the town.

I give the clothes to Sheldon, who passes them around. One man holds a shirt to the nose of the bloodhound. The hound sniffs and becomes ecstatic, tugging on his leash. Three men follow him across our yard and into the woods.

Big Joe looks at me and says, "Don't worry, Mrs. Crane. We're going to find your son and bring him home."

I can't respond. I have no breath. The mayor nods his understanding and leads the rest of the men around the house to the waiting vehicles.

"We'll be back soon," Sheldon says as he hurries off with them.

I stand motionless, watching them leave. I hear the dogs barking, the engines starting up, the rumbling voices of men as they toss words of advice and instruction to each other.

In another moment, Linda is by my side. "Miss Purcell just put the cake in the oven," she says quietly. "I hope she has it iced by the time Digger gets home."

The trucks crunch over the gravel drive and caravan down the side of the mountain. The sound of engines and barking dogs recedes and then the yard is quiet.

Linda takes my arm and leads me back inside. The kitchen is a hive of activity without words. Silent women cook, clean, dry dishes. We must stay busy because our busyness will somehow help bring Digger home. And perhaps the movement of my hands will keep me from losing my mind.

42

Linda
Monday, September 9, 1968

ALL THOSE MEN spent all those hours searching for Digger, and in the end they all came back empty-handed. They spent the whole day yesterday looking and even into the night. One group went back out this morning. None of the bloodhounds even picked up a scent. They didn't find a single thing of Digger's, not the cloverleaf necklace, not a shoe … not a body. Nothing. He's disappeared without a trace.

There hasn't been a ransom note either. Not in the mail. Not tacked to the front door. No phone calls from strange men, voices distorted by handkerchiefs held over the mouthpiece of the phone. No demands for money in exchange for Digger's life. Nothing.

Since they say enough time has passed, the police will start their search now. What—better late than never? Bunch of useless jerks. They're the ones who are supposed to help, but their job or the law or something kept them from doing what the men of the town did. They should have gone out and looked for Digger right away. So now that forty-eight hours have passed they can put out their APBs, but big deal. Too little, too late. It won't do any good. What can they find that the men and their hounds didn't find?

I can't believe this is happening. Digger's been gone for forty-eight hours. Mom's been in bed for the last twenty-four. She's sick with grief. No matter where I go in the house, I can hear her crying. Dad is wandering around like he's in shock. I feel so sick myself, I can't eat.

Dad let me stay home from school today. I didn't think I could go and face everyone, since the story hit the papers this morning and now everybody knows about it. "Black Mountain Boy Missing." So now the phone's been ringing all day, practically nonstop. That old preacher down at the church called and talked to Dad for a long time. Gail called and asked if I wanted company, and though I thanked her, I said no, I needed to be alone. Vernita Ponder called wanting to talk to Mom, but when Dad said she was unavailable, she asked to talk to me. Dad put his hand over the mouthpiece and asked if I wanted to take it. I almost said no, but then I did. The old lady spent about fifteen minutes talking about the write-up in the paper and telling me how sorry she was that Digger was missing, and then she finally said, "You've got to remember, though, that that house is a good place, and whatever's happening there is a gift," and I ended up slamming the phone down—though not before telling her that if we'd never come to this stupid house, Digger wouldn't be gone.

I always acted like I hated Digger, but the fact is, I love my brother. And if he's dead or something, and I never see him again, I don't know what I'm going to do.

Dad wouldn't let me help search for him. I begged him to let me, but he said no. He said he's not going to lose me too, and he wants to know where I am at all times.

He was crying when he said it—not weeping or anything—but his eyes were glassy with tears, and he turned away pretty quick and pretended to be busy with something else. I almost wanted to hug him and tell him he wasn't going to lose me, but I didn't. I didn't, maybe because I'm even more mad at him for bringing us down here and now something this awful has happened. If we were still in Abington, Digger wouldn't be missing.

Uncle Steve and Aunt Donna are here tonight. Again. Just like last night. Aunt Donna's upstairs trying to comfort Mom. Dad and Uncle

Steve are in the living room talking with the sheriff again. From where I'm standing in the kitchen, I can hear their voices, but they're talking so low, I can't make out what they're saying. I'm not sure I want to know.

Uncle Steve has left his pack of cigarettes on the kitchen table. I know I shouldn't, but I can't help it. I have to have something to calm my nerves. Man, I can't believe how my fingers are shaking as I take one from the pack. I find a book of matches in a kitchen drawer and run out the back door.

I go just beyond the edge of the woods and sit behind a tree. My hands are shaking so bad I can hardly light up. I'll tell you what, if Digger ran away on purpose, I'm going to kill him with my own two hands if we ever find him. But I can't believe that. Digger wouldn't run away. It just isn't like him to do something like that.

I take a long deep pull on the cigarette. As the smoke enters my lungs, I shut my eyes and savor the feel of it. Man, I've needed a cig so bad for so long. I can get them at school, but not here at home. I haven't had a smoke since Digger disappeared.

So I'm thinking, if Digger didn't run away, what happened to him? Did he really just wander into the woods and get lost? It's possible I guess, the stupid kid. He talked about looking for gold in the mountains, but good grief, who'd thought he'd ever do it? I mean, he wouldn't just run off looking for gold, would he? Well, if he did, and if he's lost, then he's probably still alive. He's probably trying to find his way back. But then, with the search parties that went out, how come they didn't find anything? They would have found *something*, wouldn't they? If Digger was just out there looking for gold?

So, what, maybe a bear came and dragged him out of the yard? Yeah, but even so, if a bear ate him, wouldn't they find something? A sneaker or some bones or something? Does a bear eat a whole person lock, stock, and barrel? I'm thinking probably not. I mean, even with a bear there's got to be something left over.

I take another long drag and let the smoke out slowly. My forehead drops to my knees. I don't want to think about what I really think happened, and I sure don't want to say it out loud because then it might be true. But the only thing that really could have happened was that Digger was kidnapped. And I'm thinking it wasn't just a kidnapper, but it's the person who killed those people over in Asheville and who hasn't been caught yet. I think that murderer kidnapped Digger, and he took him somewhere, and now he's going to kill him too.

I crush out the cigarette in the dirt because it's too hard to smoke it when you're crying.

Oh Digger, if you'll just come home, I promise I'll never say anything mean to you again. Please, Digger, please try to come home.

43

Sheldon
Monday, September 9, 1968

I SAY GOODNIGHT to Steve and Donna, fully aware of the irony of it. Goodnight? How can the night be good for them or for me, with Digger missing? How can any night—or any day, for that matter—ever be good again, without my son?

Sheriff Fields left an hour ago, taking the largest portion of my hope with him. He said he'd felt certain that Digger would wander home on his own. Or else he'd call from somewhere in town and ask to be picked up. What the sheriff didn't say, though I saw it written on his face, was that now that two days have passed, the situation has taken on a whole new dimension. Upped from code yellow to code red. He's put out APBs to all the surrounding towns. He's organized teams that will begin searching tomorrow at dawn. He understands that the men of Black Mountain have already done their own search with no success. The lawmen and volunteer firefighters will be covering ground that has already been covered. But he will keep us posted at regular intervals. We should remain optimistic, he said, while understanding that our chances go down with every hour that goes by. Our chances of finding Digger alive. Or at all.

Do some children who go missing just never show up again, I asked? Oh yes. Not that it happens much around here but across the country—

yes, it's a far too common scenario. One minute they're there, and the next they're gone, and that's it.

The end of a life. The end of everybody's life as they once knew it.

I watch the taillights of Steve and Donna's Chevy disappear down the mountain before I finally shut the front door. Digger is out there somewhere, in the dark, maybe alone. He's out there somewhere, and I don't know where he is or how to find him, and I've never felt so helpless in my life.

Wandering aimlessly, I circle through the downstairs rooms and out the back door. Where can I go that the fear doesn't follow me?

Donna said she left Meg in a fitful sleep. They were talking quietly, and Meg was crying but was so exhausted she drifted off in the midst of her tears.

I'm not sure I'll be able to sleep, for the third night in a row.

Digger. Where are you, son?

"Dad?"

I'm startled by the voice that comes out of the darkness. But it isn't Digger. Of course it isn't Digger. Linda is walking toward me across the yard.

"What are you doing out here, honey?"

"I don't know. I just had to get out of the house."

I nod my understanding.

She asks, "Did Uncle Steve and Aunt Donna leave?"

"Yeah, they've gone home."

"What are the police going to do now?"

"Start looking."

"Do they think there's still a chance of finding Digger?"

"Of course."

She looks at me a long time, like she's trying to decide whether I'm lying. Finally, she says, "Where do you think he is, Dad?"

"Honey, if I knew I'd be there and not here."

She frowns and her eyes grow small, like she's thinking. She seems to want to say something else, but she doesn't say it. We all have fears that refuse to be put into words.

She turns her head and looks up, and when she does I catch the faint scent of cigarette smoke. She thinks I don't know she smokes. She thinks I think she quit after we grounded her that time when we were still up in Abington. But I know she still lights up. Occasionally. When she can find a cigarette. At the moment, it seems a small thing, so small as to be insignificant. She is here, and I will cherish my daughter always, no matter what she does.

"Dad?"

"Yes, Linda?"

"Did you notice that weird star up there?"

I look toward where she's pointing in the sky. The star is so large I don't know how I didn't notice it before.

She asks, "What do you think it is?"

I shake my head. "I'm no astronomer, but sometimes stars and planets cross each other's paths, I guess. When they get close enough to each other, it probably looks like they're one big star when they really aren't."

"So, maybe that's a planet like Venus that's lined up with some big star or something?"

"I guess so."

"The really weird thing is, this is the third night it's been out."

"It is?"

"Yeah. The first night was the night Digger disappeared. Mom and I both saw it. You didn't see it?"

I shake my head again.

She says, "Well, maybe you couldn't see it because you were in the woods."

"Maybe," I say. "But last night when I was out with the search party, we were in some open stretches of land with a full view of the sky, and I didn't see it last night either."

"You didn't?"

"No."

We're both quiet a moment. "Well," she says, "I guess you just didn't notice."

"Kind of hard not to notice something like that."

"Maybe you just didn't look up at the sky."

"Oh, I did." Every time I prayed, every five minutes, I looked up at the sky.

"Well, anyway." She shrugs slightly. "Maybe they'll write something about it in the paper. Maybe some reporter will explain what it is."

"Yes. Maybe."

She takes a few steps toward the house, like she's ready to go inside. But suddenly she stops and says, "Dad, this may sound really weird …"

"What is it, Linda?"

Her head is tilted upward, and I can see the light of the star reflected in her eyes. "I just now got this feeling that Digger—wherever he is—he's looking at the star too and wondering what it is. So, you know, he's looking at it, and we're looking at it, and it's kind of holding us all together."

I can't speak for the lump of emotion that's lodged itself in my throat. Linda seems to understand. I hear her draw in a deep breath and let it out in a sigh.

"Well, goodnight, Dad," she says.

"Goodnight, Linda," I manage to whisper, and then I go on gazing at the star.

44

Meg
Thursday, September 12, 1968

DIGGER IS GONE. But I am a mother, and if Digger were dead my heart would tell me. I don't believe he's dead. I don't know where he is, but he is *somewhere,* and he is alive. That's what my heart tells me. I will hold on to hope for as long as I can.

Life in the town goes on as always. I sit here on this bench watching cars pass, people walking by. I've come into town to run some errands, but after the simple act of driving down the mountain, I am too weak to move. I must rest first, then see if I have the strength to walk into the bakery to buy some fresh bread.

For five days, I've barely eaten. For five nights, I've barely slept. I have lain in bed, consumed by fear. I remember people coming in and out of the room—Donna, Steve, Sheldon, Linda. Did we speak? What did we say? I don't know. I can't remember. My mind was circling down to a place of no sound and no light. Nothing.

But I couldn't stay there. I had to get up and try to go on living. So this morning, I did. I got up, showered, had some coffee, and came into town where I am now, sitting on this bench. An indifferent sun shines overhead and no one notices me when they pass by. For that, I am thankful. How could I speak to anyone as though I am whole? I'm fragmented now, broken apart by the disappearance of my son.

Digger, where are you? I know you are somewhere. Will you come home? *Can* you come home?

Last night I walked by Sheldon's room and, through the half-open door, saw him on his knees by the side of his bed. Beseeching God for Digger's safe return, no doubt. Prayer was always Sheldon's refuge. I quietly envied him that place of comfort.

Is there any hope for me? Oh God, do you have any words of comfort left over for me?

But then, I've never known where to find you. Or whether you might even be found. My eyes can't see the unseen, and my ears don't hear voices that don't speak.

A police car driving by send waves of fear over me. The officer inside is probably one who searched for Digger. He probably was among those who climbed these mountains calling for my son without getting an answer.

How will I live without you, Digger?

I reach into my pocketbook and pull out a tissue, already crumpled and stained with tears.

Unseen God, can you see these tears?

I wipe my eyes, blow my nose. I take a deep breath to steady myself. I must get up from this bench and make my way to the bakery. I must go on living somehow.

But I don't rise, and in the next moment a little girl appears and sits down on the bench beside me. She is licking a vanilla ice cream cone, a two-scooper. Of course, the ice cream parlor is right behind me. She has gotten her treat and stepped outside to enjoy it.

Is she alone? She can't be any older than five. She wears a short-sleeve plaid dress and scuffed patent-leather shoes; she swings her feet as she licks the cone. Her stiff dark hair is tied up in numerous braids and held together with colorful clips. She has managed to give herself a creamy white mustache that highlights the rich chocolate color of her skin.

She stops licking and turns her face to me. Our eyes meet. Hers are startlingly clear; luscious brown drops on a white platter.

She smiles. And when she does, I can't help it. My eyes fill up with tears again. With that, her smile vanishes, her brow furrows and her bottom lip sticks out. "Oh, ma'am," she says, "don't cry. Here." She holds up her cone. Little rivers of ice cream drip over the ridges of her fingers. "Would you like some? It'll make you feel better."

"Oh, I—"

"Celeste!"

The little girl turns and looks over her shoulder. "I'm here, Mama!"

"I thought I told you to wait for me inside!" A woman comes out of the ice cream parlor with a double dip of chocolate on a cone and a scowl between her eyes.

"I couldn't help it, Mama," the little girl exclaims. "The sun was calling me!"

"The sun must be as naughty as you are then, asking you to come outside when I told you not to. And here you are bothering this nice lady." She turns to me. "Is she bothering you, ma'am?"

"Oh no, not at all. I—"

"I just wanted to let her have some ice cream, Mama. I was trying to be nice."

The woman laughs. "Well, I'm sure she's not going to want to be eating after some little ole colored girl. Come on, Celeste honey, let's be getting home."

The woman holds out her free hand. The little girl looks back to me. "I'm sorry," she says, "but I have to go."

"That's all right," I say. And then I add, "Celeste." The name is wrapped up in a measure of wonder. But of course, the child Celeste would be here in Black Mountain on a September day in 1968.

She smiles at me. I smile in return.

"I'll see you later," I tell her.

She hops off the bench and walks off hand-in-hand with her mother. I am strong enough now to get up and walk into my day.

45

Linda
Monday, September 16, 1968

MY BROTHER IS missing and probably dead, and I'm sitting here watching *Rowan and Martin's Laugh-In.* Mom and Dad are both upstairs—no doubt in their separate rooms—and I'm down here watching Dan and Dick present the Flying Fickle Finger of Fate Award while what I really want to do is get up and scream and punch the walls or something. These have been the worst ten days of my life, and I don't believe there's ever going to be an end to them because I'm starting to think we're never going to see Digger again. At first I thought he might find his way home if he somehow just wandered off in the woods and got lost. I even imagined him escaping a kidnapper if that's what happened to him. You know, he manages to cut the ropes around his wrists with a piece of broken glass or something and runs away while the kidnapper's asleep. I pictured him showing up on the front porch all out of breath from running about a hundred miles from wherever he was taken, and him knocking on the door and me opening it and hollering, "Mom, Dad, Digger's home!" And then we'd all hug him at once with everybody crying and laughing and everything.

Your mind can come up with all kinds of stuff if you want something bad enough.

At least I know Digger wasn't killed by the ax murderer that killed those people over in Asheville. There was a big write-up in the paper yesterday about how the guy was found hiding over in the Tennessee mountains. Yeah, his cousin, some bottom-of-the-barrel lowlife living in a dirt-floor cabin over there, was playing host to the ax murderer. The two of them were drop-dead drunk on moonshine when the cops pulled the raid that nabbed them. Figures. Two of the south's finest, now behind bars. The killer's name is Lloyd Drucker, and his cousin is Ernest Drucker. The thing is, Ernest claims Lloyd has been with him for more than two weeks, and he had no idea ole Lloyd had gone around killing anybody. Said he'd have turned Lloyd in himself if he had known, though he's probably just trying to make himself look like he wasn't harboring a fugitive. Who knows, but that's not what I care about anyway. The thing is if Ernest is telling the truth, then Lloyd was in Tennessee when Digger disappeared. So there goes that theory of Digger being taken by the ax murderer, and I'm glad to be rid of it.

At school, I see the way the other kids look at me. They're afraid of me. I'm a freak now, the girl with the missing brother, and everybody's thinking it better not happen to them. Gail walks with me everywhere like she's my bodyguard, and she's ready to beat up anybody dumb enough to say anything stupid. Not that everybody's being weird about Digger. Some of the kids are real nice and go out of their way to say nice things. And I have to admit the teachers have been pretty cool through this whole thing, telling me they understand if my assignments are late and things like that. I'm not going to take advantage of it though. I'm trying to stay on top of my work and not use Digger as an excuse. I mean that'd be like dancing on my own brother's grave, and the thought makes me sick.

I can't believe they've got that Richard Nixon guy who's running for President on *Laugh-In* saying "Sock it to me" and looking like he has no idea where he is or what he's doing, like he's landed in some sort of loony bin. And now, Goldie Hawn is talking about looking that up in your Funk and Wagnalls, and the audience is laughing, and maybe the whole world out there is laughing right about now, but I don't think any of it is funny at all. I don't think I'll ever laugh again.

I get up and turn off the TV and walk around with my hands balled up into fists, and then I'm crying so hard I'm sobbing. I beat my fists on the couch and bury my face in the cushions and cry till I'm exhausted. Then the house is quiet, and I know I should get up and finish my homework for school tomorrow, but I don't want to get up. I want Digger to come home. I want life to be the way it was before.

"Linda?"

Oh great. Dad's here. I don't want to lift my head to look at him. "What?" I mutter.

"What's the matter?"

It isn't Dad. I sit up, brushing tears away with the palms of my hands. Austin is sitting in the chair beside the couch.

"Austin!" I say. I sniff loudly, wishing I had a tissue. "I haven't seen you in a while."

He shrugs. He leans forward, looking at me intently. "Why are you crying?" he asks. "What happened?"

"Digger's gone!"

"Gone?"

I nod. I'm crying again. "He just disappeared into thin air. We can't find him."

"You can't find him? When did he disappear?"

"Ten days ago now."

"Ten days?" His eyes widen. We both know ten days is too long. Who can hold on to hope after ten days? "Has anyone searched the mountains for him?"

"Of course. Plenty of people. The police, Dad and Uncle Steve, volunteers. No one can find anything. Not a clue."

"What do you think happened?"

I shake my head. "I don't know. Nobody knows. But if I had to guess,

I'd say he's probably been kidnapped. Just taken by some crazy person, you know?"

I can't say anymore. Austin holds out a hand to me, but it dangles in mid-air. He looks at it and lets it fall back in his lap. We both know he can't touch me.

He stands and starts to pace the room. He runs a hand over his hair, and his fingers are trembling. He's mumbling something I can't understand.

"What are you talking about, Austin?" I ask.

He stops abruptly and turns to me. His eyes are shining like he's about to cry. "I can't believe this happened, Linda," he says. "I feel so helpless. I can't move ahead fifty years and do something to help you."

For a minute, I can't say anything. What I really want to do is throw my arms around him and thank him for caring enough to want to help. And I'd like to have him hold me while I cry out all the terrible feelings inside because I think if anyone can help me feel even a little bit better, it's Austin. But I can't touch him, and he can't hold me. Finally, I just say, "No one can do anything anymore, Austin. I think it's too late."

He swings one fist into the other and starts pacing again. While his back is turned to me, he rubs his face with both hands and sniffs loudly. Then he turns around and says, "Maybe it's not too late. Maybe you'll still find him, or he'll find his way home. Maybe … "

As much as he wants to comfort me, and as grateful as I am, he's clutching at straws, and we both know it. No little kid is going to survive in the mountains for more than a week. And if he's been kidnapped—I don't even want to think about that.

I wipe at my own eyes again and take a deep breath. "Well," I say, "you know what it's like to lose a brother, don't you?"

"I do?" He looks puzzled.

"Yeah, well—" Then I remember. It isn't 1919 there yet. Mac is still alive. I'm afraid I've crossed the line, and Austin is going to disappear, but nothing happens except he goes on staring at me, waiting for me to say something. "No, I mean, I'm thinking of somebody else. Not you. Sorry, Austin, I'm not thinking straight." I stand. "Listen, I'm going to step outside and get some fresh air. Want to come with me?"

He hesitates a moment. He takes a deep breath like he's trying to calm down. Finally he says, "All right." He follows me through the kitchen and out to the backyard. We stand close to the big rock where Digger used to play.

I get a thought. "You know, Mac and Digger used to play together. Digger didn't tell Mac anything, did he?"

"Like what?" Austin asks.

"Like, he didn't say he was going to run away or anything, did he?"

Austin thinks a moment, then shakes his head. "No, Mac hasn't said anything. I mean, I knew he'd met Digger, but he hasn't talked about him in a while. I was assuming he hasn't seen him for some time."

"Yeah," I say. "I guess he hasn't. None of us has. That's the problem. The police say there's usually some clue left behind, something that gives you a lead to work with. But with Digger, there's nothing. Except for his stuff still in the house, it's like he never existed."

Austin frowns and looks up at the sky. We both just stand there a long time, lost in our own thoughts. Finally, Austin says, "Holy cow. That's one huge star up there."

I follow his gaze. I'm used to the star by now. "Yeah, it's really weird. It's been there every night since Digger disappeared."

"It has? I haven't noticed it before tonight."

I nod. "It's been there, all right. I've seen it every single night, and I've been wondering what it is. It reminds me of the star you see on Christmas cards, you know? The star of Bethlehem."

"Oh?" Austin is quiet a moment. "It's got to be a bunch of stars lined up, or a star and a planet or something."

"Yeah," I say. "That's how my dad explained it. But since planets move through the sky, how come it hasn't moved out of the path of the star?"

"Maybe it's just moving really slow."

"Maybe."

"There's got to be some explanation. We just don't know what it is."

"I guess so."

"An astronomer would know. Science can explain everything."

"Yeah. I guess so," I say again. "But I wonder whether science could explain this?"

"What?"

"You and me talking to each other."

"You mean since we live in different times?"

"Yeah."

He thinks a moment, then says, "I guess science hasn't gotten that far yet. But it will. Someday. What about that physicist over in Germany, the one who writes about relativity ... what's his name?"

I raise a hand to my lips in thought. "You mean Albert Einstein?"

"Yeah, that's it. Does he have a theory on time?"

"He might, but if he does I never heard of it."

"Well, maybe he will. Maybe he'll figure out how people can talk between different times."

"I don't think so. He died before I was born. If he had some sort of theory about this, it seems to me everyone would be talking about it."

Austin rises up on his toes and goes down again. "Well, if Einstein didn't get to it, then somebody else will figure it out. That person probably just hasn't been born yet."

"You think so?"

"Yeah. Someday science will give us all the answers we need."

I think about that. After a minute I ask, "Even about where Digger is?"

His eyes get small. He doesn't say anything.

46

Sheldon
Saturday, September 28, 1968

THREE WEEKS, O Lord.

Three agonizing weeks, and every night I drop to my knees and ask you to bring my son home, but you are silent. If ever I've needed an answer, the time is now. And so I kneel here beside the bed, fingers twined, forehead pressed firmly against the quilted bedspread, waiting.

The words of the prophet Habakkuk come to mind. How can they not? It's my own prayer now, the only one I have. *O Lord, how long shall I cry, and thou wilt not hear!*

The silence is all-encompassing. There is nothing besides the silence.

Angrily, I push myself away from the bed and begin to pace. The search has been called off. Everyone has given up. But I'm his father. How can I not go on looking for him? I'll drive the same back roads again if I have to. And again and again, hoping the car's headlights will catch a glimpse of something. In the morning, I'll walk again into these hills, calling my son's name, hoping for an answer. I'll—

"Sheldon?"

I whirl around. Gavan is sitting at the desk. I realize I've been waiting for him to show; I have longed to speak with him these past three weeks.

"Digger is missing," I say.

He nods. His face is impassive, telling me nothing.

"But then, you know that, don't you?" I take a step toward him, notice that small blinking line on his machine, the computer.

"Yes," he says. "I am aware."

Another step. "You are like God. You know the future."

He moves his head slowly from side to side. "No, I know the past and the present. My present. That's all."

"But your present is my future, isn't it?"

He looks at me but doesn't answer. I feel another surge of anger swelling in my chest. I lift a hand to the computer. "Can you look in that machine of yours and tell me where my son is?"

His eyes become tender with sorrow. "No, Sheldon. I can't do that. I'm not allowed. You know I'm not allowed."

I drop to the bed and put my face in my hands. The frustration is greater than any pain I've ever known.

"Tell me this one thing, then. Should I resign myself to his death?"

He puts his hands together and lifts them to his lips, as though in prayer. "Sheldon—"

"I know. That too is somehow against the rules."

He sighs and drops his hands. "I wish someone could tell me my wife will come home. I long to know she comes home safely, but that's something God alone knows. God alone, Sheldon."

I think about that, and I remember what Mcg said when we first learned the legend of the house. "The Alpha and the Omega," I say quietly. "The one who knows the end from the beginning."

"Yes." Gavan nods.

Still, I long to tap into Gavan's mind, to siphon out what he knows about Digger. "Gavan?"

"Yes?"

"Can you tell me anything at all about my son?"

He frowns. He picks up a pencil and taps the eraser on the desk. "I can tell you honestly that I don't know what happened to your son. That is, I don't know in the sense of understanding. I *can't* understand."

"You can't understand?"

"No. I'm not sure anyone can."

I tremble. I take a deep breath. "Can you give me any hope?"

Gavan nods, but almost imperceptibly. "I can tell you this: God is with Digger. And if Digger is dead, he is with God."

Ah yes, I remember now. That is how he lives with his own uncertainties. "Either way," I say, repeating his earlier words, "God is there."

"Yes," he says quietly. "And so we trust the one who knows what we can't know."

I rise from the bed and once more pace the room. "Still, under the circumstances, it doesn't seem enough. There must be more. More I can know. More I can do."

"But there isn't, Sheldon. You're limited, just as I am."

"Yes, I'm limited. I understand that. But if only I could know the why of it all, the reason God allowed Digger to be taken from us. Do you think I'll ever know the reason?"

"Yes, I do believe you'll understand someday."

"But not in this life, I suppose."

"No." He shakes his head. "For as long as we hear the ticking of the clocks, we'll know only in part. Later we'll know more. Until then, we either bow to God's sovereignty or we kick against the goads. The latter, as you know, is always a hopeless endeavor."

I stop pacing and look at Gavan. "And the former?"

"The only hope we have."

I take a deep breath, nod. He turns away, disappears. I fall to my knees by the side of the bed.

Three weeks, O Lord.

Three long weeks. You know where Digger is, but I am not privy to your thoughts. Heaven remains silent.

I press my forehead against the quilted bedspread and go on waiting.

47

Meg
Wednesday, October 9, 1968

THE LEAVES FALL down, tumbling through the evening light as a sure sign autumn is here. Soon it won't be leaves but snow, and we will find ourselves in winter. What was it C.S. Lewis said about Narnia? Always winter, never Christmas. We will live out our lives in Narnia now because for us, there will be no more Christmases. No Christmas and no spring. No Easter, no May Day, no midsummer nights. Only endless winter, our hearts frozen in time because our son is gone.

I sit by the hearth in the kitchen, rereading the letter from Carl. He asks if we can postpone the funeral until he gets home because he wants to be there for his kid brother. Carl's words hold a certain sweetness, but the idea of a funeral is repugnant to me. How can I bury my son before I know he is dead? How can I bury him when my heart clings to hope that he's alive?

How can I bury my son, at any rate? We have no body. Can you have a funeral for someone who has simply disappeared?

I close my eyes, wanting to drift off, but am startled by a voice nearby. "My, my, you sure can tell fall is here. Look at those leaves."

Celeste moves from the kitchen window and sits in the rocker across from me. She looks at me placidly, her brown eyes tender. Sheldon has told me about his conversation with Gavan. Those in the future know, but they cannot tell.

"You know what's happened, don't you?" I say.

"Digger has disappeared."

I nod.

She begins to rock slowly. "I know it's been more than a month now. I wish I'd been allowed to see you sooner."

Then I remember. "I did see you," I tell her.

"You did?"

"Yes."

"When?"

"I saw you in town. You were about five years old."

She looks puzzled. "Really?"

"Yes. I'm sure it was you. The little girl was named Celeste, and she was eating an ice cream cone."

"Ah." Celeste smiles. "Mama used to take me for ice cream often. We both had a weakness for it."

"You had vanilla and she had a double dip of chocolate."

Celeste's eyes light up. "Yes, that was us. Were we in the shop?"

"No, I was sitting on the bench out front, and you joined me."

She looks beyond my shoulder as though she is gazing through the years, back to 1968. "I don't remember that," she says. "We went to the ice cream parlor so many times, they all run together. Did we speak, you and I?"

I smile weakly. "I was crying, and you offered me some of your ice cream."

"Did I?"

"Yes," I say. "I didn't accept your offer, but thank you. It somehow strengthened me."

Celeste turns her gaze back to me and nods. "I'm glad then, Meg. I've been wondering why I haven't been allowed to see you, but it seems I did see you after all. At least that once."

We're quiet for a moment. Then I say, "Who makes the rules, Celeste?"

"The rules?"

"You know, to all of this." I wave a hand languidly. "Who allows us to see each other? Who decides when we see each other and when we don't? Sheldon says it's God. He says something about God being the Eternal Now. What do you think, Celeste? Do you think it's God?"

"Yes," she says. "Yes, I do. Mr. Valdez and I have had long talks about it. I know all about the Eternal Now, and I agree. This is somehow a gift from God."

"Why, though?" I ask. "Why do you suppose it's happening?"

"For the sake of love, I should think."

"Love?"

"Everything God does is for the sake of love."

"It is?"

"Of course."

Of course? Everything? Even Digger's disappearance?

I rise from the chair and walk to the window. The leaves fall down. I watch as though mesmerized by the colors drifting from the sky. I lose track of time until Celeste asks, "What are you thinking about, Meg?"

I turn to look at her. "I'm thinking that spring will never come again. Not really. Not without Digger."

"Ah," she says. Her eyes widen, and her brows go up. "Now I understand."

"Understand what?"

She doesn't answer. She rises too and takes a step toward me. "I wish I could put my arms around you and comfort you, but I can't. But I've asked Gavan to help."

"Gavan? How can he help?"

"I have asked him to give a message to Sheldon. Apparently, I am not allowed to see your husband. I can see only you."

"A message?"

She nods. "I have to go check on Nicholas now. But I hope I'll see you again soon."

Before I can respond, she is gone. I hear footsteps on the stairs, but they are coming down, not going up. In another moment, Sheldon enters the kitchen. But of course, it is suppertime. I have let the afternoon get away, and I have nothing in the oven.

"Meg?"

"I'm sorry, Sheldon. We have some cold cuts in the fridge. I'll have some sandwiches ready in a minute."

"Oh no, it's not that. It's ..."

"What, Sheldon?"

He is frowning, as though perplexed. "I've just been talking with Gavan. He said to give you a message from a Mrs. See."

"Mrs. See?"

"Yes. Apparently, your friend Celeste works for her. She lives in Asheville."

"Yes, I know who she is. You have a message from her? For me? She knows about me?"

"She must, yes. She told Celeste who told Gavan who told me. And I am to tell you."

"Tell me what?"

"Simply that spring will come. She says it may not seem like it now, but spring will come."

The breath catches in my throat.

"Does that mean something to you?" Sheldon asks.

I try to nod. "I'm not sure what but, yes. Yes."

He takes a step toward me, hesitantly. "There's something else."

I look at him expectantly. "What is it, Sheldon?"

"Something Celeste asked me to give you."

I wait. He takes another step.

He says, "If you don't mind, I—" He opens his arms. "She asked me to hold you."

I gaze at him standing there, arms inviting me to him. "She did?" I whisper.

He nods.

I hold my breath and blink my eyes, but it is no use. The tears escape. "Is it all right?" I ask.

"Please." He nods again.

I move to him, this stranger, father of my son. I lean my head into his shoulder, and his arms encircle me. Grief binds us because the grief is ours, his and mine. But we haven't carried it together until this moment. Now, the weight lessens and comfort rushes in, rattling the chains and locks and tombs, and unearthing the memories of what our love had been. For the first time in months, I wonder whether someday we might know that love again.

48

Sheldon
Friday, October 11, 1968

THE YOUNG COUPLE considering the '63 Chevy Impala hasn't been able to make up their minds so far. They've come over from Asheville three times since last week, have taken the car out for a test drive twice, and, even now, the husband is poking around under the hood like he's looking for verification that the car somehow, in some way, has his name on it. It's a nice vehicle, the SS 409 with four-speed manual transmission, which apparently is at the root of the problem as far as my making this sale goes. The wife keeps insisting they'd agreed to buy an automatic, a pact the husband apparently forgot the moment he set eyes on this sleek red Impala.

She's sitting in the driver's seat, using the rearview mirror to freshen her lipstick while her husband eyes every inch of the car's inner workings.

"Remember what I told you, Lenny?" she hollers out the open window. "I've never driven a manual before, and I don't want to start now. It's too much extra work."

"It's a cinch, honey," Lenny says. "Nothing to it. You'll see."

"But I just don't understand this clutch thingy. I mean, I've only got two feet. How can I be working three pedals at once?"

"You don't work three at once." Lenny stands and slams the hood shut.

He wipes his hands on a handkerchief dug free from his pants pocket. "Listen, honey, I'll teach you everything you need to know to drive it. Once you've got the hang of it, you'll love it."

She frowns. She closes up the lipstick tube and drops it in her purse. "Yeah, well, you've got to promise me you won't yell if I make a mistake." Her freshly painted bottom lip pokes out in a respectable pout.

"Aw, honey, you know I'd never yell at the most beautiful woman in the world," he says.

Newlyweds, I'm guessing, or else this guy just really wants this car.

He leans in through the open window and kisses her. "What do you say, sweetie? Shall we take her home?"

From her smile, I assume he's won her over.

"I guess she *would* look pretty sitting in the garage."

The man lets go a whoop. "Now you're talking," he says, slapping the roof happily with an open palm.

He helps his wife out of the car and kisses her again as though I'm not standing right there, awaiting their decision. With one arm around his young wife's shoulders and looking as though he's just won the grand prize on "Let's Make a Deal," he turns to me and says, "Where do I sign?"

As I lead them to the office, my thoughts turn to Meg. We were just like this young couple once, she and I. In love and full of hope. I can almost remember what that was like. I can almost remember believing it would never change.

We step into the trailer, and I usher them to my desk. Ike Kerlee is out on the lot with another customer—though a still-smoking cigarette is slowly burning itself out in the ashtray on his desk. One of these days, he's going to burn the trailer down and years of paperwork with it. I can't say I'll be sorry to see it go, though it might leave Steve in a bad frame of mind and Ike Kerlee without a job.

The husband and wife settle themselves in the two gray metal folding chairs across from me while I remove the proper paperwork from the drawer. I tap the bottom edge of the papers on the desk to form a neat pile, then lay them down in front of me at a slight left-leaning angle. Picking up my ballpoint pen, I click open the retractable nub and am ready to gather the information I need to make this sale. I raise my eyes to the couple and notice that the woman looks quizzical. Her eyes go from my nameplate, to my face, down to the nameplate, back up to my face. It has been in the Asheville paper, and she has made the connection. I see the pity and the fear in her eyes. Hesitantly, she says, "You're the one with the son ..."

That's all she says—though perhaps she should have said, *without* the son—but we all know what she means.

"Yes," I say, nodding slightly.

The husband coughs, looks at his shoes. She glances at him, back at me. "We don't have kids yet, but I can only imagine. I'm ... I'm sorry."

"Thank you."

The man pulls out a cigarette, lights it. "The police still looking?" he asks.

"Not actively," I say, "though the investigation is still open, of course."

He takes a deep pull on the cigarette. She clutches her hands together in her lap. I suppose we all wish she hadn't brought it up.

"Mr. Crane?" she says.

"Yes, Mrs. Sanderson?"

"Will you give your wife my condolences?"

"Of course. Thank you."

"I don't know how she can—" she stops herself, eyes roaming the room—"possibly manage," she finishes.

I put the pen down and fold my hands on the top of the desk. I lean closer. "Well, you see," I say, "there's something my wife and I are both holding on to." This may not be necessarily true for Meg yet, but I will speak for her.

They too lean closer, looking at me expectantly.

"There is one thing we know for sure," I go on. "God is with our son or our son is with God. Either way, God is in this with us."

The man clears his throat, takes one last nervous pull on the cigarette, crushes out the half-smoked stick in the ashtray. The woman's eyes have come to a standstill on my face. Her mouth is open slightly, her brow furrowed. I can only guess at the thoughts passing through her mind, but I have a sense that they are tumbling, somersaulting over themselves in a bid to understand what I have said.

And then she smiles. So small, it almost isn't there. But that, coupled with a growing light in her eyes, tells me she has heard what I was trying to say.

I have just preached my first sermon in the used car lot of Birchfield Chevrolet.

49

Meg
Tuesday, December 24, 1968

AND SO TIME passes. Minutes and hours. Days and weeks. And now months.

I will always figure time now from the day Digger disappeared.

A light snow drifts down from the night sky. Winter is here. Tomorrow is Christmas day. No one can survive four months alone in these mountains, especially a child.

Why then does my heart still hope?

Simply because I wouldn't otherwise be human?

Sheldon tells me, "God is with him, or he is with God. Either way, God is holding Digger in the palms of his own two hands."

That is what Sheldon says. And part of me believes him.

We stand here now, the three of us, in the backyard where I last saw Digger. Bundled up in coats, scarves, gloves, and knitted hats, Linda holds one of my hands, Sheldon the other. We lift our faces to the sky, to the shining star that has been here since that day. The day everything changed and from which we measure our new lives.

We've been quiet for several long minutes, but finally, Sheldon says, "The people who sat in darkness have seen a great light.'"

Then, silence again as we consider that. It's cold enough that our breath forms small clouds in the air.

"Dad?" Linda asks.

"Yes, honey?"

"Do you really think it could be the Star of Bethlehem?"

"Yes, honey, I do."

"But, I mean … that was two thousand years ago."

Sheldon nods. "That seems to be the gift of this house, doesn't it? If you go into town, or anywhere else, you can't see the star. Only here."

"But why?" I whisper. "What is the star supposed to mean for us?"

"I don't know for sure."

"Do you think we'll ever know?" I ask.

Sheldon nods again. "Yes. At the right time."

"When will that be, Dad?"

Sheldon's profile lights up with a small smile. "You're asking the wrong person, Linda. God alone knows the answer to that. Right now, all I know for sure is if we could peel back time, go through yesterday and the day before that and the day before that, all the way to two-thousand years ago, we'd come to the moment when God put skin on and entered the world."

Linda sighs heavily, her breath drifting off into the night air. "I never really thought of it as true," she says. "It just always seemed like another story; something somebody made up."

Sheldon nods but says nothing. I wish the angels would appear to us the way they did to the shepherds and tell us what it means.

"What I really don't understand," I say, "is, why us? Who are we that such an extraordinary thing should happen to us; that we'd be the ones chosen to look into time? You'd think God would pick people who are—I don't know—famous, or important somehow."

Sheldon doesn't look at me, but I can tell he's thinking about that. Finally, he says, "Maybe we're more important to him than we think."

I feel Linda squeeze my hand. "Well, Merry Christmas, Mom and Dad."

My heart lifts with an unexpected joy. "Merry Christmas, Linda," I say.

"Merry Christmas, honey," Sheldon adds.

We need to go in now. It's late and we're getting cold.

But Linda thinks of one more thing. Looking up at the star one last time, she says, "Merry Christmas, Digger."

The star twinkles overhead. The heavens are silent and yet, we go to bed carrying something like hope in our hearts. It shines like a point of light in an otherwise dark place.

Part 2

What then is time? If no one asks me, I know what it is. If I wish to explain it to him who asks, I do not know.

—Saint Augustine

50

Linda
Sunday, April 6, 1969

It's nearly midnight, but I can't go to bed until I've finished writing this stupid English paper that's due tomorrow. All year the teachers have treated me kind of special, in a good way I mean, because of what happened. They've always said if I needed extra time to get an assignment done, I should take it. But I never have. Not once. And I'm not going to start now. I couldn't do that to Digger.

Mom and Dad went up to their rooms a couple hours ago. I'm sitting here at the dining room table with books and papers spread all over the place. I'm trying to write about what an Emily Dickinson poem means, and I don't know if what I'm saying makes any sense. When I chose this poem, Mrs. Crowell looked at me all funny and asked if it was really the poem I wanted to write my paper on, and I said yes, because it's one poem of Emily's I may actually identify with. I mean, I know she's talking about someone dying in their house, and how she has to sweep up her heart and put her love away because she won't want to use it again until eternity—yeah, I think I understand that. I just hope what I'm writing makes sense to Mrs. Crowell, since she's the one grading it.

Mom won't accept that Digger's gone. She says she thinks he's still alive. I wish I could say I agree with her, but I don't see how he could be alive after all this time. I mean, really, what kind of miracle could be keeping an eight-year-old kid alive out in the wilds by himself? Digger wasn't even a boy scout, for crying out loud. It's not like he knew how to make a fire or scrounge for food or make a tent out of leaves or whatever. And if he did get lost out there, it's not like he wouldn't have wandered into a town somewhere, begged a dime from someone, and called us to come pick him up.

Face it. Digger's gone and he's not coming back. He's dead and we're never going to see him again.

I think Dad thinks the same way I do, but I'm not sure. Still, I don't see him trying to convince Mom to accept that Digger's gone. He's just kind of letting her go on hoping if she wants to.

Carl will be coming home from Vietnam soon. Maybe he can get through to Mom, help her to accept what's happened. At least she'll be happy he's home.

The house has been mostly quiet since Digger left, as far as that time thing goes. The star still shows up every night, but we don't see people very often. I've seen Austin a few times, and Mom and Dad have seen their own people a couple of times. But that's it. If it's God who's running this show, he's playing out a pretty long intermission.

Okay, I've got to wrap up this final paragraph and get ready for bed. How to sum up what I said Emily's saying, which may not be what she's saying at all, but who knows what anyone's saying when they're speaking in poetry? I—

"Hello, Linda."

I jump about a foot at the sound of my name. "Austin!" I holler, and it comes out so loud I wonder whether Mom and Dad will wake up. But I can't help it. I'm so happy to see him. "What are you doing here?" I ask.

It's probably a stupid question. He's not doing anything other than sitting across from me at the table. He's drumming his fingers impatiently on the tabletop.

"I wanted to see you," he says. "I was hoping I could … somehow."

"Is something wrong?"

He stops drumming. "No. I mean … well, listen, Linda, I'm going to war."

"You're going to war?"

"That's right. Today President Wilson called for war on Germany and the Congress declared it. I'm going to sign up."

I knew it was coming, but I don't want to believe it. "But aren't you a pacifist, Austin? You told me yourself, you don't believe in war."

"I don't." He shakes his head hard. "I don't. But now that it's here, I can't run from it like a coward. I've got to go."

"Well, why don't you at least wait until you're drafted?"

He's still shaking his head like he can't stop. "I'm going now. I'm not waiting."

I can't change the past. If I say anything wrong, he'll disappear. So all I do is nod.

"Listen," he goes on. "I know you know who wins this war, and I also know you can't tell me. So I'm not here to find out."

"All right," I say. I feel stupid, but I don't know how else to respond. Anyway, I don't care about telling him who wins. I just want to beg him not to go. Because I know he's buried in France, and he'll never see America again.

"So I'm here to say good-bye," he finishes.

We look at each other a long time. There are tears running down my cheeks. His face looks calm enough, but his hands are clenched up into fists like he's already looking for a fight.

"I'll miss you, Austin," I say. I'm so choked up it's no more than a whisper.

"I'll miss you too." Now his eyes shimmer, and I think maybe he'll cry, but he manages not to.

"What do your parents think about you signing up?" I ask.

"I haven't told them yet."

I nod. "Guess they'll find out soon enough though, huh?"

"I'm going into Asheville to sign up in the morning."

I pick up the pen that had fallen out of my hand when he appeared and tap it nervously on the notebook in front of me. "I wish I could ask you to write to me but …" I finish by lifting my shoulders.

He understands. "Of course I can't. So I wanted to give you something. To remember me by."

"How?" I ask. "How can you give me something?"

"I left it somewhere for you to find," he says, nodding toward the kitchen. "On the hearth there's a yellowish colored stone shaped like an oval. If no one has fixed it between my time and yours, then it may still be loose. Lift it up, and you'll find what I left you."

"Should I look now?"

"Yes. I want to know whether you get it."

I nod and push my chair back from the table. He follows me into the kitchen where I kneel at the hearth and look for the stone.

"There," Austin says, pointing. "To the right."

I follow the line of his hand and find a stone that is yellow and oval. I touch it with my fingertips. "Is it this one?"

"Yes. See if you can lift it."

I can. It slips easily out of place. Beneath it, I find a piece of cheesecloth wrapped with a white ribbon. I lift it gently.

"You left this for me, Austin?"

He laughs lightly. "Open it, silly, so you can see what it is."

My fingers tremble as I pull on the ribbon and unwrap the cloth. I lift a necklace by its long chain until a slightly tarnished heart is dangling over my palm. "It's beautiful," I say.

"Can you put it on?"

I look at the lobster claw clasp. "Yes, I'll try." In another moment, it is fastened around my neck. I rise and smile, holding Austin's gaze. "Thank you."

"Don't forget me, please."

I'm crying again, softly. "How could I ever forget you?"

He lifts a hand to his mouth, blows me a kiss. I press my fingers to the necklace that lies against my chest.

"Good-bye, Linda."

"Good-bye, Austin."

And with that, he literally fades and disappears, like a dream that goes away when you open your eyes.

51

Meg
Monday, April 7, 1969

"JUST TWO AND half months and I'll be a married woman." Celeste smiles at me as she fingers the diamond ring on her left hand.

"I haven't seen you in awhile," I say. "Is everything ready for the wedding?"

"Almost." She nods and sighs happily. "Just this morning I picked up my dress from the seamstress who did the alterations. You should see it! It's just beautiful."

"I wish I *could* see it," I say. "I wish I could be there at the ceremony. I know it's going to be lovely."

"Oh, don't worry, you'll …" She pauses a moment, as though brought up short by a thought. Finally, she says, "I'll fill you in on all the details afterward. I have a feeling I'm not going to be able to stop talking about it for some time to come."

She radiates joy, and I'm surprised to find myself warmed by it. It's good to remember that joy is possible.

Linda left for school in tears this morning. "Austin's gone," she said. That's all she would tell me. Even then, the words came out in a choked whisper, as though her heart was breaking.

After Linda left, I sat down here by the hearth in the kitchen to have a cup of coffee and to go through my morning ritual of calculating time. Today is April 7, 1969. Digger disappeared on September 7, 1968. This marks the seventh month. I have not seen my son in seven months. Still, the sheriff calls once a week, sometimes twice, to give us an update. What he says is always the same. No fresh leads. No clues. Nothing.

I was also thinking this morning that I hadn't seen Celeste in nearly six months when suddenly she was there, sitting in the other rocking chair, holding a cup of tea. She was smiling dreamily to herself, so I greeted her by asking what she was thinking about. The wedding, of course.

I try to smile at Celeste now as I ask, "Will Mrs. See be there?"

"Oh yes, she'll be there. Of course." She sips her tea, and her brow puckers as though in thought. "What makes you ask about Mrs. See?"

"I don't know," I say, though actually I do. I sigh, get up, and pour myself another cup of coffee. "This morning I was remembering what she said about spring. You know, that spring would come. Now it's April and everything is budding and blooming." I turn to the window and look out. "But it isn't spring. Not really."

Always winter and never Christmas, I think. *And certainly never spring.*

I move back to my chair and sit. Celeste is nodding. She settles her empty cup and saucer on the hearth. "I wish I could tell you what Mrs. See meant, but I don't know."

"That's all right," I say. I look at the coffee in my cup and feel my stomach turn. I don't want it after all. I too settle my cup and saucer on the hearth. "Strange things happen in this house, and none of it seems to make much sense. I suppose I should be used to that by now, if one can get used to"—I wave a hand—"any of this."

Celeste rocks quietly a moment. "I think someday it will all make sense—everything that's happened and is happening here, I mean."

"Do you?"

"Yes, I really do." She stops rocking and leans forward in her chair. "I have something to tell you. It's another message from Mrs. See. I'm not sure it's proper for me to be passing along messages but ..." Her eyes roam the room as though she's waiting to see whether something or someone will stop her from speaking.

"How does Mrs. See know about me?" I ask quickly, in case she disappears.

"Oh, I know for sure I can't tell you that," she says, shaking her head.

"Okay. Well, can you tell me the message?"

Her warm eyes come to rest on my face and she smiles. "She says there must be forgiveness where Sheldon is concerned."

I draw back in surprise. "How does she know I haven't forgiven Sheldon? Did you tell her?"

"No. I promise you, I didn't tell her."

"Who is this Mrs. See then? Is she some sort of clairvoyant or something?"

Celeste laughs lightly. "Oh my, no. Nothing like that."

"Well, you must have told her *something* about me."

"A little. Not much, really." She pauses, then adds, "I can tell you only that she's a woman who cares about you."

"Cares about me? She doesn't even know me."

"Well, she has a good heart."

"And does this Mrs. See have a first name?"

Celeste chuckles again. "Yes she does. Her name is Margaret."

"Uh huh."

I'd like to tell Celeste to tell Margaret See to mind her own business. But I don't.

I don't because I know Margaret See is right. A year has passed since Sheldon first asked me to forgive him, and I haven't done it.

I rise and go back to the window. I look out at all the blooming things, the newly unfurled leaves on the trees, the crocuses and daffodils budding near the edge of the yard. Behind me, I hear Celeste say, "Mrs. See, she's like most old folks, you know? They're always talking about how fast time goes, how fast their lives have gone by. She says young folks think they have all the time in the world, and the next thing they know, it's all gone. The sure thing about time is that it always runs out."

I think about that a moment. Then, still looking out the window, I say, "All right. What's that have to do with me?"

"She wants to know what you're waiting for," Celeste says. "Because if you wait too long, it'll be too late."

What, in fact, *am* I waiting for? When will the moment come that I'll finally forgive Sheldon? Will I ever be willing to forgive him?

A cloud shifts and sunlight slants across the yard, falling softly on the grass. Winter has indeed ceded to spring, no matter how I feel about it. In all the calculating I've done these past months, I never figured into it the fact that time runs out. I know that Mrs. See is right, and I must find it in myself to forgive my husband, in spite of the lingering heartache. Maybe not today and maybe not tomorrow, but soon. This is something I must do very soon.

I turn back to say as much to Celeste, but the chair where she was sitting is empty and her tea cup too has disappeared from the hearth.

52

Sheldon
Friday, April 11, 1969

"SOMEBODY HERE TO see you, Shel." Ike Kerlee takes the butt of a cigarette out of his mouth and, with a flick of his wrist, sends it airborne. It lands on the hood of a '62 Nova. He doesn't seem to notice. He's too busy lighting up another.

"Who is it?" I ask. I'm out on the lot putting price tags on windshields.

"I don't know. Never seen her before, and she wouldn't give me her name." His wrist is flapping now like a panicked bird as he extinguishes the match and lets it drop to the ground. I'm about to remind him Steve has asked us to keep the lot free of litter, but he interrupts by saying, "She's a looker, I can tell you that much."

I'd be more than happy to hand this customer over to Ike. It's nearly quitting time, I'm tired, and I'm not sure I have the patience to talk to someone who probably doesn't know the first thing about cars. "You sure she asked for me specifically?"

He exhales, squinting at me through the smoke. "Your name's Sheldon Crane, ain't it?"

Wiseguy. Sighing, I offer Ike what I hope is a respectable look of annoyance, then turn and head to the office. On the way, I glance at my watch: 4:24 p.m. Depending on what this lady wants, I may not be out of here by 5:00.

My feet reluctantly carry me up the two cinderblock steps to the door of the trailer. I open it to find a blonde-haired woman gazing out the window, her back to me. She's wearing a pillbox hat and a blue tailored suit, like she's dressed to go somewhere special.

"Good afternoon," I say. "Can I help you?"

When she turns around, I feel myself punched in the gut. I am sent reeling. I clutch the doorknob to steady myself.

"Charlene!" I say.

"Hello, Sheldon." Her voice is cool, confident. She takes a step toward me, and only then do I notice the tiny, bundled child in her arms. One glance at the sleeping baby sends me into a cold sweat. I swipe a hand across my forehead and find it moist. "I know you weren't expecting me," Charlene goes on.

"No, I …" I am shaking my head dumbly. The room seems to fluctuate as though the earth is tilting at odd angles.

"I decided I had to come. I had to see you," she says.

I must sit down. I wave a trembling hand toward the metal chairs by my desk. "Won't you have a seat?"

She chooses a chair, shifts the sleeping child from the crook of one arm to the other. She smiles wanly up at me.

I somehow make it to my desk chair, collapsing into it. I clasp my hands together on the desktop to try to still them. My eyes keep moving to the door.

Oh God, if you've ever answered my prayers, hear me now. Please don't let Ike Kerlee walk through that door.

"I heard about Digger," she says abruptly. My eyes shift from the door to her face, that lovely young face. "I want you to know how sorry I am. He was a good boy."

"Yes. Thank you. He's a good boy," I repeat, changing her past tense to present almost without thinking.

"Mother told me back in October, back when it happened. You know, when Steve was calling the news around to family. He told Mother, who told me. I could hardly believe it. I still can hardly believe it."

Oh yes, Charlene's mother was Steve's aunt, Meg's aunt. Of course, yes, family call family in the face of tragedy. People needed to be notified.

"I would have come then," she continues, "but I wasn't able to travel." She drops her eyes demurely and settles them on the face of the child. The baby is so small I recognize it as a newborn, no more than a month old, maybe two.

"Are you here to see Meg?" I ask hopefully.

The blue eyes rise to meet mine; they are full of something I don't quite understand. "No, Sheldon," she says slowly. "I'm here to see you. I thought you ought to know." She lifts the child a fraction of an inch. "He's yours."

"Mine?"

"Yes. Yours and mine. This is our son."

Now I'm certain the earth has tilted precipitously, and I'm hanging on to the desk for dear life. If I let go, I will go floating off without a tether into space. "Are you sure?" I ask dumbly. "Absolutely sure?"

Now the look in her eyes tells me distinctly that she's hurt and a little angry. "Of course, I'm sure." She shakes her head. "You were the only one."

I stare at my hands clenched on top of my desk. I don't want to see the child, don't want to see its face. Certainly, I don't want to believe it's mine. "But when we parted," I say, "I had no idea."

"When we parted, I didn't want you to know. I wasn't sure I was going to tell you at all. But then …"

"But then what, Charlene?"

Her shiny red lips form a small line. "Then I heard about Digger. I didn't know what to do at first, but after he was born"—she glances again at the child—"I thought … well …"

I wait. She looks at me expectantly as though I already know what she's going to say.

After a long and painful silence, she finally says, "I've come to ask you to marry me, Sheldon. We have a child. You lost Digger but … you have a new son. You can start over. The three of us—we can make a family."

Perspiration explodes along my brow. "But Charlene, I *am* married. I have a wife—"

"But you don't love her, Sheldon."

"No, you're wrong. I love Meg. I always have. I—"

Suddenly, the door flies open, and Ike Kerlee comes barreling in. He must see the look of horror on my face because he stops in mid-stride. His eyes roll from me to Charlene, and then for once he does something right. He backs up and leaves without saying a word.

I take several deep breaths, thanking God for the interruption. Finally, I look back at Charlene. "Do you have a lawyer?"

"No." Her voice is small. She shakes her head.

"Find one," I say. "Find one and put him in touch with me. We'll make arrangements for child support. I can promise to help you financially, but that's all I can do."

The blue eyes become glistening ponds. I am overwhelmed by a sense of my own wrongness. What have I done to this young woman? In how many ways have I hurt her? The evidence of my wretchedness lies in her arms.

"Charlene," I say, "if only I could undo it all. If only you had never known me."

"I'm not sorry, Sheldon. I loved you. I still love you." She stops. She's waiting for me to respond. I can't. Timidly, she asks, "Do you … don't you still love me?"

I feel the sudden urge to tear at myself—my arms, my legs, my face— to rip away the flesh that has brought me to this moment. "No," I say, voice trembling. "No, I'm sorry. But no."

Her eyes well up and then a single tear rolls down each cheek. And yet, she tries to smile. "I didn't think so," she says. "But I had to ask. I wanted to know for sure. I didn't want to go through my whole life wondering. I mean, you can't blame me, can you?"

I shake my head slowly. "No, I can't blame you."

"I was hoping, maybe you'd change your mind about things. Especially, once you saw the baby and all."

"I am sorry," I say again. "I really am. So very sorry."

I wait for her to explode. I wait for her chastisement to fall down on my head. Surely she's furious, isn't she? What woman wouldn't be? If she were to lash out verbally, even physically, I would feel it was my due.

But she doesn't. She simply reaches for a scrap of paper and a pen, scribbles something, pushes the paper across the desk at me. "This is my address and phone number," she says quietly. "In case you change your mind."

She stands to go.

"Charlene?"

She pauses. She won't look at me.

"Promise me you'll call that lawyer. You have my word, I'll help you financially."

She nods.

"And listen, if you ever need anything … extra … for the boy, anything at all, you must let me know."

She glances at me, nods again—one small lift of her chin—and walks to the door. She hesitates a moment, her hand on the knob. "Sheldon?"

"Yes, Charlene?"

"Before I go, wouldn't you like—you know—just to look at him? Don't you want to see how beautiful he is?"

I drop my eyes and shake my head. "No. Please, it'd be best if I didn't. I'm sorry. Please try to understand."

I hear her sigh. The door squeaks open slowly. I raise my eyes to her again to find her looking back at me over her shoulder. "Your son's name is Gavan," she says. "At least you should know that much about him."

With that she leaves, closing the door quietly behind her.

53

Linda
Friday, April 11, 1969

ANOTHER FRIDAY NIGHT scooping up ice cream. There's that group of seniors from school laughing it up over in the corner. Half a dozen of them, three boys and three girls. I know their names, and I know a couple of them are real snobs, but that's about all I know. The school year's practically over, and I haven't made any real friends besides Gail. Mostly because it got off to a bad start. From the outset, I was the new girl with the missing brother, the strange kid from the North, who had tragedy and rotten luck and probably all kinds of curses clinging to her like a bad smell. Wherever I went, there it was. And no one wanted to hang with a girl like that in case the bad might rub off, and their own little brothers or sisters might suddenly disappear or some other rotten thing might happen.

I don't blame them, really. I mean, when we first came down here, all I wanted was to get out. Finish high school and move back north to get away from these backwoods yokels. So I haven't exactly been Miss Congeniality, and when the yearbook comes out, I'll probably find I've been voted most likely to live and die alone. That's all right. Let them think what they want. When I leave Black Mountain, I'll know I had two good friends here, Gail and Austin. That's enough.

At the thought of Austin, I find myself touching the necklace. Again.

I haven't taken it off this whole week, not even to take a bath. Gail asked me in school on Monday, who gave it to me. I told her it was from an old boyfriend I used to know. She asked what happened to him, and I said he went to war. She thought I meant Vietnam. How could she know I meant the First World War? She asked if he got killed over there. I said yes. She was surprised I'd never told her about him before, and she asked his name. I said I didn't want to talk about it because it was too hard. As it was, I had to turn away and pretend I was looking for something in my locker or I would have ended up crying.

"Hey, Linda! Another large chocolate malted here, will ya?" The guy that's hollering raises a hand and actually snaps his fingers, like I'm a servant.

It's Jimmy Barton, one of the seniors, trying to impress his girl Arlena Jo. She's got her hair puffed up so high, she's probably got to duck through doorways, and I bet she found those eyelashes on the sale table at Woolworth's. She's never so much as given me the time of day, and I'm thinking it's because she's a cheerleader and I'm not. She and Jimmy are two of a kind; both stuck up and probably more in love with themselves then they are with each other.

"And bring two straws, will ya?" Jimmy hollers.

I sneer at him, but he doesn't see because I've already bent over the tub of vanilla ice cream in the freezer.

"He's a jerk," Gail whispers in my ear. "And she's not much better."

That's not exactly news to me, but I nod anyway. I toss the ice cream, milk, and chocolate malted powder into the stainless steel cup, and I'm thinking I should maybe add something gross like raisins or cigarette ashes or maybe even spit but I decide not to—only because I don't want to lose my job.

But never mind. I stick the cup on the milkshake machine and switch it on, and while I've got my back to the door, I hear the bell tinkle and Gail says, "Well, hey, Grandpa! Hey, everyone! I was wondering whether you guys were going to come in."

Yeah, it's 9:00 and usually the perverts are here by 8:00, drinking coffee and playing checkers. I glance over my shoulder at them and wonder what took the old geezers so long to get here tonight. Maybe they stopped by a bar to try out their luck picking up women or something. Obviously, they struck out. Big surprise there.

I am not in a good mood right now. I feel like I hate everybody.

I carry the chocolate malted with the two straws to Jimmy's table, and the whole time I'm walking across the shop, I have a feeling someone's watching me.

"That's fifty cents," I say to Jimmy.

He digs around in his pants pocket and pulls out a couple of quarters. "Here ya go," he says. "Keep the change." He winks at Arlena Jo, who bursts out laughing.

I glare at them both and decide next time I'm not going to hold back. Chocolate-flavored Ex Lax in their two-straw chocolate malted. See how that plays out at the end of their romantic evening.

Okay, so I'll admit it. I'm jealous of them, of what they have in each other. I'm jealous because I'm alone. The one I cared about went to war, and now he's dead.

I'm walking back to the counter when I realize it's Bim watching me with his watery old eyes. As soon as I get behind the counter, he leaves the table where the perverts are sitting and comes over.

"What can I get you, Gramps?" Gail says.

"Would you mind mixing me up some hot cocoa, honey?" he asks.

"Sure, Grandpa. It'll just take me a minute."

Gail gets to work, and I'm standing there wishing another customer would come ask for something because I can see the old man's staring at my necklace. Just to make him mad, I cover it up with my hand, like I'm doing it without thinking while I'm looking around the shop and not paying him any attention. The bell tinkles again and a couple of married folks come in, and I have to dish them up some strawberry ice cream.

While I'm doing that Bim leans closer to the counter and says to me, "Nice necklace you've got there, Linda," and as soon as he says it I find myself breathing out a bunch of hot air because he's really annoying me, and I just want him to go away.

"Thank you," I say without looking up at him, though I want to tell him it's none of his business, and if he wants to know the story behind it he can just ask Gail. Not that she knows the real story either. Only I do. And Austin. That's it.

Gail hands Bim his hot chocolate. He gives me one last look before heading back to his table. Good riddance, old man. You can just keep your eyes to yourself.

Two hours until I can go home. I don't want to be here. Somebody let me out of here so I can go home and cry.

***

10:30 p.m. I can't stop yawning. Sadness wears you out. If I had just one wish, I'd wish I could go back in time and not be so mean to Digger. Regret is always bugging me. It's like some little animal with sharp teeth gnawing at my brain, so that sometimes all I can think about is how rotten I was to that kid. If I could see him again, I might even tell him I love him, though if I did he'd probably look at me like I'd lost my mind. Who cares? I'd tell him anyway. Just so he'd know. Then maybe that little beast in my head would finally go away.

Thirty minutes till I can get out of here. It's been a long night. My right arm aches from scooping up ice cream. My head is a dam about to burst. But this isn't the place for waterworks, Linda. Buck up. No bawling in front of the customers.

I'm wiping down the counter with a rag that smells like ammonia when Bim rises and pushes his chair under the table.

"Goodnight, all," he says. He shuffles over to the counter. "See you at home, Gail. You've got your key, right?"

"I've got it," Gail says. "If you want to wait another half hour I can give you a ride home."

He shakes his head. "No, I want to walk. The exercise will do me good."

"All right, Gramps. See you later."

He nods in my direction. "Goodnight, Linda."

I lift my gaze only long enough to say goodnight, then go back to cleaning. I sense the old man's eyes on me, but when I look up again he's heading out the door.

"Hey, Bim!" One of the perverts hollers, the one named Buford. "Your glasses! Hey, you forgot your readers!"

He waves a pair of dark-rimmed glasses in the air, but the door is already closed, and Bim is passing in front of the plate glass window. Buford bangs on the window, waves the glasses in the air. "Bim! Hey, Austin, old man! Your glasses."

I look up sharply. Bim acknowledges the glasses with a nod and turns back, but Buford has already moved to the door. He meets Bim in front of the shop and hands him the glasses. Bim tucks them into the pocket of his shirt. The two men nod at each other and go separate ways.

"Gail," I say. My hand stops making circles on the counter with the rag. I'm following Bim with my eyes. By the time Gail says, "Yeah?" he's already gone.

"Why'd Buford call your grandfather Austin?"

"That's his real name." She shrugs. She's cleaning the milkshake maker and is too busy to look at me.

"His name is Austin Leland?"

She laughs a little at that. "No, silly. His name is Austin Buchanan."

I feel like she slapped me, and I'm almost mad. "Are you sure?"

"What do you mean, am I sure? He's my own grandfather, isn't he? I ought to know what his name is."

"But why isn't his name Leland?"

"That's my mother's married name. Before she was married she was a Buchanan."

"So your grandfather is Austin Buchanan?"

"That's right. Why? What's so strange about that? I mean—hey, Linda, where are you going? What—"

But I don't hear the rest of what Gail's saying. I'm already out the door and running down the sidewalk. I haven't even bothered to take off my dirty apron. Waving a hand, I holler, "Wait! Hey, wait a minute, will you!"

Finally, he stops and turns around. He's standing under the light of a streetlamp, and when I reach him we're staring at each other, and I'm searching his face for something ... something to tell me this is him.

"Austin?" I finally say. "Austin Buchanan?"

He gives one terse nod. "That's right."

I squint and lean in closer to inspect his face and, even though the eyes are the same—yes, those are Austin's blue eyes—still I say, "I don't believe it. Your name may be Austin Buchanan, but you're not the one I know."

He sniffs at that, points to my necklace, and says, "You found that wrapped in a piece of cheesecloth under a stone on the kitchen hearth."

And when he says that I think I might faint because I know it must be Austin, but I can't believe this old man is that beautiful young kid I'm half in love with. And anyway, he went off to war and got killed somewhere over in France.

"You can't be Austin!" I cry. "Who told you about the necklace?"

He holds one gnarled-up fist to his chest. His face looks stern, and he's frowning like he's tasting something sour. "I *am* Austin, Linda," he says. "I am the Austin Buchanan who gave you that necklace. I'm in here." He taps his fist to his boney chest and says again, "I'm in here."

I'm shaking all over, and I want to scream until my vocal cords explode because I can't believe this is happening. I shake my head, trying to understand. "But you're dead," I say. "Austin Buchanan is dead."

He frowns even more, and his head kind of cocks to one side. Then he smiles, and I think he almost chuckles when he says, "I know I might *look* dead but—"

"But you are. You're buried over in France."

"Buried over in France? How'd you get an idea like that? I'm not buried anywhere, Linda. I'm not dead yet."

"But, didn't you die in the war?"

"No." He shakes his head slowly. "No, I didn't. I came home. I came back home, got married, had children. And I grew old. That's all that's happened. I just grew old."

Even as he's speaking, I understand something. "Gail's your granddaughter and Linda's your daughter, and I'm thinking ... I'm thinking ..."

"That's right, Linda. I named my daughter after you."

"You never forgot me, then?"

"Of course not."

"But what did your wife think about you naming your daughter after me?"

"She never knew our daughter was named after anyone. How could I have explained? Should I have told her I named our daughter after a girl I once knew who wasn't even born yet?"

None of it makes any sense to me, and I just keep shaking my head and thinking, *My God, what happens to people? What happens to people?* I never knew before that old people really had been young people once because I've never known a young person who turned old. The old people I know have always been old and all the young people will always be young and aren't going to end up old like that and ...

"Why did you think I was buried in France?" Austin says, interrupting my thoughts.

"Oh, um." I keep feeling like Rod Sterling's going to show up any minute now and start saying, *You've just crossed over into the Twilight Zone,* because I can't believe Bim has been Austin all this time. I rub my forehead and tell myself to keep talking. "I found your family's gravestones in the cemetery by the church," I say. "There was a stone for your mother and father and one for Mac. Mac died as a kid. Mom thought it was probably the flu epidemic that killed him. And since you weren't there, we figured you had died in the war and were buried over in France."

"Well, I'm still very much alive, even if that appears questionable to you. And as for Mac, no, it wasn't the flu epidemic. It was …"

But he doesn't finish. I'm waiting, but he's looking over my shoulder like he's just seen Mac himself walking up behind me. His eyes get wide and his mouth kind of drops open. I turn around to see what he's looking at, but the sidewalk is empty from where we are to the corner. Nobody's there. I turn back to him and wait. Finally he says, "I have to go, Linda," and he starts walking away. I yell after him, "But where are you going, Austin?" He doesn't answer me. He just walks off into the night, the same way he left me a week ago when he disappeared from my life forever.

54

Meg
Saturday, April 12, 1969

I'VE BEEN BAKING since 5:00 a.m. It's nearly 7:00 now, and the two circular layers of cake are cooling while I mix up the frosting. Chocolate, of course. Chocolate cake and chocolate frosting. I eye the box of candles on the kitchen counter, and as I stir the frosting, I ask myself again what I've been asking myself since I awoke: *Why am I doing this? Have I finally completely lost my mind?*

But I will frost this cake, and I will put the candles in it. I will do it because of what I've resolved. As long as the star shows up, I'll hold on to hope. When the star no longer appears, I'll give up. I don't know what the star means, but it must mean *something*. And as long as it shines, I'll know that this isn't finished yet. There's something else.

I wonder whether Sheldon remembers. Surely he does. Maybe that's why he didn't look well when he came home from work yesterday. Maybe that's why he went straight to his room and stayed there. When supper was ready I found him lying on his bed with one arm thrown over his face. "I'm not hungry," he said. "I'm sorry. You go ahead and eat without me."

"Are you sick?" I asked.

He seemed to have to think about that for a long time. Finally he said, "Yes." Just that, nothing more.

"Can I get you anything? Some aspirin or Pepto Bismol?"

"No," he said. "I don't think anything will help. I just need ... time."

"Time?"

"To rest. I'll be all right."

I never saw his eyes. He didn't lift his arm from his face. I closed the door quietly when I left.

The cake isn't quite cool enough to be frosted. I pour myself another cup of coffee and sit down in one of the rocking chairs to wait. I find myself wishing Celeste would show up. It would be nice to talk with her. I find it restful to be with one who is just "spending time."

I sip the coffee and rock quietly. I shut my eyes and rest my head against the rim of the rocker. Digger's face rises up in my memory, as real as if he were here. I feel him as though he were solid. Time diminishes nothing. My heart aches with fresh longing, but also with fresh hope. Hope is unseen and tenuous, but at the same time more solid than flesh, stronger than bone. I find it's what holds me together. More than that, this hope—from wherever it may be coming—tells me everything is happening as it should.

Footsteps approach. I open my eyes thinking I'll see Celeste but it's Sheldon. He enters the kitchen still wearing the shirt and slacks he was wearing last night. His hair is disheveled, his face dark with a day's worth of stubble. He looks as though he hasn't slept all night.

"Sheldon?" I say.

He sits in the rocker across from me and sighs heavily. He looks down at his hands, clasped together between his knees. I feel my pulse quicken.

"What is it, Sheldon?"

He lifts his eyes to me; they are red-rimmed and bloodshot. "I saw Charlene," he says.

The cup in my hand trembles so violently, coffee spills over into the lap of my housedress. "Where? When?"

"Yesterday. She just showed up at the lot."

"Why? What did she want?"

"She had a child with her, Meg."

"A child?"

"A baby."

An iciness takes hold of me. I shiver. "What are you saying, Sheldon?"

"She claims the baby's mine."

I feel as though I'm falling, though in fact I'm rising and walking, weak-kneed, to the sink. I drop the cup and saucer into it, china clinking against the porcelain. Both hands clutch the edge of the sink for support. "Do you think she's telling you the truth?"

"Yes." The rocking chair squeaks as Sheldon rises out of it. "I believe the boy is mine."

"Boy?"

"Yes, the child's a boy."

I hear myself wail, one sharp cry of grief climbing up my throat. It is a year ago all over again, only this time the anger is deeper and the pain is worse. Unfaithfulness is one thing, but a child ...

My eyes fall to the cake, the bowl of frosting. With trembling fingers I grasp the spatula and angrily spread frosting over one layer of the cake.

"I'm sorry, Meg," Sheldon says, so quietly I almost don't hear him.

"Do you know what today is?" I ask. Tears are streaming down my face. I keep my back to Sheldon so he doesn't see.

"Yes, I know."

"Digger is nine years old."

"Yes."

I lift the second layer of cake and put it on top of the first, drop a mountain of frosting on it. "And now you're telling me you have a son with Charlene."

He doesn't answer. I sense him drawing closer, and then his hand is on my shoulder. "Meg," he says.

"Don't touch me." I pull away.

"Meg, please, I—"

"So, now you have someone to take the place of Digger?"

"No, Meg, no. Never."

The grass outside grows dark with shadow; a cloud must have passed across the sun. I wipe my tears with a dishcloth and take several deep breaths. "What will you do now?" I ask, still not looking at him. "Do you intend to leave me for Charlene, now that there's a child?"

"No, Meg. I don't intend to leave you. I'll pay child support, but that's all."

I think about that a moment, consider the strain it will put on our already depleted pocketbook. My anger is a hard knot in my chest. "How much?"

"How much what?"

"How much will you pay every month?"

"I don't know yet. I'll have to talk with her lawyer."

"And what did Charlene say?"

"She ... she thought I should know about the boy, but she knows my place is here."

I swing around, look Sheldon in the eye. "Is it?"

"I hope so, Meg," he whispers. His eyes are wide and full of fear. "I have no desire to leave. Unless you want me to."

I turn away, finish frosting the cake. I have nothing to say to him that will take away his fear. Pulling nine candles out of the box, I plant them on top of the cake. "I'll never forgive you, Sheldon," I say.

The room is so quiet, I can hear Sheldon breathing. Finally, he says, "I understand. I won't ask it of you."

His footsteps in the hall tell me he has left.

I begin to sob, tears dripping on the cake. My offering to my son, baptized with sorrow.

55

Linda
Monday, April 14, 1969

This morning, Mom and Dad called me into the living room with this look on their faces that told me something really bad had happened. I'm thinking maybe they finally found Digger's body, or what's left of it, but it had nothing to do with Digger.

So, you remember Charlene, don't you? they asked.

"Um, sure," I said, but I'm thinking, you've got to be kidding, right? Like I'm so stupid I would forget Mom's cousin, someone who lived with us for I don't know how long. Someone who's the reason we came down here and set up camp in boonie land. Oh yeah, I remember Charlene, all right.

Well, she's had a baby. Dad's baby. He's your brother.

I had to leave for school in ten minutes, and they think it's a good time to tell me I have a baby brother? I couldn't believe it. I mean, talk about proof that one of your parents has been fooling around. A baby adds a whole new dimension to the picture. But it kind of explains why Dad's looked like death warmed over all weekend, walking around like he just stepped out of the morgue. Mom hasn't exactly been in a good mood either. I should have figured something was up.

"So, what, is he going to come live with us or something?" I asked.

"No," Dad said. And he didn't waste so much as a second in saying it. "Charlene will raise him."

"So he's got nothing to do with us, right?"

"Well, in a sense, no, but we thought you should know about him."

Yeah, well, I think I'd rather not have known, thank you very much. I mean, the whole idea of it is enough to give me the creeps. Mom's cousin is the mother of my brother? Sheesh! That's got to be some kind of incest going on, isn't it? And even if it isn't, it's kind of like Dad's cheating is carved in stone now. We'll never be able to sweep it under the rug and forget about it.

I asked, "So what's the kid's name?" and that's when things got really weird. Evidently Mom hadn't bothered to ask, and Dad acted like he didn't want to tell us. He wouldn't look either of us in the eye. "Well," I finally said, "didn't Charlene tell you his name?"

"Yes, she did," he said. And then he kind of mumbled, "The boy's name is Gavan."

"Gavan?" Mom said, and her eyes got real big.

And I asked, "Isn't that the name of the guy you see around here who's living in the twenty-first century?"

Dad nodded. Still wouldn't look us in the eye. "It doesn't mean they're one and the same. The last name of the Gavan I see in this house is Valdez, not McMurphy."

So? Charlene probably snags herself a husband somewhere along the way. Why shouldn't his name be Valdez? Hopefully he's not a loser like you, Daddy-o.

I didn't say that out loud, but I was thinking it. And from the look in Mom's eyes, my guess is she was thinking it too.

Good going, Dad. You have an affair, so we come down here to this godforsaken place, and next thing we know Digger disappears. Just when we think it can't get any worse, you tell us you have a son with your lover, who happens to be Mom's younger cousin. Well, that's just great.

Something tells me you're not going to be winning the Husband of the Year award this time around, huh?

I sure don't feel like being at school today. I wish I could go somewhere and get quietly and thoroughly drunk.

I drive into the student parking lot, find a space, and cut the engine. Instead of getting out of the car, I'm going to sit here for just a minute to try to pull myself together. The bell's going to ring any minute now, but I don't even care if I'm late. Wish I had a cigarette. A person can only handle so much. I don't want a baby brother. I want Digger back.

Okay, get it together now, grab your books and move. Pretend like everything's honky-dory, like your life is as good as everyone else's. Right, that'll be the day.

Get out of the car. That's it. Get out and start walking. Try to get through the day without having a nervous breakdown.

"Hey, Linda! Wait up!"

I recognize the voice. Gail is running up behind me.

"Hi, Gail," I say, hoping I sound nonchalant.

She's out of breath by the time she reaches me. "Listen," she says, "I've got some bad news."

You too? Well, it can't be any worse than mine, though I'm sure as heck not going to tell you *my* bad news. "What is it?" I ask. I frown like I'm trying to look concerned.

"Bim's in the hospital," she says. "He had a heart attack."

I stop and stare at her. Now I really *am* concerned. "When?"

"Saturday," she says. She pushes her hair out of her eyes and shifts her books from one arm to the other. "I'd have called you, but I've been at the hospital most of the time and I've been too scared to do anything more than just sit and wait."

"Is he going to be all right?"

She shakes her head. "Yeah, they said as heart attacks go it was pretty mild. But he's going to need a lot of rest."

"What happened?"

Her eyes get wide. "That's the really weird thing, Linda. You're not going to believe it. He—"

Inside we hear the bell ring. Gail makes a move like she's going to go in, but I grab her arm and hold on. "What happened?"

"He was looking for your brother."

"What? He was looking for Digger? What do you mean?"

"He kept saying his brother didn't listen to him. He said Mac promised not to go out looking for gold, but he did it anyway. One summer when they were down here, Mac climbed up into the mountains and fell into a mineshaft somewhere. Grandpa said that's what killed Mac. He thought maybe Digger had fallen into the same shaft. So the old fool went walking up into the mountains and wore himself out."

"Did he find the mine? What was there? What'd he find?"

"Nothing. He found the mine all right, but Digger wasn't in it. After that, he just came home and keeled over. Mom had to call for an ambulance, and they hauled him off to the hospital. I swear, Linda, I thought he was going to die. Crazy old guy, going up in the mountains like that."

She's shaking her head and telling me to hurry up and get to class, but my mind is already somewhere else. It's with Austin, wherever he is right at this minute. My heart's squeezed up tight because I'm not seeing Bim; I'm seeing Austin, going up into the mountains, looking for my brother. I'd have loved him—I know that for sure—if we'd shared the same time. If only we'd shared the same time. I'd have grown old with him, and who knows, maybe if I was old too I wouldn't be so creeped out by him. I'd still love him, and we'd be old together, and it'd be all right.

"Can I visit him?" I have to holler because Gail's already on the front steps of the school.

"What?" she calls back.

"Can I visit Aus—" I stop myself. Gail doesn't know I knew her grandfather when he was young. "Can I visit Bim in the hospital?"

I'm moving toward the steps. She lifts her shoulders and looks a little surprised. "Sure, if you want. He's at the VA. You know where that is?"

"I'll find it."

"Okay, but listen, don't go today. Let him rest a few days before you go see him, all right?"

I nod. Next Saturday, then. Saturday I'll drive over to Asheville and wander around the VA till I find Austin. And God, please don't let him die between now and then. I've got to thank him for trying to find my brother.

56

Sheldon
Monday, April 14, 1969

I AM NOT a sinner; I'm sin itself.

Flesh, blood, bone—all of it sin. I'm filled with self-loathing. And there's no escape.

Not unless I can crush it out, the way Ike Kerlee over there crushes out his cigarette in the ashtray. The stub of the thing, head bent, stilled under the weight of Ike's tobacco-stained index finger.

How good it would be not to exist.

I find myself glancing continually at the office door, wondering whether it will open and Charlene will be there with the child in her arms. My child.

The weight of my wrongdoing bears down. It *will* crush me. It's crushing me now. One son is dead. One son should never have been born.

The words on the loan application in front of me are senseless marks, without meaning. I pretend to read, to be absorbed by this paperwork, even though no customer sits at my desk. If I look busy maybe Ike will go on reading the newspaper and not try to talk to me.

I have nothing to say to him or to anyone. I am a dead man, without words.

There was a time when I thought Meg might find it in herself to forgive me. I don't believe that anymore. Hope is nonexistent. I have one too many children, and now I will never have a family.

I wonder, God, how you might have let this happen and then I remember—it wasn't your fault, it was mine. When I'm tempted to be angry with you, I remind myself of that, and my anger comes back around to where it belongs. I dug my own grave with my own shovel without any help from you, and now I will lie myself down in the dark, and I will shut my eyes and you can shut yours. We are through.

I start when Ike laughs out loud. "Hey, Shel," he says, "get this. You know that guy that was arrested for killing those people over in Asheville last year?"

I say yes even though I don't remember.

"He's saying he killed those folks because he heard voices telling him he had to do it. He said he had to listen to the voices or *they* would kill *him*. So that's his defense, that he was just obeying orders so he wouldn't be killed! Like you can't blame him for doing what he was told to do."

He laughs loudly again, shakes his head. I look at him with leaden eyes.

"Yessiree, nothing like copping the old insanity plea, huh?" He folds up the newspaper and slaps it down on his desk. "You get caught committing murder, and all you have to do is say you've lost your mind."

The thought of losing one's mind has some appeal.

I will never forgive myself. There is no clemency, and I'll expect no mercy.

57

Meg
Thursday, April 17, 1969

HE'LL BE HOME soon. My son will be home safe and sound.

I press Carl's letter to my heart and breathe deeply in relief. He's already stateside and will be coming to us on the train. I'll be able to put my arms around him and hold him once again.

I'm standing on the upstairs porch, looking out over the newly greened mountains. In this one sense, at any rate, spring has come. Carl is returning home safely from the war.

I find that I'm thankful, and the words rise up in my mind: thank God.

Are you the one to thank, then? You who did not keep my other son safe?

"Hello, Meg. A letter from Carl?"

I'm not surprised to find Celeste standing on the balcony beside me. Only glad. "He's coming home, Celeste," I say. "He should be home in about a week."

"Thank God."

I nod happily. "Yes."

We're quiet for a moment. Finally I say, "Celeste, I would like to ask you something."

"All right."

"That man you work for …"

"Mr. Valdez?"

"Yes. Gavan, isn't it?"

"That's right."

"What was his mother's name?"

"His mother? I have no idea. Why do you ask?"

"I think he may be Sheldon's son."

She looks at me with puzzled eyes. "His son?"

"How old is he?"

Celeste thinks a moment. "He must be in his mid-thirties somewhere."

"That would be about right."

"I don't understand, Meg. Why do you think he's Sheldon's son?"

I feel my grip tighten on Carl's letter. "Sheldon has a child with Charlene. She's the woman he had an affair with. We've just found out."

Celeste sighs. She looks out over the mountains as though looking for the answer out there. "I really don't know much about Mr. Valdez's personal life," she says.

I want to ask her to ask Gavan if he knows who his father is, but somehow it doesn't seem right to make Celeste a go-between in this. "What's he like?" I ask. "Gavan. What can you tell me about him?"

She nods. "He's a very good and kind man. A wonderful father to his son. He's a theologian. He teaches at one of the colleges here."

"A theologian." I laugh lightly. "Well, that figures."

"I'm sure it must have been hard on you, Meg," she says, "to learn Sheldon has a son."

I feel the tears well up. I don't want to cry. "It somehow makes the infidelity more complete, doesn't it?"

Seconds pass. I bite my lip to stifle the tears.

"Meg?"

I don't respond.

"I'll tell you truth, Meg," she goes on. "If Cleve does the same to me after we're married, I will be tempted to quietly and tenderly kill him."

I give her a sideways glance and a crooked smile.

"And what would our Mrs. See say to that?" I ask.

Celeste smiles too now. "She would say what she has said to me a thousand times. Forgiveness is the road between heaven and earth."

"I see." My eyes grow small. "Is that what she thinks?"

"It's what she knows."

"And was her husband ever unfaithful to her?" My words taste bitter; I have to look away from Celeste.

"Well, like you, she's had some hard things happen in her life," Celeste says. "She's had to learn to forgive."

I sigh heavily. "The funny thing is," I say, "I had felt almost ready to forgive Sheldon. It had taken me a long time, I know, but I was finally there. And now, this. He and Charlene have a baby together. And now, I'm not sure I can forgive or even want to forgive. Not when it comes to the child."

She nods. "Even though I understand your feelings, Meg, I'm not sure we have the luxury of choosing."

"Choosing what?"

"Which debts to forgive and which to demand payment on."

I have to think about that. I know she's referring to The Lord's Prayer: *Forgive us our debts as we forgive our debtors.*

"I suppose Mrs. See would still think I need to forgive Sheldon, even though there's a child."

"Hmmm." Celeste nods. "She's a stubborn one. So yes, even with a child in the picture, she would probably hold out for forgiveness."

I sniff out a small laugh. "All right then," I say. "Any other words of wisdom from your elderly employer?"

"As a matter of fact, yes," Celeste says. "She told me to tell you that as long as the star is shining, you must not give up hope. You must rest in it because everything is happening as it should."

The words of Margaret See make me shiver. It's as though that woman can read my mind.

58

Linda
Saturday, April 19, 1969

THE WEIRD THING about all the old geezers in this hospital is they were young once. I know that now. And I know it was time that dragged them to this awful place where they're shriveled up, glassy-eyed, sitting in wheelchairs or shuffling around like a bunch of zombies. If they hadn't been caught up in time, they'd still be young. And, for the first time, I realize there's something wrong with this whole thing—I mean, this growing old and dying. Like we should all be living outside of time so we can just be young and alive forever. It makes me sad, knowing I'm on the same train these guys are on, and there's no getting off. It's almost enough to make a person wish she'd never been born.

Here's the room. I have to take a deep breath before I go in. Not that I want to take in the smell of this place, which is almost enough to send me kneeling at the porcelain throne, as Carl used to say. Carl, who's coming home from the war, who survived Vietnam, who will one day end up in a place like this anyway, old and ready to die. You can't win for losing.

There's Austin, looking even more dead than usual, except he's breathing. I see the covers over his chest rise and fall. Thank God. I'm glad he's still alive. I walk across the room, and at the sound of my footsteps he opens his eyes. He looks at me like he's never seen me before, and he doesn't know who I am, but I know he's surprised because why would he expect me to come here to see him? We look at each other for a minute without saying anything until finally, I blurt out, "Gail says you're an old fool."

He smiles at that, his head bobbing up and down on the pillow like he's trying to nod. "She's probably right."

"You climbed up some mountain looking for Digger."

"Yes. Yes, I did."

"And you gave yourself a heart attack in the process."

"I'm afraid so."

"Well, listen, I think … I mean, it was nice of you, you know, to do that. I want you to know I appreciate what you did."

He shuts his eyes and smiles again. He looks like the words made him feel better for a few seconds. But then he looks kind of sad and says, "I only wish I could have found him."

"But if you did," I say, "he would still be dead. I mean, you'd have just been finding a body, and by now it'd probably be in pretty bad shape."

"But I could have at least brought the body home for burial and given your parents—and you—some sense of peace. I wanted to do that for you."

I nod. "Now I really know you're Austin," I say. "I remember how you always wanted to make everything better for people. Like you wanted to save the whole world."

"Save the whole world," he repeats real quietly. He smiles sadly and shakes his head. "I gave up on that idea a long time ago, I'm afraid. There's no saving the world. It's useless. People will keep trying, just as I did, but … well, they'll find out. Eventually, they'll know."

"What do you mean, Austin?"

He draws in a breath, and his whole body shudders. Maybe I shouldn't be here. Maybe I'm just wearing him out. I'm about to say never mind, I should just go and let him rest when he says, "Last time I saw you in 1917, I was going to war. You remember?"

I nod and lift my hand to the necklace. "Sure I do."

"Well, I went. And I saw things that"—he stops and looks me in the eye—"that I hope you'll never see in your lifetime. Things too horrible to talk about. But afterward, I still thought there might be hope. It was the war to end all wars, after all. That was it. We could stop fighting now and live in peace. But then came the Second World War, and then Korea, and now Vietnam. You knew that the last time I saw you in 1917, didn't you?"

I sniff out a laugh, even though I'm not trying to be disrespectful. "Yeah, I knew it. I mean, my own brother was over in 'Nam. I guess I never told you about that."

He's moving his head back and forth on the pillow now. "It doesn't matter. It wouldn't have mattered if you told me. It wasn't war that made me realize how wrong my thinking was and how futile my hopes were."

"It wasn't?"

"No. It was my son."

"Your son?"

"Lyle." He swallows hard, and his eyes are all watery. "He's a criminal and a murderer. He was perfecting the craft of getting into trouble when other kids were still learning how to ride two-wheelers. No matter what I did, I couldn't get him to behave and play by the rules. Every day, I see the evidence of what he did to my daughter." He lifts his hand to his forehead as if the scar is there instead of on Linda's head. "Now he's on death row. The law says he deserves to die. If I couldn't change my own son and turn him into something good, what chance would I have with the whole world?"

We're quiet for a minute. I shift my weight from one foot to the other. I'm afraid Austin might start crying, but he doesn't. He's looking out the window like he's suddenly interested in the clouds swirling around and changing shapes up there in the sky.

"Austin," I say, "when you get out of the hospital, I want to show you something."

He looks back at me. "Do you want to tell me what it is?"

"No." I shake my head. "I'd rather just show you."

"All right. The doctor says I should be out of here in a couple of days."

"That's good. So that means you'll be okay, right?"

"Sure, I'll be okay," he says. Then he adds, "For a few more years, anyway."

Yeah, I guess none of us lives forever, huh? But then, that's kind of what I want to talk to Austin about, once he gets out of this place where everyone's dying.

59

Sheldon
Sunday, April 20, 1969

I STEP INTO my room and find him sitting there, staring intently into that machine of his. His profile in view, I see now what I didn't see before. He looks familiar because he looks so much like me. He is my son.

"Hello, Gavan," I say.

He turns from the machine and smiles. "Hello, Sheldon. Haven't seen you for a while. How are you?"

It seems the most redundant of questions in the face of what I have to ask him, but I answer anyway. "I'm fine, thanks. And you?"

"Doing well. I'm reading another letter from my wife. She's coming home soon."

I nod slightly. "Wonderful news. My son Carl is coming home from Vietnam himself this week."

"Very good," he says. "We have much to be thankful for, then."

"Yes." I move to the bed and sit. I am so close to him I could reach out and touch him, if I were able. If he were solid to my touch. But he is not. "Gavan?"

"Yes, Sheldon?"

"You're my son, aren't you?"

I hear his sharp intake of breath. He leans his elbows on the arms of the chair and clasps his hands together. "So you know, then."

"Yes. Your mother told me."

His head moves up and down as he thinks about that. "Yes, I knew she would come. I just didn't know when."

"Why are you here?" I ask. "In this house?" I wave a hand.

He leans toward me. "I wanted to meet you."

"You never meet me in your time?"

"No."

I don't ask him why. "How did you know I'd be here?"

"Linda told me."

"Linda? My daughter Linda?"

He nods. "She sought me out. We've become friends," he says. Then he adds, "In my time, not yours."

"How did she find you?"

He nods toward the machine. "Internet. Something called Facebook."

"Facebook?"

"Yes. It's fairly new. It—"

My raised hand stops him. "Never mind," I say. "Your world is too much for me. I just want to know why you chose to come to this house."

He frowns, moistens his lips. "Well first of all, like I said, I wanted to meet you." He looks at me a moment; I nod for him to go on. "And second, I wanted to tell you something you otherwise wouldn't know." He looks down at his hands, swallows hard.

"I'm listening."

His eyes find mine, and he smiles. "I just want you to know that I'm glad to be alive."

I have to stop everything, even the sheer act of breathing, to let those words sink in.

"You see," he goes on, "I know the circumstances surrounding my birth, that it was something of a surprise. Well, I suppose that's an understatement." He pauses to smile apologetically before going on. "I imagine it was very hard for you, something you wish had never happened. But I can't help being thankful that it did, of course. Mother married Aidan Valdez when I was four years old, and he was a very good man and a very good father. He gave us a comfortable life. But I knew early on he was my stepfather, and I always wanted to know who my biological father was. Just to meet you and to tell you that as hard as it was for all of you, I'm glad to be here. I'm trying to live a life that would make you proud of me."

So many feelings rise up in me that my chest aches trying to hold them all. I wish I could touch my son, clasp his hand, put my arms around him. And yet, this seeing him, this hearing his words—this is a gift, and it is enough. "I *am* proud of you, Gavan. More than I can say."

He smiles fully now. "Thank you."

"And your mother? Is she ... was she happy?"

"Yes. Very. She's still alive, still married."

"Do you think she forgave me?"

"I know she did. She's the one who taught me to love you."

"She did?"

"Yes. It took her some time, but she came to respect you."

"Respect me? For what?"

"For not leaving your wife, when you might have easily done so."

"I find that hard to believe."

"You can believe it because it's true."

I rise from the bed and walk to the window, shaking my head. Staring out at the night sky, I can scarcely gather my words, but at length I manage to mumble, "I wonder why we were chosen? Meg, Linda, and I—we've all wondered why we were chosen."

I turn around to find him looking at me quizzically. "Chosen for what, Sheldon?"

"For this house. For this gift. I know now beyond all doubt that's what it is."

He shrugs and shakes his head. "I have no answer for you there, I'm afraid. Sometimes gifts are simply given out of love."

"Because the giver loves us?"

"Yes."

I raise a hand to my chest, feel the pounding within. "Grace," I whisper.

He cocks an ear. "What was that?" he asks.

But I don't respond. I am thinking about the gift. "Think of how it would be if we could all see into time and know the things we need to know, to know all that God knows."

"But we can't." He cocks his head. "We've been allowed to come here and to see in part, but not fully, not the way he does. Still, we don't have to know what God knows. We only have to know God."

I nod slowly. "And so we trust the one who sees all."

"Yes. It's called faith."

"I know of faith. I remember it."

"You'll know it again." He stands, pushes the chair under the desk. "Sheldon, come with me. I want to show you something."

"All right."

I follow him into the hall and next door to Digger's room. In the quiet glow of a night-light, I see the sleeping child in the bed, a boy about three years old. Gavan and I stand beside the bed and listen to him breathe.

"Nicholas, my son," Gavan says. "Your grandson."

"My grandson," I repeat, a measure of awe in my voice. "He looks very much like my own son Digger."

Gavan nods, smiles. "As a very wise man once said," he whispers, "'God makes all things beautiful in his time.'"

60

Meg
Tuesday, April 22, 1969

WE STAND ON the station platform under a cloudless sky, waiting for the train to pull in. It should arrive any minute now. I'm wearing a new dress, a sleeveless blue eyelet, and a pair of new white pumps bought especially for the occasion. I need things to be new. I need life to begin anew when I welcome my son home.

Linda is sitting on the bench, her long legs crossed, one leg swinging nervously as she looks out over the rails. Sheldon is pacing. He keeps looking at his watch. There are others on the platform and inside the small station house. They look bored, caught up in routine. Maybe they're meeting someone, or maybe they're waiting to take the train themselves; either way, the day is an ordinary one. Unlike mine. For me—and for Sheldon and Linda too—today is a day of joy. God knows there are only too few of those.

Sheldon stops abruptly. "I think I hear it," he says.

Linda rises and walks toward me. I listen. "Which way is it coming from?" I ask.

"That way," Sheldon says, pointing.

My gaze is riveted to the tracks as though I'm willing the train to appear. And then, there it is. The engine comes into view, leading the way. Inside one of the cars that follows is Carl.

Linda slips her arm in mine and rests her chin on my shoulder. "I never thought I'd want to see Carl so much," she says with a laugh. I nod and draw in several deep breaths to steady myself. Sheldon takes my hand and squeezes it. I allow it because for the moment, I'm happy. I imagine Carl watching for us from the train window. He will see the three of us here together, waiting for him. I hope it's a picture that fills him with happiness.

The lights of the train engine draw closer. The wheels clack over the rails, steel against steel, rattling, easing themselves into the station. The platform trembles under our feet. A gust of wind, the clanging of the engine's bell, a squeal of brakes, and the train sighs to a rest.

Men and women begin to disembark. My eyes scan the crowd for a familiar face. For one terrified moment, I wonder whether he didn't come, whether he missed the train, whether it was all a lie and he never came home from Vietnam at all. But then ... there he is: the tall young man who seems to tower over everyone.

"Carl!" Linda calls. She waves both arms excitedly.

I drop Sheldon's hand and take a step forward. Carl sees me. He waves, smiles, rushes toward me. All else around me falls away as I find myself in his arms. He lifts me up; my feet are off the ground. My heart floats.

Thank God, my son is home.

61

Linda
Thursday, April 24, 1969

GAIL GIVES ME a strange look when she answers my knock on the door. "So why are you taking my grandfather up to your house?" she asks.

"I told you," I say. "I want to show him something."

"How come I can't come?"

"I told you that too. This is between me and Bim."

"How can anything be between you and Bim? You've never even acted like you like him."

"Yeah, well, this has nothing to do with whether or not I like him. Even though I do. Like him, I mean. Well, you know, as much as I can like an old guy."

Her scrunched up face scrunches up even more. "You're acting really weird, Linda," she says.

Yeah, well, I'd like to see how you'd act if you could talk to your grandfather when he was eighteen years old and living in 1916. Weird happenings make people act weird.

"Is he ready to go?"

"I think so." She looks over her shoulder and hollers, "Grandpa, Linda's here. You ready?"

I'm still standing on the front step under the porch light as she hasn't invited me in. Not that I mind. I want to get going.

Finally, I see Bim shuffling down the hall, his daughter fussing over him and insisting he wear a sweater. The daughter named Linda who was named after me.

"All right," Bim says, "I'll wear the sweater if it'll make you happy." He slips it on, walks to the door and says to me, "Let's go before she tries to make me wear galoshes too."

"I'm just looking after your health, Dad," the other Linda says. "The nights are still chilly, and you're just getting over a heart attack, you know."

"Thanks for the news flash, darling," Bim says. "I'll keep that in mind."

Bim steps out into the night, and together we head to my car, parked at the curb. Or on the curb as usual. Before we're halfway down the walk, Mrs. Leland calls to me from the front door, "Don't keep him out too late, Linda!"

Sheesh! Like we're going on a date or something. "I'll bring him home in half an hour," I holler back.

Once we settle in, and I start the engine, he says, "You know, I haven't been to the house in fifty years."

"No?" I say. "Well, it looks pretty much the same, except probably older and more run down."

"And just what is it you want to show me, Linda?" He looks at me, and once again I see Austin's blue eyes. They sparkle when they catch the headlights of passing cars.

"I'll show you when we get there," I say.

He settles back in the seat. "All right. Will I get to meet your parents?"

"No, thank heavens," I say. "They're over visiting with my uncle Steve and his family. My brother Carl is there with them. I was there but left to come get you. They think I went home early to finish my homework."

"You didn't want them to know I'm coming to the house?"

"Not really."

"Why not?"

"I'm just not sure how to explain."

Out of the corner of my eye, I see him nod. "So Carl's come home," he says.

"He's been home two days now."

"And he was in 'Nam, you say?"

"Yeah, that's right."

"War changes you, you know. When a man comes home, he's not the same man who left."

"Yeah? Well, Carl spent his time typing up reports, so it wasn't like he was blowing people up or anything. And I'll tell you what, Bim, right now he's facing something a whole lot harder than anything he ever faced in 'Nam." I glance over at him and see that he's looking at me. He doesn't say anything, but he's just sitting there waiting for me to go on. So I say, "He knows now that Digger's really gone."

Bim swallows hard, his huge Adam's apple going up and down his wrinkled old throat. He still doesn't say anything, but his face looks like somebody died. Which I guess somebody did. Even though we've never seen the body or had a funeral.

We're winding our way up the mountain toward the house. "Have you told your brother about what happens in the house, as far as seeing into time?" he asks.

"We haven't told him yet. Mom and Dad plan to, but they want to give him a few days to settle in before they hit him with that one. Meanwhile, we're hoping he doesn't bump into somebody who's not really there, if you know what I mean."

"Yes." He manages to chuckle. "I know what you mean. I remember the first time I ran into you. You were lying out in the sun in that little bit of a bathing suit."

"You thought it was my underwear."

"I'd never seen anything like it. Not in 1916. I thought you were the most beautiful woman I'd ever laid eyes on."

At first I want to be creeped out by that, but then I remember the way he looked standing over me. Young and handsome and alive. "Really?" I ask. "You really thought that?"

"Yes, Linda, I really did."

"Thanks," I say. Then I add, "Austin."

We pull up in front of the house, and I turn off the car. "Come on in," I say.

Bim gets out of the car slowly, like his joints don't work quite right. As we move up to the porch, he says, "You used to wait for me here on the steps."

"Yeah, I guess I did."

"Seems like a long time ago."

"For you, it was. Not so long ago for me."

I open the front door for him, and he steps inside. I follow. He's looking around like he's mesmerized by the place. Finally, he says, "You're right. Not much has changed."

"Come on," I say, nodding toward the kitchen.

"Where are we going?"

"Outside."

"Outside?"

"That's right. Come on."

He follows me through the kitchen and to the back door. I notice he draws his sweater more tightly around him when we step out back. I remember then that old people are always cold. Suddenly I want to yell at him for growing old on me, as though he did it on purpose. I know he didn't, but still I want the old Austin back—or the young one, rather. I want the Austin who gave me the necklace, but I know I can never have him.

We stand in the middle of the yard with the stars shining overhead. "Well?" he says.

I point upward. "Remember?"

He tilts his head back. "Remember what?"

"That," I say. "The star. Remember we looked at it together before?"

He doesn't say anything for a long time. Finally, he shakes his head. "I don't remember. What is it?"

"It's the star that showed up the day Digger disappeared. It's been here every night since—but only here. You can't see it from anywhere else. So it's got to be from another time."

"Another time?" he echoes.

"Yeah. I brought you out here to see it once when you were still back in 1916. Don't you remember that?"

He squints and moans like all of a sudden his head hurts. He's looking up, but I know at the same time he's thinking back, trying to remember. "Oh yes," he says. He's speaking so quiet I can hardly hear him. "Now I remember."

"Well, back then you were sure science could explain it. I thought you might be right, but now I'm not so sure anymore."

"So why did you bring me here tonight, Linda? Why did you want to show me this now?"

"Because I think it's the Star of Bethlehem. Remember, I told you that before. I was wondering what you might think now. Do you think it could be the Christmas star?"

His eyes grow small, and his head moves slowly up and down. "Well, I don't know," he says. "If the star can be seen from nowhere else but right here, then it's got to be something that happened in another time. But the Star of Bethlehem?"

"Well, if it *is*—and I say it is, because it's got to be something pretty important—then wouldn't the whole thing be true? I mean, the whole thing about God coming to earth? I always found it hard to believe, like it was just a story or a fairy tale or something. But with the star showing up every night, I kind of have to wonder."

He stops looking at the sky and looks at me. He's rubbing the back of his neck like it's aching from looking up too long. "I've never believed in any of it, Linda. You know that. Not in God. Certainly not in God coming in the flesh."

"But the star?"

He takes a few steps forward, looks up, looks down. He paces in a small circle, finally coming back to me. "It's real, isn't it? The star is real."

"Yes," I say. "Of course it's real. We can see it, can't we?"

"But that doesn't mean it's what you think it is. It doesn't mean ..." He stops talking and starts pacing again.

"Dad said something about, if we peeled back time, we could go back to the day Jesus was born. He says it was a real event, you know, something that really happened."

He stops pacing. He looks at me, and he looks angry. "What are you getting at, Linda?" he asks.

I shrug. I'm beginning to be sorry I brought him here. "You just sounded so sad in the hospital. I thought if I brought you out here and showed you the star and told you it just might all be true, that would give you a little hope."

He stares at me a long time like I've said something terrible, but then he tilts his head back again and looks up at the star. "Such foolishness," he says. "But perhaps you're right. Perhaps it's a glorious foolishness. It would be worth considering."

I don't really know what he's talking about. But as he's standing there in the light of the star, I can see that some kind of sadness slips off his face. He breathes in deeply like he hasn't been able to catch his breath in a long time. He looks at me again and says, "Thank you for bringing me here tonight, Linda."

I give him a nod. "You're welcome, Austin."

"Maybe I'll come back and look at it again sometime. You've given me much to think about."

"All right."

"For now, I'm tired. I think I'd better go home."

"Okay. But Austin?"

"Yes, Linda?"

"Just speaking for me, I'm finding it easier and easier to believe."

He nods but doesn't say anything as we walk across the grass to the house.

62

Sheldon
Saturday, April 26, 1969

CARL LOOKS AROUND the dining room table, his eyes shifting from me to Meg to Linda and back to me. His fork hovers over his plate, interrupted in its otherwise frantic journey toward the next bite. Finally, he says, "You guys been dropping acid or something while I've been away?"

"I wish," Linda says, but when I look at her she shrugs. "Just kidding, Dad."

Meg says, "Listen, Carl, I know it sounds crazy. And heaven knows we didn't believe it at first either. But it's true."

Carl's eyes narrow. The fork still hangs motionless over the chicken fricassee Meg has prepared for lunch. "So you're telling me you see people in this house that are living in different times?"

"That's right, son," I say.

"Well, what? Are they ghosts or something?"

Linda shakes her head. "They're not ghosts. Some of them aren't even dead yet. Heck, some of them aren't even born yet, for that matter."

"Not born yet?" Carl echoes. "Like who?"

"Well," Linda says, "Dad said he saw Gavan's son, Nicholas, who isn't born till the twenty-first century."

"The twenty-first century?"

I lift a hand. "It's impossible to understand, Carl," I say. "But I can tell you this much. It's a gift. For whatever reason, God is allowing us to see in part what he sees in full. He's giving us at least a glimpse into the Eternal Now."

"Yeah?" Carl sounds skeptical. "How come?"

For love's sake, I think.

Before I can speak, Meg says, "We don't really know, Carl. We just wanted you to be prepared in case you see anything out of the ordinary."

"You mean like somebody suddenly appearing on the couch next to me when I'm trying to watch TV or something?"

"Exactly," Linda says.

The fork reluctantly stabs a piece of chicken and carries it to Carl's mouth, where it is slowly consumed. Once Carl swallows, he says, "Peyote, right? Or magic mushrooms? Listen, I've heard 'shrooms can distort time and make you see things that aren't really there. Not that I'd know from experience—"

"Sure, Carl," Linda interrupts.

"But really," Carl goes on, "you're making me nervous here, folks. I mean, I come home from 'Nam thinking things are finally going to be somewhat normal, and I find my family's been turning on with Timothy Leary or something."

Meg sighs heavily. She looks at me, hoping I'll have an answer for Carl. I take a long drink of water to give myself a moment to think.

"Listen, son," I say at last. "Surely you know us better than that. We wouldn't take drugs, and we certainly wouldn't lie to you. At the same time, we don't necessarily expect you to believe us either. Maybe you'll see for yourself, and maybe not. For now, we'll just let it rest, all right?"

But Carl's not quite ready to let it rest. "And anyway," he says, his eyes making the rounds again, "what's so great about the place where we lost Digger? How can that be a gift?"

His words silence us. I for one feel momentarily chastened, as though

I've forgotten what happened here. Not that I could ever forget.

"Listen, Carl," Linda says, "why don't we go down to the ice cream parlor where I work? I can get us a couple of free banana splits."

"All right. Sure." Carl lays down his fork and pushes away from the table. He steps around to Meg and kisses her forehead. "Great lunch, Mom. I've missed your cooking."

She smiles up at him and pats the hand that has momentarily alighted on her shoulder. Then Carl and Linda are gone, and Meg and I are left to gaze at each other across the table. There was a time when what we wanted most was to be alone, she and I. Now, it leaves us feeling awkward and afraid. Her face has grown pale, and her lips are slightly parted, as though she wants to say something and at the same time doesn't want to say it. I try to swallow but my mouth is dry. My heart sinks in my chest like a stone.

63

Meg
Saturday, April 26, 1969

WITH CARL AND Linda gone, the room is so quiet I can actually hear a clock ticking, the clock on the mantle in the kitchen. The seconds fall away, telling me it's time. No more waiting because the number of seconds is finite and someday there will be an end to them. So says Mrs. See, and I know she's right.

I feel the words at the base of my throat, but I can't seem to find the strength to carry them to my tongue. I squeeze my hands together in my lap and pray for courage, but several more seconds tick off and the moment passes. Sheldon is speaking.

"Well," he says, "I guess we really couldn't expect Carl to react in any other way. It's a little, um—beyond the pale, so to speak." He tries to smile, but his lips tremble.

I nod. This isn't what I wanted to talk about, but I need to respond. "I suppose he'll simply have to experience it to believe it," I say.

"Yes, I suppose so. At least if something happens, he won't be caught completely off-guard."

"And if nothing happens?"

"Then he'll go on thinking we've lost our minds."

Sheldon and I look at each other and, suddenly, we laugh. Together.

Loud and long. As though our son thinking us crazy is the funniest thing in the world. Because somehow, in this moment, it is.

When the laughter trails off, I know it has taken something with it. Something bad that had been hanging in the air between Sheldon and me for far too long. And when the room is quiet again, I'm no longer with the man who wronged me; I am with an old friend.

"Sheldon?"

"Yes, Meg?"

The words are there now, and it's not too late. "No matter what else happens, we need to be a family again."

"We do?" His right hand shakes as he reaches for his water glass. He starts to lift it but changes his mind. "I mean, of course we do. For the sake of the children."

"No, Sheldon," I say. "Not just for them, but for our own sake too."

His eyes narrow slightly, like he's trying to understand. "For our own sake?" he repeats.

"Yes. I'm tired of being alone in our marriage. I want us to be together again, like we were at the start of things."

He sits up a little straighter, and his face brightens. "Do you think we can be?" he asks. "Together again, I mean?"

"I don't know. But I believe we have to try."

"You want to try, Meg?"

Just as he says that, I picture Charlene and the baby. A sharp pain strikes at the heart of my resolve. I take a deep breath and let the pain roll through me. I can't follow the lingering hurt because it's headed in the wrong direction. Forgiveness, Mrs. See said, is the road between heaven and earth. It's a difficult first step, but I decide again to take it.

"Yes, I do want to try," I tell Sheldon. "What I don't want is to grow old alone. I want you with me."

Sheldon is smiling now, tentatively, as his head moves from side to side. "I don't even know how to begin," he confesses.

"You must begin by forgiving me."

"Forgiving you? I don't understand. I'm the one who—"

I raise a hand. "You must forgive me for holding on to my anger so long, for not being willing to forgive you when you asked me to; and you must forgive me for being a pastor's wife for so long without ever really believing what you believed."

Sheldon is silenced by that. A long moment passes before he says, "I never should have asked you to be a pastor's wife. I never did ask you, and maybe that's the problem. I did what I wanted to do, even though my decisions didn't make life easy for you."

"No, you never did ask me," I agree, "and maybe you should have, but what's done is done. If you were to ask me now if you should be a pastor, I would tell you yes. You made the right decision. That was how you were meant to spend your life. I know that now."

Sheldon's eyes glisten at me down the length of the table. He nods slightly and moistens his lips with his tongue. "Thank you for saying so, Meg. That means a lot to me. And of course I forgive you if there's really anything to forgive, but the more important question is, can you forgive me? I'm the one who did the greater wrong."

"Oh, Sheldon." I sigh and shake my head. "I'm not going to try to weigh your wrong against mine. We were both wrong, and now we have to put it behind us and try to move forward."

Sheldon drops his eyes. "You do understand that the Gavan in this house is my son, don't you?"

There's the pain again. I push it aside. "Yes, I understand. So he came and found you."

"Yes. He wanted to meet me and to tell me he's glad to be alive."

I think about that a moment. It never occurred to me that this person who wasn't meant to be might in fact be happy to be alive. I cock my head and look at Sheldon. "That's good, then, isn't it?"

"Yes. Yes, it is."

"And you said his son, the boy Nicholas—you said he looks like Digger."

"Very much so. There's a little bit of Digger living on in him."

Oh Digger. That is one pain that I will allow to settle in my heart. I couldn't push it away, even if I wanted to. Of Nicholas, I say, "Life springs up even from our mistakes, and there's something good to be said about that."

"Only because God makes it so."

I feel the pressure of tears at the back of my eyes. I lift my gaze to the window so they don't spill over. "I'm willing to believe that now," I say. "I'm not even quite sure why, except for the strange happenings in this house and the chance to see something of what God sees. Still, I don't consider either Gavan or Nicholas a substitute for Digger."

"Of course not," Sheldon agrees. "Neither do I."

"He is ... Digger is gone. I've been trying to hold on to hope, but as the days go by I'm finding it harder and harder to believe he'll come home."

Sheldon's mouth forms a small line as he nods. "I'm afraid you're probably right, Meg. I don't think Digger will be coming home. It's time to let him go."

Time again. I give in to the tears and allow them to roll down my cheeks. "You know, I had come to believe that as long as the star was shining over our house every night, there was hope for Digger's being alive. But that's the thing. Maybe the star is telling us that he *is* alive, and we'll see him in heaven. I want to believe that at least."

"We can believe it," Sheldon says, "because it's true."

Of all the hundreds of sermons that Sheldon has ever preached, he has just given the first message of hope that I actually believe.

I nod and smile at him. "Then it's enough," I say.

64

Sheldon
Saturday, April 26, 1969

THERE'S A DREAM-LIKE quality to the moment, when what you have been hoping for happens and yet things don't seem quite real. You have to pause and wait for your heart to catch up with your mind so that both are in the same place.

"Meg," I say quietly, "if you don't mind, I would just like to hear you say the words."

She looks puzzled. "What words, Sheldon?"

"That you forgive me. I mean, that's what you're trying to tell me, isn't it? That you forgive me?"

She is crying still, silent tears rolling down her cheeks, and yet as I look at her waiting for an answer, she smiles. "Yes, Sheldon," she says. "That's what I'm trying to tell you. I forgive you."

I am like air. Weightless. Unconfined. Free to move about for the first time in a very long while.

I push myself away from the table and stand. "I've so longed to comfort you, you know."

She wipes her tears with the back of one hand as she rises from her chair. She hesitates a moment so I take the first step. My legs are weak, and I can't move fast enough. The distance from my end of the table to hers seems endless and yet, in the next moment, she's in my arms.

65

Meg
Saturday, May 10, 1969

CARL HAS BEEN home for almost three weeks, and the house has been quiet. That is, no sudden appearances from anyone who isn't really there, no talking with people from other times. Only the star remains, but it seems smaller somehow and dimmer, as though its job is done and it's sinking back into history.

Maybe all of it is finished. Maybe the house has accomplished what it was meant to do for us, and now it'll lie dormant till someone else needs it. Another family, maybe. Or maybe Gavan Valdez in the unimaginable year of 2005. Meanwhile, we settle back into life, grateful for what we have, trying as ever to accept what we have lost. Looking ahead to what we will find again.

Sheldon is talking about going back into the ministry, finding a small church to serve as assistant pastor or something. It would be a second profession, in addition to the dealership, because we must pay the bills and provide for Charlene's child. As it should be. We prepare for the future we know is coming.

I think I'm ready to be a pastor's wife this time around. Sheldon says all it takes is a little bit of faith, and that's a good thing because a little bit of faith is all I have—though that's more than I had before. At least it's a place to start and a place from which to move forward.

I stand at the kitchen sink, a cup of coffee in one hand, its matching saucer in the other. The grass outside shimmers with dew in the early morning light, and the leaves of the trees rise and fall with the wind. Upstairs I hear footsteps. Sheldon is getting up, getting ready to go to work. Another Super Saturday Sale—*Prices that can't be beat.* And so it goes. He doesn't complain. He says the used car lot is a sanctuary of sorts, his customers the sheep of his flock. He is a pastor because he can't be anything else. I understand that now, and accept it.

Margaret See was right. Forgiveness is the road between heaven and earth. I am able now to love Sheldon without the constant anger and pain. Those continue to fall away while the love grows stronger. In that regard, time is our ally and will bring us where we're meant to be.

Carl's presence in the house is a great solace. He plans to stay with us a while, and I'm grateful. I'm not ready to let him go again. Not so soon. He plans to apply to the University of North Carolina in Asheville, which he can attend on the GI Bill. One reason I think he wants to stay here is to see if the house has anything for him—anything to tell him, anything to give him. I hope he won't be disappointed, but I think we've gained all we're going to gain, and—for me, at least—that's enough.

Linda will graduate from high school next month and plans to follow Carl to UNCA. She too will continue to live with us. Her choice. Imagine. I have my daughter back.

I lift the cup to my lips and sip; the coffee has grown cold. I must start Sheldon's breakfast anyway. Scrambled eggs, toast, bacon—I want to send him to work with a full stomach. It may be a long tiring day. Maybe I'll send a thermos of coffee with him too.

The dregs of cold coffee swirl in the bottom of the cup. I'm reluctant to move away from the sink and start the day because it takes a certain strength to live, sometimes more than I have. It's still hard to get through the days without Digger.

But we do. We will live through today and tomorrow and the day after that, and maybe one day it won't hurt so much.

I will allow myself one more look out the window before I turn to the stove. One more glance at the morning before I begin the day. Lifting my eyes to the glass, I gasp and forget to breathe. Both cup and saucer fall from my hands and shatter in the sink.

"Digger," I whisper.

My knees weaken, and I have to clutch the edge of the sink to keep from falling. I shut my eyes, open them again; he is still there.

Digger is playing in the backyard, his arms extended as though they are wings. He climbs up the big rock, bends his knees, leaps. His laughter fills the air.

My right hand briefly settles over my heart then rises to my lips. He's wearing a white-and-green striped shirt, brown shorts, white socks, blue sneakers, and a clover chain necklace. He is wearing what he wore on the day he disappeared. And I know what that means. I'm seeing that day all over again. I am seeing into time, seeing him as he was on the day he left. I'm incredulous and sick at the thought. Of all the good this house has done, this one thing is cruel beyond words. I don't think I can bear it.

His arms outstretched, he climbs the rock, leaps, laughs. Then he sees me. He sees me watching from the window.

"Hi, Ma!" he hollers as he waves.

My hand drops from my mouth; I rush to the door and into the yard. But what if he isn't real? What if he too is only seeing into time?

I stop and look at my son. "Digger?"

He stands still and looks at me. His arms fall to his side. "Yeah, Ma?"

"Digger?" I say again.

"What? What's the matter, Ma? You don't look so good."

I'm trembling, terrified he will disappear. "Digger, give me your hand."

"But why?"

"Just do as I say, please." I extend my hand, reaching for him.

"You're shaking, Ma. Are you cold?"

I bend down, both knees on the grass. *Please God, let his hand be solid. Let him be real.*

Digger looks at his hand. "I got dirt on me."

"It's all right. Really it is. Just—just let me touch you."

My hand hangs in the air, waiting. Digger rubs his palm against one hip. Then he reaches for me, his dirty little-boy hand slicing through air, his fingertips sliding down my fingers until his palm comes to rest in mine. I grab hold. His flesh is solid. He is alive.

Crying out, I pull him to me, hold him tight against my breast. "Digger! Digger, you're here! You're really here."

He struggles against my embrace. "Let go of me, Ma. What's the matter? You're smothering me."

I let him go, cup his dusty, dirty, beautiful face in my hands. Tears run down my cheeks. "Digger, where have you been?" I ask. "Where have you been?"

He looks puzzled. He's trying to pull his face from my hands, but I don't let go. "What do you mean, where've I been? I've been right here playing. Where do you think I'd be? Why are you crying, Ma? You act like I been gone forever."

Oh Digger, you were. You were gone forever, and you don't even know it.

I lift my apron and wipe my eyes. "I'm sorry, Digger. I'm just so happy, is all."

"What are you all happy about? Did something good happen?"

"Oh yes, something good. Something very, very good."

He shrugs. "Did Marjorie go home? 'Cause if she did I can take this stupid necklace off."

"Yes. Yes," I say, laughing. "She went home a long time ago."

He tugs at the necklace and tosses it aside. "I'm hungry. When are we going to eat?"

"Soon, but first, I have a surprise. Carl came home. Carl's here."

His eyes grow wide with surprise. "He is? He came back from 'Nam?"

"Yes, he came home. That means we're all together now."

Digger throws up his hands. "Hooray! Let's celebrate and have a party with cake and everything. Can we have a chocolate cake, Ma? Can we?"

"Of course we can. But first, let me call Carl out to see you. And Daddy and Linda. All right?"

"Sure! I'll holler with you."

He begins to holler. I turn back to the house and see Sheldon standing in the doorway, motionless and wide-eyed. He looks at me with fear on his face. "Is he ..."

"He's real, Sheldon. He's back. Digger's back."

Sheldon gives off a cry that almost sounds like a cry of pain, but in the next moment he's in the yard, and Digger is in his arms, and they are both talking and laughing at once.

Once Sheldon loosens his grip, Digger leans back, puts two fingers in his mouth and fishes out a small white pearl. "Look, Daddy, you knocked me around so much you knocked my loose tooth clean out! Can I put it under my pillow tonight and get a nickel?"

Sheldon takes the tooth, bloody at the root, and lays it in the palm of his hand. He gazes at it for a long while as though it's something unknown, something he's never seen before. And indeed, maybe it is. Because it is evidence that while time passed for us, it didn't pass for Digger. Sheldon lifts his eyes to me. We share a look of puzzlement and wonder. "I don't understand, Sheldon," I say quietly. "Where has he been?"

"I don't know," Sheldon admits. "Outside of time, maybe? But I don't know where that would be."

"He told me he hasn't been anywhere, that he's just been right here all along. I think he thinks it's the day he disappeared."

"You suppose he has no memory of ... anything?"

"He doesn't seem to."

Digger tugs on Sheldon's sleeve. "What are you guys talking about?

Why are you saying I disappeared and don't remember?"

His wide eyes flit between me and his Dad, looking fearful. Sheldon kneels in front of him and puts a hand on his shoulder. He starts to say something, stops, shakes his head. "We have some explaining to do, Digger," he says quietly. "Something has happened, and we'll tell you all about it. But don't worry, everything's all right. Everything's fine now."

Digger's face relaxes and he shrugs. "Okay," he says. He points to the tooth in Sheldon's hand. "So do I get the nickel or don't I?"

Sheldon closes his fist over the tooth and laughs. "Of course you do, Digger," he says, hugging the boy to himself again. "We'll put the tooth under your pillow tonight."

Our joy is interrupted by a scream and Linda running toward us in her nightgown. "Digger!" she cries. "Digger, you're here! I can't believe you're really here!"

She too kneels in the grass and throws her arms around her brother. Digger scrunches up his face and tries to wiggle away. "Hey, knock it off," he mutters. "What's the matter with you anyway? You're—" He stops and his eyes grow wide. "Carl!"

Carl is coming toward us now, walking barefoot across the grass, wearing only a pair of shorts and an undershirt. Instead of shouting like Linda, he is quiet, like someone in shock. He reaches Digger and drops to the ground, his naked knees making dents in the grass. He looks from Digger, to Sheldon, to me. "Then it's true," he says. "About the house."

"Yes," Sheldon says.

Carl smiles and takes Digger's hand. "Hey buddy, you're home."

"*I'm* home?" Digger replies. "You're funny, Carl! You're the one that came home. I didn't even know you were coming back. Why didn't somebody tell me you were coming?"

"I don't know, Digger. I guess we wanted to surprise you."

"Well, you sure did! And now we're all here and we're all together! Isn't that great? Ma says we can have a party!"

Carl reaches out and ruffles his little brother's hair. And then he pulls Digger to him and wraps him up in a hug so tight it looks like he's never going to let go.

Sheldon reaches for me and takes my hand. Linda's arm is around my shoulder. My sons are hugging each other; their laughter fills the morning air.

Thank God. Thank God.

We are all home now, and we are all together.

Epilogue

To God let votive accents rise;
With truth, with virtue, live;
So all the bliss that Time denies
Eternity shall give.

—John Quincy Adams, The Hour-Glass

Celeste
Summer 2007

DIGGER SOMEHOW SLIPPED in between time or out of time or above time or perhaps even below time—we don't exactly know, and it doesn't much matter. What matters is that he came back, or was allowed back or was brought back. We're not sure of that either. Digger had no memory of what happened for a long time. When he was grown, his mind began to offer up snatches of something he said was beyond his ability to describe, though he did say it was like nothing he'd seen before or has seen since. I for one believe that from his vantage point somewhere out of time, what he saw was heaven—from a distance, of course, just a glimpse of things to come.

Digger's unexpected return made him something of a legend in his own time as he slipped back into the routine of life in Black Mountain. The townsfolk were understandably amazed that, after so many months, he was alive, unharmed, and very much the same little boy who had disappeared without a trace. Not only in our own town but also across the county, he became known as The Miracle Boy Who Survived the Mountains. Of course, it wasn't that at all, but who could explain? His parents—rather like the mother of Jesus—had to ponder certain mysteries in their hearts without giving too much away to others.

The day Digger came home was the day the star disappeared for good. That night, as a family, the five of them stepped out after dark to take what would be their last look at the star. The star had already faded some, like Meg said, as though it were being pulled back into history. But that night, even as they gazed at it, its light simply vanished like a candle blown out. It had finished what it came for.

The Cranes stayed in the house until 1974 when Sheldon accepted the call to pastor a church full-time in Asheville. After that, he left the used car lot for good and never looked back. He and Meg moved with Digger to Asheville, where Sheldon served the church until his death in 1999. Over the years, the house in Black Mountain was rented out to a number of folks, but no one spoke of anything strange happening there, and thankfully Vernita Ponder was able to die without her hometown being overrun by curiosity seekers. Not until 2005, when Gavan Valdez bought the house, did anything unusual happen within its walls, but Gavan for one wasn't about to let the news get around town. When Mrs. See sent me to him and he hired me to take care of Nicholas, I assured him I would keep the secret.

I worked for Mr. Valdez until the summer of 2006 when his wife came home from Iraq. Having fulfilled her duty, she left the National Guard to raise her family, which came to include two more children over time.

That same summer I got married and went on working for the elderly woman in Asheville, who Meg thought of as Mrs. See. Funny thing was, it wasn't Mrs. See—it was Mrs. "C," which was what I always called her. The C was short for Crane. For Margaret See was, and is, Meg Crane; for some reason the Meg of 1968 was allowed to speak to the Meg of 2005, through me. Or perhaps vice versa, as Mrs. C was the one offering advice to Meg, knowing full well she was talking to herself—or rather, the person she had been some thirty-five years before.

Which was a gift perhaps many of us could use, if only we were allowed to hear words of comfort and advice from our future selves. But we are not, most of us. Most of us must live by blind faith, so to speak, because these temporal eyes of ours can't see the future. We can live in the now and remember the past, but we have to trust the future to the One who is already there, and who has at least told us in his Word that we're moving toward a happy ending. That's all we're allowed to know, but it's enough, don't you think?

So now I'm pouring a couple of tall glasses of sweet tea for Mrs. C and myself, as it's a hot summer day, and she's already waiting for me to join her in the rocking chairs on the porch.

"Celeste?" I hear her call.

"Yes, Mrs. C?"

"Digger just sent some more pictures of the grandkids to my phone. You've got to come out and see them!"

"I'll be right there!"

I carry the tea to the porch where I find Meg Crane peering at her cell phone and smiling over the grandchildren that once upon a time she thought she would never have.

"Well now, aren't they the fine-looking crew," I say as I sit in the chair beside her.

We will no doubt be out here for much of the afternoon where we like to drink our tea and talk and remember and wonder and marvel and just spend time. So long as the clocks are ticking, we will spend our time gratefully, knowing the hours have wings that carry us home.